STRYKER

LEXI BUCHANAN

Copyright © 2018 by Lexi Buchanan

All rights reserved.

No part of this book may be reproduced in any form or by any electronic or mechanical means, including information storage and retrieval systems, without written permission from the author, except for the use of brief quotations in a book review.

DEDICATION

To Abigail,

As you leave school and embark on a new chapter of your life, if I could give you three things, they would be confidence to always know your self worth, the strength to chase your dreams, and the ability to know how truly, deeply, loved you are.

Love Mum x

PROLOGUE

STRYKER (10 YEARS AGO)

"DAD, I'M NOT SURE this is such a good idea." My heart raced in my chest as though it would explode. My palms went slick as fear coursed through my veins.

I'd already thought Dad's late night plans were a bad idea…and they seemed worse the minute I saw the dark, deserted alley. It gave me the chills.

Nothing good was up that alley.

Even at fourteen I knew it, but my dad was determined so I followed him across the street. Something shouted for me to run, which gave me pause, but my legs had a mind of their own and followed him.

My dad turned, and then frowned when he noticed the slight hesitation in my usual eagerness to follow him anywhere. The nervous twitch in his right eye went crazy. "It isn't, but it's the only thing I can do."

Before I could work out what he meant, my dad

grabbed my arm as though he was afraid I'd run. He dragged me to the mouth of what I considered a nightmare.

The stench of rotten food made me want to hurl. Every creak, even the wind howling around us, had my eyes constantly straining to see through the pitch black. I half expected someone to jump out brandishing a gun, or knife, or some other weapon.

Head down, my eyes landed on the hold my dad had on my arm. Something wasn't right. In fact, nothing about the evening felt right.

I knew my dad constantly bet on the fighters in the cage, winning and losing on a regular basis, but what that had to do with tonight, if anything, I didn't know. My dad never took me to the fights no matter how much I begged. I wanted to hang out with dad… wanted to be like the fighters—tough, strong, fearless. One day, that would be me standing in the cage with the crowds shouting my name. Then my dad wouldn't have any choice about keeping me away from that life.

I'd never understood the obsession my dad had for the fights, but they'd put him on a high for days afterwards… unless he lost.

Pulled to a stop, I felt the shake of my dad's hand as his grip tightened. He turned to look at me and the fear I saw in his eyes was something I'd never expected to see. My blood turned to ice and the wrongfulness of the night felt all too real as a large vehicle headed down the alley from the opposite entrance.

Caught in the headlights, my first reaction was to run and hide. The tension jumping off my dad was high. His breathing was frantic and sweat beaded on his forehead.

With my free hand, I shoved the black hood of my sweatshirt from my head so I didn't miss anything.

My pulse hammered in my neck and all I could hear was my heartbeat thrashing in my ears.

When my dad's only reaction was to stand and stare at the approaching vehicle, I knew then, that they where here because of him.

What had he done?

"Dad?" I turned and hoped he'd offer me an explanation as fear and anger knotted in my gut.

He didn't and wouldn't meet my gaze until the purr of the SUV's engine cut off. "Son, I'm sorry. If there was any other way I'd have taken it, but there isn't…I love you. You won't believe those words soon, but I mean them with every breath I take."

"What?"

Before he could say more, the doors of the SUV opened and a large man climbed out, moving behind us. Three other men emerged and stood in front.

The one in a dark suit stepped forward, his steely eyes on my dad. "Peter."

"Mr—"

"No names tonight…*Peter*." His gaze slid to me and my breath caught at the back of my throat. He looked me over—assessing. "He'll do."

What did he mean?

"Dad?"

My dad didn't explain and, seconds later, I felt his grip on my arm loosen as the large guy stepped closer.

None of this made any sense, but I'd known something was wrong the minute I'd stepped out of our apartment.

It was obvious that my dad had done, said, or agreed to

something, but my brain worked overtime trying to work out just what.

Then I felt my wrists clasped tightly before they were pulled behind my back in a grip so strong that I knew even as I struggled that I wouldn't get free.

"Dad," I shouted, my eyes begged him to help me, but he just watched while they dragged me away.

The suit held his hand out and halted the guy who had me. He spoke with a threat inflected into his voice to my dad, "With this exchange, you can consider your debt paid in full. You stay away from him and me, and, you never step foot near the cage again…in any city. You won't like the consequences if you do." The man in the dark suit stepped in close to my dad, and threatened, "Am I clear?"

My dad's body quivered in fear and his eyes nearly bugged out of his head while the man threatened him.

Fear trickled from my belly and gradually spread throughout the more I listened to the conversation around me.

Until now, I had no idea just how serious my dad's gambling habit had become. I should have though. But surely he wasn't giving me over to the men to settle his debt. Was he? What did they want with me?

What… No!

The hold on me tightened as I started to struggle. The man behind me wasn't like the others. He was big and strong, and wore jeans and shirt as opposed to the others in suits. His scent was trouble, and even though I continued to struggle, I knew that he wouldn't release me.

My heart pounded as sweat ran down my face, mingling with the tears I couldn't control as my situation sank into my brain.

My dad, who I loved, who I thought loved me, had sold me in exchange for his gambling debt to be wiped clean. How could he do that?

My dad glanced at me one last time, pain in his eyes, before he turned and ran down the alley.

The man behind, tugged me toward a black SUV, but I struggled and tried to dig in my heels, my eyes still on my dad as he ran and left me with these assholes.

At the SUV, another man tried to grab my legs, but I kicked out and heard him curse as my booted foot slammed into the man's jaw.

"Hold that fucker," the man growled, grabbing me around the neck while more hands held me down.

My vision started to dim but then the man in charge forcibly removed the hands. "I don't want the fucker dead." He stepped back straightening his jacket. "Get him in the truck. *Now*."

No way!

In a last ditched effort to get away, I yelled, "*Dad! Help me!*"

My dad paused.

They all did.

Then my dad took one step toward me…hesitated. A bullet hissed from beside me—a silencer muffled the sound—and I watched as my dad disappeared around the corner seconds before I saw brick from the building fly off.

He did it!

He left me!

"I'm not going with you," I raged against everything. The fact of what my dad had done, the restraints holding my wrists, the hands gripping me. I struck out, blindly, as I struggled and kicked. My teeth sank into the soft flesh of the hand covering my mouth and I felt a moment of triumph as the man cursed in pain. Seconds later, the triumph was gone as the man's fist flew into my face. I felt the pain blossom, starting on my nose as my mouth filled with the metallic taste of blood. The pain ricocheted through me as I turned my head to the side and spat out blood. It felt like my jaw was on fire while I breathed through the pain.

I sucked in a breath to fight harder but my body tensed as fingers dug into my cheeks as a hand clamped around my face. The man in charge leaned forward, his eyes burning with anger as he loomed over me. "You're mine now lad. You're going to become my fighting machine. No more fucking nursemaids. I'm going to make you a man, and you're going to make me money to pay off your father's debt."

I couldn't talk with the hand clamped around me, but I memorized the man's face, and made sure that I would never forget it.

That close to me I noticed the scar to the right side of his face that ran a good few inches. I thought that he was an American at first, but now I wasn't sure. Something else was in him, and his accent, one I couldn't place, slipped with his anger.

I hoped that when I woke up in the morning the memory of tonight would still be there. Because one day, when I was a man—stronger—I was going to get even with everyone involved…including my dad, the one person I always thought would be there to love and support me—the one person who was supposed to protect me from evil.

How wrong was I?

EVIE (10 YEARS AGO)

WHILE MY MOM AND dad were partying with friends, and supporters of my father, I was on the sidelines trying to pretend my life didn't suck. I'd tried to fake a headache so I'd be allowed to stay home but it hadn't worked. I'd been told to sit and sip water regardless as to how late it had gotten.

I was twelve years old and hated that my father had just been elected as a state senator. My mother told me that I was selfish for thinking about myself all the time; that I should be more supportive.

How could I be more supportive when the new job meant my father would be away from home even more than he already had been? I really didn't see me wanting my dad at home as being selfish. I loved him, and missed him when he wasn't home.

But now, he would be gone more and school would be even harder to deal with. The other kids loved to make fun of me because of my family and my father's ambition.

I wanted to be part of a normal family. I couldn't even remember the last time we all ate around the table at the same time. I would only have my dad for family vacations now. He'd promised more but I knew that wouldn't happen. He loved his work, and really I should stop being ungrateful because I had everything I would ever want... apart from the one thing I *really* wanted...my father home.

My one best friend, Millie, was the only one who truly knew my fears, and she was the only person to know how much I hated my life.

Over the past few months I'd spent so much time at Millie's house that it felt like my second home. I loved being there. Her father was larger than life and, although he'd scared me at first, I'd finally gotten used to him.

My mother still tried to keep me apart from Millie when she wasn't lost in a world of her own making, and actually paid more attention as to what I was up to.

Like now.

I sighed as I spotted her walking toward me with a sour expression on her face, as though she'd eaten a lemon. It soon changed to a smile when Mrs. Grant appeared to her right.

Mom certainly had something on her mind though because her path continued toward me. I hated being center of attention, which she knew so I hoped that I wasn't expected on stage or anything while my father made his speech, even though I knew I wouldn't get away without.

"Evie dear." Mom took the cup of water from my hand and tugged me up. "Straighten your dress. Your father is about to make his speech and we both need to be at his side to show our support." And then she had to go and ruin it all. "We'll be on the front page of the newspaper tomorrow."

My heart sank and I wanted to run. I would have except her grip around my wrist tightened…almost to the point of being painful.

"Just be pleasant for the rest of the night, and," her lips twisted with annoyance, "I'll let you go on the trip with Millie and her family."

While her words sunk into my shocked brain, I let her lead me across the room to where my father stood with his team.

Mom knew how to get her way but I didn't for one

minute believe she'd just thought about that to get me to do their bidding. She'd have something else up her sleeve and need me out of the way so that she didn't have a child to supervise. I wasn't about to complain because I wanted to go to Chicago with Millie more than anything. When I'd brought it up to Mom, she'd scoffed at the idea because she considered Millie's family beneath her. I couldn't see why she couldn't treat everyone the same.

"Smile," she hissed between her teeth.

And like the world's most lifelike puppet, I did exactly what she wanted. My smile was full of love and support as we greeted Father.

"There she is." His smile was real as he enclosed me in his warm embrace and I felt a pang of guilt that mine wasn't. "My princess," he whispered against my ear before he kissed the top of my head.

CHAPTER ONE

STRYKER (PRESENT DAY)

"WHO'S THE BEST?" COACH yelled into my ear causing my head to pound as hard as I punched the bag in front of me.

Instead of replying to the old bastard, I grunted and took all my anger and hatred out on the bag. Sweat glistened on my skin with the furious pace I'd set...the one that I'd been doing since seven that morning...the one that I'd usually still be doing at seven in the evening but not today.

Tonight I had a fight.

Thud. Thud. Thud. Kick.

Each strike pushed a worry away from my mind and reminded my body that I was ready. I'd have to work hard during the fight but I'd win. My stamina would hold longer than any opponents they placed me against.

I had no life outside of the gym or the East Coast Martial Art Fighters Club (ECMAFC), and I hadn't since I was fourteen. It had been beaten into me over and over again that I could be the best if I accepted my fate.

Thud. Thud. Thud. Kick.

Beaten down, I took it, and now, those same money hungry fuckers wanted even more out of me...to throw a fight.

Not once in my fighting career had I thrown a fight, and regardless of what they wanted, I planned on winning. It was my name that would be talked about, not theirs.

My one time dream had been to be a fighter so I could share something with my dad. They took my life and made sure I accomplished the first. The second would never happen.

At twenty-four, I was so fucking tired of them, the life, and every damn thing.

I wanted a life...

A family...

I learned at an early age that opening my mouth could cause a whole lot of trouble. So silent I stayed—most of the time. Which had always pissed the men in their ivory fucking towers off because I refused to talk to the media about upcoming or past fights. What the press really wanted to know was about me—where I came from, who my family were, and, most of all, they wanted to know my true identity. Scoop of the century for them would be to discover the *real* name of *Stryker*.

As I glanced at Coach, who hovered in my peripheral vision, I was so fucking pissed with him and everyone else. I always had been but nothing like I was now. If Coach weren't so fucking old, I'd have knocked him down years ago.

He knew it as well.

Sucking in a breath through my nose, I let it out slowly as I paced my hits to my breath but it didn't work. Each blow filled me with anger and I hit harder…faster. So they thought that by telling me to throw a fight, I would with no questions asked. They could think again.

The fuck who had decided the loss was going to discover that I didn't always do as they ordered. And the pissant who'd decided they needed a fight throwing had been too fucking scared to come and tell me to my face.

Hiding behind Coach.

Well fuck him!

With one final punch, the bag came loose and flew into the wall before it dropped to the floor with a heavy thud, narrowly missing Coach.

The only sound was my heavy breathing, as I clenched my fists to lose the anger that still held me. I screwed my eyes closed, trying to breathe before the headache really knocked me on my ass.

In…two…three…and out.

I felt my heart rate gradually slow. I refused to let my anger continue to consume me. They had me on a fucking leash and instead of fighting my way out, I let them keep it around my fucking neck.

"You got it outta your system?" Coach asked, unmoved from where he'd been watching me beat the shit out of the bag. "Because you need to take a break before the fight."

I turned away and slung a towel around my neck before wiping the sweat from my face and out of my eyes. The water Coach passed me felt good going down my throat, and I drank another…ignoring the eyes that were on me. Most guys in the gym gave me a wide berth, but they still watched me…waiting for that weakness to exploit. I hated them…this constant power struggle. I crushed the empty bottle in my hands and tossed it into the trash. I needed something…I needed more.

I'd never admit that to anyone because then, they'd have more of a hold over me. There was one guy at the gym who would always bring his girl with him. She'd sit on the sidelines and watch while her guy worked out. I'd watched them, and the way she looked at her guy made me crave to have someone look at me that way.

One thing I'd always refused from them had been women. They'd brought them to me since I was seventeen. That first time, the woman had stripped naked, and I'd briefly gawked at her like any adolescent boy would. Her big tits and bare pussy had caused my dick to punch up in the air before I'd turned my head away. She'd known and had moved into my line of sight before starting to play with her tits and finger herself. I'd come in my sweats; embarrassed as fuck.

After that first time, I'd switched off and had refused to participate. But then I'd become the man that I am today; older, wiser, full of ripped muscle that they'd found intimidating. They'd stopped for a time, but then it started again when I won fights. Won them money.

It was my reward.

I'd be lying if I said I hadn't been tempted. So damn tempted to wet my dick, but I hadn't. Ever. My hand had had so much use over the years, I was surprised I still had the strength to punch…or that my dick hadn't fallen off. But, no fucking way was I going to fuck a whore. I certainly never met anyone else, but I dreamt and kept my one and only longing to myself. The longing was my weakness and, in part, I dreaded the day, if ever, that I gave my heart to anyone because then, they'd have the biggest hold over me that they'd ever had.

I needed to run...

The words popped into my head the same as they always did at unexpected times.

If I listened and acted then they'd come after me. They were the only ones to know my real name. They knew everything about me, and even watched every fucking dollar that was spent for my keep, which wasn't much. In fact, during my whole fighting career, the most I'd insisted be spent and refused to back down from was on my apartment. I'd always dreamed of living high, where I could look out over the city at night, at the sun setting and rising. I'd wanted to watch how the heat would rise during the morning, until it was at its fullest strength around noon. And I had that. I could sit all day on my balcony and just dream of freedom.

I'd be laughed at by outsiders if they knew how much of my life was controlled by others and the reason why. Considering my strength and ability that I now had, I sometimes wondered why I hadn't fought for my freedom from their clutches. They'd given me the chance to live alone because I told them that I couldn't concentrate otherwise. They'd believed me, but I was watched.

You know why you haven't run though...they hold you under the threat of kidnapping another boy to replace you if you leave.

I'd been through hell over the years, and I'd never wish that hell on anyone else.

Since the night my life changed, I'd never seen the suit again, although I had the feeling that he was the one running the show. I would find him one day. There was no question about that. When I did, it would be his turn to pray.

"Fuck!"

I was supposed to be calming down, but I needed the anger for the ring in a few hours.

Coach jumped at my angry cursing, and when I glanced at him he rubbed the back of his neck. A sure sign he was agitated. "I'm sorry, Stryker." He glanced at his bright green sneakers before he shook his head, and gave me his back. "I'm calling it. Go home and relax for a bit before you're picked up."

Go home and relax.

What a joke.

I was supposed to be a machine. I was no longer the sniveling boy too afraid to ignore the demands on me. After the initial beating, I did everything. I let them lead me by the fucking balls, and still did. Sometimes I think death would have been the better option to have taken when they'd given me the choice.

But go home and relax—as if that was an option.

Heading toward the showers, I thought of the one place where I wasn't known. It was difficult to hide my size, but with a beanie pulled low I could sit in a dark corner while I watched the world around me. I wanted that world…a life away from the ring. I'd been going there for a few weeks, but it had become the only place that I could really think. It was the only place I'd ever managed to disappear and not been found until I was ready to be.

The small bar was crowded on the weekends, and where I would normally shy away from crowded areas, I relished being at the bar. No one bothered me there, not even the ladies, which was fine with me. I may have started craving the soft touch of a woman, but I didn't want anyone right now. No way would I give *them* the opportunity to use someone else against me.

Assholes!

The lot of them.

Even hours later in the locker room at the arena, I felt my anger simmering.

The hum of the fans that filled the arena reached me, and the noise helped my concentration. It was a sound so familiar and reassuring that I'd started to crave it a few years ago. It made me feel like I could accomplish anything with my fans…that crowd…behind me.

Coach had already taped my hands and held my gloves in his. I wouldn't put my gloves on until the last minute before entering the ring.

Ring, cage, it didn't matter to me which I fought in because I was a cocky *sonofabitch* and always won.

Coach moved into my line of sight, which was his way of saying, "Let's go."

I stood and let Coach fasten the robe around me. I hated the feel of the silk against my skin, but the size of it swallowed me in fabric. It kept my eyes focused on the ground as I moved down the tunnel, past the fans, until I was at my corner.

Coach shoved my gloves on and held my gaze. "You've got this, Stryker. You win and show those assholes."

I knew I had this, just like I'd known at every fight. I also knew that I'd win regardless of what they wanted.

Climbing into the ring, I shoved the hood free and ignored my opponent. They hated to be ignored, which made the fight more difficult. I'd still win, but I'd feel like

I'd won fairly, instead of being pissed around by an opponent who was scared shitless of me.

Coach grabbed the robe from around me as I took in all the shouting and frenzy that surrounded these fights.

I slowly started to turn and stared out at the crowd, the fans…and felt like my stomach had dropped to my toes.

All I saw were a pair of emerald colored eyes alight with passion. Heat pulsed in them and I found myself taking a step toward her before I caught myself…my hands itched to keep moving toward those eyes but I fought the urge.

Her gaze burned into me and I felt that craving again… for something I couldn't have and the bitterness was like oil on the flame of my anger.

I'd win tonight.

Not for me.

Not for them.

But for the beauty with the emerald eyes.

EVIE

I SAT WITH A bottle of warm water in my hand, surrounded with people who I was supposed to call friends. I didn't know them. Well, not really. My fiancé, Patrick, knew them, but me, not so much. I'd tried so hard to join in with their conversation, but they were really all a group that didn't want me included. Patrick laughed when I told him how I felt and commented that they didn't know how to hang with a senator's daughter. I'd found that damn weird and hadn't bothered again. My father might hob nob with the president, but I didn't.

Since we'd arrived for the fight, Patrick had ignored

me. I was stuck with a total stranger on one side, and one of *his* friends on the other. Patrick was at the end of the row, his head leaning toward another guy, Oliver, who he was deep in conversation with.

I knew that he ignored me because I'd badgered him about getting me a ticket for the fight when he'd rather keep me away. I'd pointed out that I needed to do research for the book I planned on writing. He'd laughed until he realized I was serious. That hadn't gone down too well with me.

I should have gotten myself a ticket and gotten my best friend, Millie to tag along with me, but I knew Patrick went to all the fights so he'd have seen me in the crowd. It would have been easy for him to spot me as my red hair stuck out like a sore thumb.

So, anyway, here I was, effectively surrounded by strangers, waiting for two guys to come out and kick the hell out of each other…all for research.

The crowd hummed with a restless energy that was hard to ignore. I felt it pulsing inside of me and then the hum stopped as the lights went out and a hush fell over the arena.

My belly quivered with nervous energy.

A booming voice crackled over the sound system as they announced the first fighter, Damien "Rockman" Kelly. The crowd grew rabid as they booed their displeasure.

My heart started to pound and my ears buzzed as blood rushed around my head. I wasn't sure if it was through fear or excitement as an air of danger spread throughout the place.

And then, I was sure my heart stopped altogether as "Stryker" appeared following his announcement.

I couldn't see him clearly because he kept his head dipped and he was wrapped in a long black robe. So my reaction to him was odd to say the least.

My seat was close to his corner and I had no trouble seeing him as he prepared to climb into the ring.

He towered over the other men by inches, and when he removed the hood, his unruly black hair gleamed in the lights. The crowd, on hearing his name went wild but it was nothing compared to the cacophony that erupted when he climbed into the ring. But I was frozen in my seat as the crowd cheered and writhed around me in their excitement.

Muscles rippled under his silk robe, quickening my pulse, and when he shucked the robe, I was sure I whimpered out loud. His stance emphasized the force of his thighs and the slimness of his hips.

His whole body rippled with tension as he slowly turned in a circle to greet his fans. Facing his corner, he stood there, devilishly handsome.

My eyes refused to leave his beautiful face. The set of his chin suggested a stubborn streak and his lips looked firm but sensual. His dark eyes didn't miss anything and when they met my unwavering gaze, my heart stopped altogether. He carried on past me, but, seconds later, his gaze returned to me and held.

I couldn't look away as my face heated with arousal, although it should have been embarrassment. Even when his coach spoke to him, I felt like he struggled to move his attention away from me. When he finally did, I felt bereft, sad even, though my eyes stayed on him.

And then it was like he had switched off in the ring.

Everything that had caught his attention was gone and he was focused solely on his opponent. I gasped as the bell rang and the two men closed the distance between them. His fists flew like lightening and I clung to my seat unable to tear my eyes from the bloody scene as the two men grappled around the ring. I wanted to stop it but a part of me wanted to watch as the excitement of the crowd beat through me.

I cried out when Stryker took a strong cross to his chin, his head reeling to the side before he planted his feet and swung back. The crack could be heard over the crowd and Stryker's opponent swayed on his feet before he toppled to the mat.

Throughout the fight he held my attention and when the announcer held his arm up in the air to state that he was the winner, Stryker's eyes scanned the crowd until he found mine.

Our gaze was only broken when Patrick stood in front of me. "Let's go." He took my arm and led me out of the arena, much to my disappointment.

I had so many questions but knew I couldn't ask them of Patrick. He kept glancing my way, but I refused to acknowledge him for now. My mind and body was in turmoil as I wondered about the larger than life fighter.

I certainly knew whom I would be researching when I was alone. First though, I'd have to sit through drinks with Patrick and his friends. I shuddered and stared longingly down the street at my escape. All I wanted was to be alone with my thoughts and I sighed as we headed into their favorite wine bar. For some reason, tonight's drink felt wrong being in this place with piano music softly playing as affluent men and women sat on the plush couches and chatted. After the violence of the fight, and with how raw I felt, loud music in a bar with others from the arena would have felt right.

Then again my head probably wouldn't have held up under that, because it now throbbed with just the piano music.

I rubbed at my brow and tried to catch Patrick's eye, but his back was toward me, which I was sure he'd done deliberately.

Sighing, I leaned back and watched the group around Patrick. He threw his head back and laughed at something someone said...clearly he was in his element. I, on the other hand, wasn't. It was a bone of contention between us and I was never as social as Patrick would like me to be with his friends. It always took a lot of persuading on his part to get me to go out as a group. I had no interest but I'd discovered that it was so much easier just agreeing. I mean it was only a few hours, and half the time I wasn't even sure Patrick wanted to be with them, or me.

Tonight had been different though as I'd practically begged to go to the fight. I'd never been included on fight nights before so I'd probably thrown a wrench into Patrick's usual plans.

With a heavy sigh, I glanced around and realized that although I was in the group, it was like I was on the outside looking in. At least that was how I felt...alone in a sea of people. What made me sad was that the one person I should be able to talk to, was the last person I wanted to.

I glanced at Patrick again and smiled when he acknowledged me, he didn't come over. My smile slipped. He knew that I wanted to leave, which was why he stalled by pretending to be interested in the conversation he was currently having. *The asshole.* He just didn't want to leave and possibly miss something.

I couldn't remember the last time he actually showed some concern for my welfare, and I knew that sounded self-centered, but it was true. We were supposed to be getting married in a few weeks and both of us had left the planning to our parents. More specifically my parents. And that right there told me we shouldn't be getting married, at least to each other.

It all started a month ago when I thought to hell with it and gave in to my mom's constant phone calls. I'd had enough and told her to do what she wanted and just send me a schedule so we'd know when to be where. What I'd really wanted to say was, "The weddings off." If only it had been that easy I could have moved on with my life. But the thought of ending things made me sad. I did care for Patrick but I wasn't in love with him…I wasn't sure if I ever was. I read and write about love all the time, but I'd never felt that all-consuming passion. The one that made me ache for a person or where I couldn't imagine life without him. I stared at Patrick. The problem was I could imagine my life without Patrick and most of the times, it looked a lot better than life with him.

Neither of us had used the 'love' word, which made me wonder why Patrick would ask me to marry him. We enjoyed each other's company, at least when we were alone. Once we added anyone else, especially his friends, it was like that familiarity we had just shut off. I always felt unwelcome even when they smiled and invited me to sit and chat with them.

His mother, Rosemarie, would make me feel welcome,

but it always felt 'strange' as though there was something that underlined our being together.

Millie had a lot to say about Patrick's parents, and she was the one holding me together because I felt close to shattering.

Patrick talked about our future whenever we were alone and he had it all planned out. How many children, what I would be doing when the babies came, what he wanted for his career, and even where we would live at each stage of our marriage. I would find myself close to hyperventilating when he went on…I didn't want my life planned right down to the minute. He never asked what I wanted, never even asked if I agreed with him. Everything was about his five-year plan and knowing how fucking anal he was, he wouldn't be willing to change them for anyone.

My mother loved Patrick, and she hadn't stopped telling me what a catch he was. The only reason she thought that was because she was thinking about grandchildren and how handsome or beautiful they'd turn out because of Patrick's good fortune in the look's department.

I just wished my life was so much simpler. No private education, no family money, no mother wanting her daughter married off to supply her with grandchildren. My biggest wish as a child had always been for my dad to work a nine to five job and be home in the evenings and on the weekends. I would have traded all the wealth and privilege I'd had as a child for my dad.

My wishes never came true.

"Bunch of assholes."

Momentarily startled, a grin spread slowly across my face at the sound of my best friend's voice in my ear.

Spinning around, I wrapped her up in a hug. It was the first time I'd seen her in three weeks, and that was three weeks too long. She was the only person alive who understood me, and made me smile these days.

Millie was a few inches shorter than me with ash-blonde hair clustered into short curls around a heart-shaped face. Her hourglass figure with a slim waist and curvy hips usually had guys drooling.

"What are you doing here?" I placed my unwanted drink on a table, ignoring the glances from Patrick's friends. They could think what they wanted, which they'd do anyway.

"Thought I'd rescue you now that I'm back in town." She grinned.

I took hold of Millie's hand and dragged her with me to the back of the bar as a sigh hovered on my lips. The wine bar was a favorite with lawyers and businessmen—a place where they could do business and spend company money on entertaining.

It might make it into one of my books, but that was about it. A small bar across town had my heart. The floor plan was tiny and, on weekends, there was hardly any room to move let alone breathe as the music blared through the place. But the food was amazing, and unexpected for a hole in the wall place. To me it was the best place in the world. The one place I felt at home whenever I visited. Julio, the owner, was always welcoming and had a ready smile for anyone who stepped through the doors.

I often spend the afternoon there with my laptop in front of me while I worked away on my next novel.

If only I had the courage to put my writing out there. It just got tiring being me all the time—the senator's daughter; prim and always smiling for the camera...always pretending to be perfectly put together. The truth was I had a wild streak deep inside and it was fighting to break free.

I glanced back at Patrick and frowned. He kept me controlled to a certain degree and I allowed it. It was easier. But he'd changed. He wasn't the carefree guy I'd started dating. He'd become more serious and since he started wearing suits for work, he'd acted differently toward his outlook, and me.

I felt like I was drowning, and sinking deeper into a life I didn't want. I wanted to be free to enjoy the things I liked instead of the things he liked—wanted to be free to pursue my passions instead of presenting the front of perfect daughter for my dad's constituents. It wasn't only that because in the beginning Patrick had been charming and we'd had a satisfying relationship, although he hadn't touched me that often. But now, it felt more like a chore for him, and I guess that was how I felt. Like I was with him, he was my fiancée so he had the right to want me the way he did, and when.

I shouldn't feel like that.

"You need to pay attention," Millie snapped her fingers in front of my face, an angry frown on hers. "We need to do something to get you out of this whole engagement farce."

I blinked a few times, and watched my friend as she waved her hands around in front of my face. It was too loud to catch what she went on about, but I could guess.

Millie had never liked Patrick and thought he was only looking for a way in with my father. Their feelings were mutual though because Patrick couldn't stand Millie. She found him too controlling, and he found her too clingy.

He'd tried to end our friendship a few times and strangely, he'd sounded a lot like my mother as he went on about family connections and public image. But I'd ignored him. Millie was the sister I'd never had, and it would be a cold day in hell when I gave her up for anyone.

"Thank fuck." Millie let out an exaggerated loud sigh when the music finished. "My ears hurt."

"Do you want to leave?"

She looked stunned for a moment and then grinned. Taking my hand, she dragged me down the hall at the back, and didn't stop until we were outside, down the back alley, and on the sidewalk haling a cab.

"Where are we going?" I stumbled into the cab when she shoved me on the ass. I landed sprawled on the seat as she fell on top of me, giving the driver an address.

He shot off while we untangled our limbs. "What was that about? We're not five anymore."

"I didn't want us to be seen." Millie straightened her top before she flashed a boob.

"Okay."

"I can't believe you did that."

"Did what?" As far as I was aware, I hadn't done anything other than leave in a cab with her without letting anyone know.

Crap!

Trouble was going to stem from this.

I quickly grabbed my cell and shot Patrick a text that I'd call him tomorrow.

Steam would probably come out of his ears when he read my message. So I turned my cell on to vibrate and shoved it to the bottom of my purse. The last thing I wanted was for him to ruin my evening with Millie.

"You free now?"

"For a while." I smiled and felt like a heavy burden had lifted from my chest. "I'm so glad you found me tonight. A surprise, but an amazing one."

"No way was I going to stay out of town when it's our twentieth anniversary of the first time we met." She smiled but it didn't reach her eyes. "I'm worried about you, which is why I wanted you to myself."

I raised a brow.

"Okay," she grinned, "perhaps I always want you to myself, but seriously, this time is different."

As we passed through town, I glanced at her. "Where are we going?"

"My new place. No one has the address."

"Oh." I liked that idea. In fact, I loved that idea. "So no one is likely to come knocking for me."

"Exactly." She grinned and was probably delighted with herself.

"Millie," I started, "you didn't move because of me, did you?"

"My lease was up and, instead of renewing, I found somewhere else. I think that I did good keeping it to myself."

I chuckled. "You did."

Millie wasn't known for her patience, and usually couldn't keep something to herself for long unless it had something to do with me. In that regard, she always kept her lips sealed.

"Come on. We're here." Millie took my arm and pulled me from the cab after she'd paid the fare. She was practically dancing in excitement. "I can't wait for you to see my new place. Best decision I've made in a long time."

Five minutes later, I stood at the floor to ceiling window of Millie's new apartment. She was on the nineteenth floor and the view over Central Park was stunning. I hadn't realized we were so close to the park because my head had been elsewhere but the apartment was worth it just for the location alone.

The lights around the park shone brightly, and looking down there was a large brass band that was obviously playing as people walked by. I'd love to be down there listening, and then afterwards a hot chocolate with whipped cream, or even to sip the drink while listening.

My mouth watered and I longed for that. Patrick wouldn't be able to stand still long enough to enjoy and appreciate any of it though.

Would Stryker?

"About this research that you want to do," Millie started, "I think you need a sidekick."

I turned and faced her, forcing my longing to the back of my mind—something that I was used to doing.

Millie sprawled on one of her black leather sofas, her shoes kicked off and her blue eyes on me.

"I wasn't planning on going without you. I'm too shy to go into a gym alone," I admitted. "But I do need to tell you about tonight." Her brow rose, her curiosity piqued.

The last email we'd exchanged, I'd mentioned about needing to do some research around the Club for my next book. The idea had indirectly come from Patrick who thought my writing was a waste of time. His family owned the gym for the New York-East Coast Martial Arts Fighters Club. No bystanders allowed. Current or future fighters only. From what I'd heard, it was tough to get picked to be part of the team.

I'd never been to the gym or to a fight before tonight, and all that was changing.

I chewed on my lip and dropped down at the side of Millie's hip. "I went to a fight tonight with Patrick…and my heart stopped." I shook my head and gazed out of the window. "I'm not sure how I know this but he noticed me…the fighter that is. But only after I'd noticed him." I turned back to Millie and grabbed her hands. "Just one look had me aching, but something about him made me want to wrap my arms around him and never let go."

Millie stared at me, surprise clear in her eyes. "Um, wow."

"Just wow?"

"I'm not sure what to say. I don't remember you ever reacting to a man like that before."

"I know. I'm going to research him when I get home. Maybe have him as the main character in my book." I inhaled and went for it. "Once I have my story written, will you read it?"

She screamed. "Oh my God! You're seriously going to let me read your book?" She jumped up and tugged me into her arms. "Really? Promise me."

I grinned at her enthusiasm. "It won't be easy for me, but yes. I want you to be the first one to read it but there is a condition to you reading it."

"Figures." She continued to grin.

"You have to give me honest feedback. No, this is really good, awesome, fabulous. I want the truth regardless of what that is. I love you Millie, and that won't change if you hate my book. But you have to be honest because you won't help me as a writer if you're not."

"I hear you." She jumped up and danced in front of

me. "This calls for a celebration."

I laughed, warm happiness spreading through my body and I realized it was the first time I'd felt it in a long time. "I love you, Millie."

She stopped her dancing, her smile slipped as she really looked at me. Dropping to her knees, she took my hands into hers and held tight. "You're scaring me."

I shook my head. "There's nothing wrong," I paused, "well, nothing out of the normal for me. I just wanted you to know how much I appreciate you."

"Oh, Evie. You're my best friend. I'd be lost without you." Clambering back to her feet, she smiled. "Now, let's get rid of all the gloom and think about all those huge, sweaty men that we're going to meet at the gym...maybe *your* fighter will be there. Oh, we need wine for this."

She ran off to the kitchen while I thought about the fighters at the gym. I'd done as much research as I could from the internet and would probably recognize some of the fighters if we came across them. They all looked frightening to me with their height and strength, which gave me second thoughts about researching them...at least, until Patrick had arrived in a foul mood. He'd been pissed about something and he'd taken his frustration out on me with his verbal nit picking at everything I should and shouldn't do. I'd then decided that I'd go for it and no more hiding behind my laptop too scared to put my work out there.

In the past I'd taken more knocks than I should have for my twenty-two years. People could be evil, which was why I'd held off from opening myself up to even more criticism.

This time, however, I was more determined than ever to do something with my life.

CHAPTER TWO

STRYKER

"BEAUTY SLEEPS OVER," THE man whose voice grated on my nerves hollered.

The loud voice didn't shock me, and when I crashed last night after the fight, my dreams were teased by *my* red-haired, emerald-eyed woman. I'd imagined her touch on my skin, with my hands tangled in the glorious red locks of hair that I'd caught a glimpse of as she'd left. Just the image left me rock hard and uncomfortable as I lay unsatisfied on my stomach.

I knew that *he'd* visit me today because I'd disappeared for two hours last night. The men who watched me were lax and gave me a bit of freedom, and usually management wouldn't find out. But I guess disappearing right after a fight I was supposed to throw wasn't the wisest thing I'd done.

I never reacted to him. Honestly, I'd only ever spoken to the ass once or twice, but I stayed silent as I watched him from between my narrowed lids. I did this because I knew my silence unnerved him, and the others. They liked to act tough, but I made them nervous and after the shit I'd put up with from the lot of them over the years, I relished the fear they had whenever I met their gaze head on.

It was Sunday, which meant no training, although, I usually ignored the day of rest everyone else seemed to abide by and clocked hours at the gym. Except today, I'd probably shock the lot of them when I refused to budge. I was going to have the day to myself at my apartment. I wasn't going to do anything but lounge around and read, and think of her.

There was no television or internet in the apartment. I didn't own a cell, and only had a landline for incoming calls. It was a quiet existence, except for my life in the gym.

I gladly accepted it.

A glance through one eye toward the window told me it was a beautiful day in New York, which meant I could sit outside—my one luxury.

They spied on me from room to room except the bathroom and bedroom—the only two rooms without a way to the outside.

The living room had large floor to ceiling sliding glass doors, a large patio on the opposite side, which was my sanctuary. The access to outside and the view were two of the reasons I wanted it. The apartment could have been a hovel and I'd have insisted they bought it.

If I wanted to risk my life, then I could try and leap over to the balcony across and to the left. Chances were that I'd miss because it was just a bit too far over, even with dropping a floor. They still had a camera out here though.

The invasion of privacy was more irritating than annoying. I didn't really have any privacy to hide, and what I did need privacy for, I took care of in the shower. I wasn't exactly used to the invasion but I could ignore the cameras most of the time…life was what it was.

I rolled over to my back, now that the tension at my hips had deflated, and gazed up at the white ceiling while I kept him in my line of sight. He was new to the show. I hadn't yet figured out his position within the organization but I would. I always did.

"When you're done ignoring me," the asshole loomed over me from the side of the bed, "I need to talk to you about something."

"Training?" That's all everyone wanted to talk about… training or the fight. I wasn't going to be the first one to mention that I'd ignored them last night because I'd won.

"No." He appeared pissed as he turned abruptly and walked out of my bedroom.

I rose up on my elbows to see if he was still there or if he'd headed out.

"I'm waiting."

Fuck! I wasn't so lucky.

Why couldn't the fucker go and annoy someone else.

I kicked off the cover and strolled to the bathroom. While I took a leak, I glanced at myself in the mirror. I did that every morning and I didn't know why. I didn't pay attention to my features, which had changed a lot over the years. At one time, I looked like my father, but that soon passed. I'd grown harder, tougher than him and sometimes, if I looked hard enough, I could see some part of him in my eyes or the slash of my mouth but then it would be gone…I was not my father.

Outside of those few short seconds, my father wasn't someone I thought about, at least, I tried not to. He would pop into my head when I least expected him to.

I'd never been able to accept that he willing handed me over to them. I just couldn't comprehend how he could do that. He said he loved me, but that had been a lie. You didn't willing do what he did. I never would, and a lot of people out there wouldn't either. It was just my fucking luck to be born to one of the low percentage of people who didn't give a damn.

Yanking my sweats up, I headed into my living room and straight to the kitchen. I pulled out a carton of milk, and drank straight from the carton.

Once I'd drunk a liter, I swiped my hand across my mouth and turned to face the stressed out figure of the man.

When he realized my attention was on him, he stopped his pacing and glared, his hand running through his hair.

This was the first time I'd seen him rattled.

"What's going on?"

"The boss knew you wouldn't throw the fight…you won him a lot." He smirked, and ran his hands through his hair.

Had that been some sort of test? I wouldn't know unless they decided to tell me.

"Fuck," he cursed. "I need you to be on your best behavior at the gym during the week."

I snarled. Was he serious? "I'm not five."

He ignored me. "I've arranged for my fiancée and her friend to have access to the gym. Research." He turned and looked out of the window before he met my gaze again. "She thinks she can write, and wants to write a fictional novel surrounding the Club. She can't write and I don't want her around you guys, but it's our wedding in only a few weeks so I want to keep her happy until that's over with."

I snickered to annoy him.

His eyes met mine and narrowed.

"You," he pointed his finger, "will not look at her, talk to her, or go near her. She's completely off limits. She's been told to stay away from the fighters, only to observe, especially you, you piece of shit."

My eyes narrowed as I watched him. He thought I wouldn't hit him because he had something to do with the boss, but he was wrong. I knew that he wasn't at the top so breaking his nose wouldn't hurt me. But it would make me feel a lot better.

He slowly made his way to the front door as I tracked him. He sweated beneath his suit and knew he had seconds before the venom of *Stryker* was unleashed on him.

The asshole.

As the door banged behind him, I ran to it and growled, hoping he'd shit himself with fright.

Amusement raced through me until I slumped against the door and slid to the floor.

I was interested in seeing what the pampered princess looked like. Would she be as put together as her fiancé, or would she be worse.

She wouldn't stand out like *my* girl did. My girl? Who the fuck was I kidding? She wasn't my girl, and probably never would be. I mean what were the chances of seeing her again. She'd been a mesmerizing presence in a crowd of hundreds. If I ever got the chance to have a girl, I sure as hell wouldn't talk about her like he did.

He obviously liked to humor his fiancée, but I couldn't help wonder what kind of books she wrote. I had a good collection of novels since I spent so much time alone when I wasn't at the gym or at a fight. Most of my collection was crime and thrillers, but there were also some paranormal romance books on my shelves. I bet the *asshole* had never even read any of his fiancée's books.

Asshole!

Today, I'd piss him off again, because I'd changed my mind about staying home.

A FEW HOURS LATER, I'd managed to sneak out again, but I knew it was only a matter of time before they discovered where I went.

I pushed the thought aside and, instead relished the afternoon crowd in the small bar. I loved it so much that it was a risk I was willing to take. Julio knew who I was and realized from the first that I liked to be anonymous while I was here. He'd always pour me a tall glass of milk during the day and a bottle of water in the evening. Right from the first, he'd told me only to pay when I lost a fight; otherwise my drinks were on him.

The bar was never busy on Sunday afternoons, until around five, which was why I'd decided to ditch my plans of being alone on my balcony for this place. I was still alone, but it just felt less lonely, as though I had a place where I belonged.

I would spend my time in a dark corner and watch

others come and go. They'd come in with friends, loved ones, maybe; it was a guessing game with me. When the nights were busy I'd guess who would hook up with whom.

I wasn't always right.

There wasn't anyone here right now to grab my attention, until I glanced toward the door.

My heart stopped as the light streaming through the open door followed her inside. She was a redhead, and her hair shined like liquid fire. She looked shy and unsure as she hesitated on the doorstep. Then Julio called out and her whole face lit up with delight at seeing the older man. I felt something hit me in the chest.

Ridiculous.

Then it hit me like a ton of bricks. It was the woman from last night and she was more beautiful than I remembered. My gaze swept over her body. Soft and delicate.

Julio tugged her close to where I was hiding in the dark, and offered her the table two over from mine. It gave me an unobserved view of the delectable woman. She removed her jacket and looked around, her eyes hovered on me before they moved away.

She knew someone sat where I did, but she had no idea who. I knew that my face was completely hidden, which was the reason why I'd chosen this particular seat.

With a glance over her shoulder toward me, she reached into her large purse and pulled out a laptop. I had no idea how to use one, but I'd seen others with them.

Once she'd set her work area up, and Julio had delivered her a tall glass of milk, she started to work.

She'd ordered milk.

Was that why Julio sat her near me? Because she ordered milk and we obviously came in alone.

The young woman was distracted so I used it to my advantage and really looked while I was unobserved; no Coach or guards watching my every move.

Her hair was a rich, glowing auburn with natural curls that tumbled carelessly down her back. The urge to bury my nose into the back of her neck and inhale her scent into my lungs was strong. The dream I'd had last night had been about the feel of her silken strands as they caressed over my body. Just remembering the dream, and having her so close, had my body twitching with tension; so much so that I shoved my hand into my jeans to rearrange my hard cock into a better position.

As I watched, her fingers stilled from the rapid speed on the keyboard, and then she tilted her head to the side. The shock of having those emerald green eyes locked onto mine when I knew she couldn't see me caused my blood to thicken and pulse with arousal.

I was completely enthralled with her. The smooth skin of her face glowed with pale gold undertones was highlighted by the freckles dusting her cheekbones and over the bridge of her nose. Like cinnamon sugar. My eyes focused on her full and rounded lips while the tip of her tongue snaked out to run along them. It was clearly a nervous habit.

She quickly turned back to her computer, but her fingers stayed lax, as though she was distracted and couldn't think.

Her curves made my mouth water. She wasn't skinny like the women that *they'd* tried to award me with, she was all woman. Her breasts and ass would easily fill my hands, and the more I thought about pounding into her, the more my dick twitched and throbbed for release.

My fists clenched on the table because I desperately wanted to drag her to the back of the bar and finish what she'd started by just sitting there.

What the fuck was I doing?

I had no right to watch her, or fantasize about her touch, or what I wanted to do to her. I just couldn't look away.

I eventually inhaled, and shook my head to try and clear the lust. It eased, but refused to leave.

God, I was losing it.

Why her? I'd never felt want or need as hard before.

All of a sudden, she jumped down from the seat, closed her laptop and shoved it back into her purse. She grabbed her jacket and the straps of her brown purse before she moved to the bar.

As she leaned over it to talk to Julio, the denim stretched over her curvy bottom, which put the vision of her doing just that with me behind her back in my head.

I silently moaned, and my erection leaped with excitement.

I needed a fucking cold shower!

How the hell was I supposed to deal with that? The whole emotion behind my want was ridiculous and scared the fuck out of me at the same time. Never before.

I'd craved someone to call mine but it was a faceless idea. Just something to look toward the future for, but there was something about the girl who was now leaving. My first thought was to follow her, but I'd probably terrify her with my size. Could I let her leave without knowing her name or how to see her again?

You don't have a choice...she might not want to see you again...it's dangerous to see her again...

"Fuck!"

I needed just one glimpse before I went back to my fucked up life.

Moving quickly, I punched through the doors and caught a leg disappearing inside a cab before the vehicle took off.

Disappointment settled inside of me as I stood on the sidewalk and watched her disappear out of my life. The sad fact was that she hadn't really been in it to begin with.

Sighing, I rubbed the back of my neck and turned.

Julio stood behind me.

He smiled. "She'll be back, my friend."

I stared after him as he disappeared back inside the bar.

What was wrong with me chasing after a girl? I'd never done anything like it before, never had the opportunity to do so before, and the need settled heavily on my chest.

The way my thoughts had gone would be dangerous if anyone even suspected the longing I had. Just to feel the tender touch of a woman.

Someone who *they* didn't bring me.

Someone who wasn't paid to be nice to me.

Someone who I'd only send away.

Just once I wanted to know what it would be like to have such innocence in my life.

My head thrown back, I breathed deeply and gazed up at the sky, angry at how my life had turned out.

Would I ever get the chance at a future that didn't involve fighting?

I sneered at the irony of it all. If you had asked me

when I was fourteen, all I'd wanted was to be a fighter so I could be one of those guys my dad idolized. I'd wanted to do that so I was close to him but that changed the moment he ran from that alley...the moment I realized I'd meant nothing to him.

When everything had first happened, I didn't believe that he would leave me like that. I thought he'd come back. Every time we were in public, I looked. Every time I entered the arena, I would look for him from under my hood. I'd keep my head down but my eyes searched for him. If I was honest, they still did. I have never stopped searching and I never would.

My father was warned away from the fights, but it's been years so why wouldn't he be back after all that time? I knew him, and he wouldn't have stayed away for long. He probably spent the years since I made my debut betting on me. Had he made a fortune off me while I paid off his debt with the bastard he'd given me to?

I still don't know the *fucker's* name but I've heard people call him the "Irishman" in fear. One day he would be mine, and he was going to tell me the full story of what went down ten years ago. His men had hinted that there was more to it than what I heard that night. I'd never figured out what the more was. But I would even if it took another ten years.

With my fists clenched, I pulled my hood low over my head so I wouldn't be recognized. I glanced up and down the street before I made my way down the sidewalk and back to hell.

EVIE

I SHOULDN'T REALLY BE here, but I couldn't go home when I felt so out of sorts. The feeling had suddenly hit me not long after I'd arrived at Julio's bar, and even as I let myself into Millie's apartment my heart still beat frantically in my chest.

That was twice in two days, not even twenty-four hours between. What the heck was going on with me? Millie would talk me around. To what, I had no clue. I basically needed her to tell me what an idiot I was being. She really was the most down to earth person that I knew and she was never afraid to tell me the truth.

"What the hell." I fell into Millie's apartment mid-thought when the door was yanked out of my hands.

"Are you okay?" Millie grabbed me seconds before she tugged me inside and slammed her door closed. "I thought you said you'd never need the security card I gave you to this place." She frowned.

"I didn't even think about that." I shrugged, placed my purse on the floor and tugged her over to the sofa. "Something really weird happened and…and I think I've finally lost it. I mean," I rushed on, "how many twenty-two year olds get freaked out during the day in a bar all because I felt eyes on me, as though the person wanted to eat me up."

Groaning, I dropped my head between my knees. "God, I feel strange. Not only was there the fighter from last night, but then today."

"You're not making any sense."

For the first time since I'd arrived, I raised my head and looked at Millie. She stood in front of me, bewilderment clear on her face. "That's not surprising because I can't make any sense out of it."

"You need to calm down and start at the beginning." Millie turned me around and pushed my shoulders until I was lying down. My head fell into her lap and her fingers began playing with my long hair. It was something that she'd done since we were kids, and it always had a soothing effect.

"I went to the small bar I love. It's the only place where I can breathe. Well, except for with you, but you know what I mean."

Millie frowned, which told me that she hadn't really known what I meant.

I couldn't stay down because I was too restless after being at Julio's place, and I needed more of something. I just didn't know what.

"Okay." I breathed in and out a few times before I felt calm enough to talk. "When I entered Julio's place, he greeted me as usual…but instead of sitting me at my regular table he took me further into the bar." I watched Millie frown, and asked, "You following."

She nodded.

"He seemed to look off into a darkened corner and when I glanced there, at first, I didn't see anyone, but then I felt eyes on me. As though someone was staring at me so hard they could see through me. I know I'm not making much sense, but when I turned, the shape of a large man was visible." I paced back and forth in front of her window.

"It sounds like you need to stay away from there."

"No, I want to go back."

"Evie, are you crazy? That guy might have problems. Who sits in the dark staring at women?"

She was right. Of course she was right.

I felt something though, even if I did run to Millie's.

For a few minute, as my hands had hovered over the keys of my laptop, I'd felt his loneliness reaching out to me. It had been familiar…as though I'd felt it before and I had when I'd been sitting in a crowded arena, watching the fighter last night.

Maybe because he felt it too.

All I'd seen of the stranger at the bar was from his waist up to his chest, and his arms, which had been long, leading to large hands. I'd wanted to see more, but I'd chickened out and ran as though my ass was on fire.

I'd go there again.

I had to.

The pull had been strong.

Nothing that strong could be left to the what if's.

Even the little voice in my head, reminding me that I was supposed to be getting married soon, did nothing to persuade me that it was a bad idea.

"He could be a murderer, or an ex con. Someone that you don't want to touch you." Millie looked serious about her suggestions when I glanced at her.

"I don't think he is." I dropped into the chair by the window.

"Oh my God!" Millie jumped up and kneeled in front of me, her hands grabbed mine and held tight. "Please tell me you'll stay away."

I bit my lip. I didn't want to lie to her. But really, I knew that I would go back to Julio's. It was my escape, my bit of solitude from everything about Patrick and the wedding. Except now, I had more of a reason to go back. I wanted to see who it was in that corner.

Julio would know. I had a feeling he purposely made me sit close to the mystery man.

"Evie, stop daydreaming and promise me you won't go back there."

"I'm not going to make a promise I know I'll break. I wish I could explain it to you, but I can't." I closed my eyes and prayed she didn't think I'd completely lost it when I admitted, "He made me throb, Millie."

Her eyes widened in surprise.

"I'm serious. Full-on, panty wetting throb. That's why I ran. The feeling came over me so quickly that it scared the hell out of me so I left. But God, I squirmed when I got into the cab and my heart thudded in my chest like it was going to explode. It was so raw…so primitive, and…and I need to feel it again."

Millie dropped to her bottom. "You've never been like this before. I don't know what to say or do. I'm the wild one. The one who usually runs to you with guy problems. This…this is weird."

"I know it is." We stayed quiet for a few minutes before I admitted, "Patrick's never wet my panties."

"What?" she choked out.

"Well, I mean," I felt a blush coat my cheeks, "obviously things worked but I mean instant wet panties didn't happen before today. I don't even know what this guy looked like. Just that I got the impression he was big."

"Big," she snickered.

"I only saw his chest and hands." I shoved her over, and giggled like a schoolgirl with her. "He was all heat, Millie."

She became serious. "You really are serious about wanting to see this guy?"

I nodded.

"I was afraid you'd say that." She clambered to her feet. "I think I need to be there next time. To keep you safe." She grinned.

I groaned. "Yes, Mom. But remember he's mine. I saw him first."

She rolled her eyes. "How old are we again?"

"Stop. I've been thinking since Patrick's arranged the gym thing for us, we could go tomorrow, and I thought we could work out while we're there."

"You're kidding right? You want to work out with all those hot, sweaty bodies around us?"

"Um."

"Evie, you won't even walk into a gym on your own, how are you going to get up the nerve to work out while they watch us make asses out of ourselves?"

"Ugh! As you put it that way, we'll just do the watching." I grinned.

I was just as susceptible to a hot, sweaty guy as the next person, engaged or not.

The 'engaged' part made my heart sink. I didn't want to be engaged, and wished with all my heart that I'd had the courage to refuse Patrick when he'd asked.

My own parents had said nothing. My mother had been overtaken with excitement that her only daughter was about to get married. My mom wanted grandchildren, so any husband would do.

Patrick really had been fun to begin with. He'd made me laugh and while he didn't excite me in the bedroom, the sex had been okay, I guess. But leading up to our engagement, I sensed that his mind was constantly elsewhere. He was abrupt with me and would tell me one thing and do another. I'd started to work up to telling him that we were over when he surprised me with a trip to the Florida Keys.

I'd still felt something was going on with him while we'd been there. He didn't seem like the same man I'd started dating.

"You're thinking about Patrick," Millie commented. "You always go brooding and have this look on your face as though you've swallowed something horrid."

"I'm not that desperate." I plopped down onto the sofa, kicked my ballerina shoes off and placed my feet onto the coffee table while I thought about what to say. "It's my fault that I'm in this mess, Millie. I could have said no, but I didn't."

"That ass asked you in front of a room full of people. He knew you'd say yes in a situation like that. He knows how you think, how you were trained to act in public, which means you have to change things up."

"How?" I turned to face Millie but her gaze was still fixed on her ceiling, a grin on her face. "You have to start doing the opposite to what he'd expect you to do."

I laughed. "I'm already doing that by going to his family's gym."

"How exactly did that go down with *dear* Patrick?"

Groaning, I closed my eyes and really hated remembering. Millie would also notice the blush that I could feel creeping into my face, but what I did left me queasy.

"You didn't?" She grabbed my arm. "Oh, Evie. You did?"

I sighed. "It's not like I haven't done it before, and it

was over quickly." And wasn't that the truth. "It got us into the gym."

As soon as I'd finished the blowjob, Patrick had zipped back up and told me he'd leave passes at the door for Millie and I. I'd felt cheap as he'd walked away, leaving me on my knees—like a whore instead of his fiancée.

CHAPTER THREE

STRYKER

SWEAT DRIPPED INTO MY eyes and my heart pounded with exertion. I gripped the rope in a loose hold while my feet alternated the landing as the rope turned under them. Coach would count when I first picked up the ropes, but he soon miscounted and gave up. The ropes and the bag were my usual choice of cardio and I could go for hours if I watched my pace.

It also gave me time to think, and remember.

The redheaded beauty had teased my dreams again. I'd woken hard and aching with my legs tangled in the sheets.

Her innocent face behind my lashes, my fist around my cock, and I'd spilled all over my chest within seconds.

Thump. Thump. Thump.

My feet continued to pound on the floor as the rope slapped against the mat in rhythm and my dick swelled in my briefs at the dream of her. I didn't know her name and we'd only been in the same room for mere minutes, but I craved something about her.

I knew I'd go back to Julio's place. No way would I be able to stay away knowing that she'd be back there. Numerous questions ran through my mind. Was she married? Have a boyfriend? Wanted a boyfriend?

I laughed which broke my concentration as I stumbled over the rope much to the shock of Coach, and my embarrassment.

"Fuck," I hissed under my breath. "I'm done with this," I added to cover my blunder. "Time for the bag."

The eyes of others in the gym were on me, they always were but they were interested in that small falter. Like sharks, they circled at the slightest hint of a weakness. I grimaced, they were wrong…they weren't sensing a weakness. The isolated location of my workout meant that there wouldn't be any socializing between the other fighters and me. They loved to keep me this way since there was less chance of me saying something I shouldn't to one of the others.

A quick scan around the gym told me that whatever attention I'd caused had been forgotten as the others continued with their own training.

I reached for the gloves, ignoring a speculative glance from Coach while I tried to get my concentration back. I'd never lost it before so it unnerved me that I'd lost it so easily with thoughts of the woman.

Shoving my hand into a glove, I tightened the strap and as I pulled on the other glove a hush fell over the gym.

My eyes met those of Coach before we both looked across the gym. The strap of the glove dropped from my mouth as my gaze fell on those of *my* redheaded beauty. She blinked, then focused her gaze on me, recognition, and then fire blazed from her gorgeous eyes.

She quickly turned away to her friend, and acted like she had tuned in to whatever Carter said to them.

Carter, otherwise known as Carter "The Rocket" Stone, was another fighter at the gym. He seemed friendly enough with the others and always keen to spar or offer advice. I couldn't help the slice of jealousy that hit me at the attention he showed her and her blonde friend.

While Carter showed her friend how to use a piece of equipment, *my* girl slyly glanced back in my direction and a light blush coated her delicate cheekbones when our gazes collided again.

The heaviness in my chest felt like a fist squeezed my heart while I struggled to stop staring.

Insane.

I took one step toward her, and had Coach step into my line of sight. He hid his amusement with a cough behind his hand. He coughed again. "Better look elsewhere, son." He shook his head. "The one you can't take your eyes from is Patrick's fiancée." He frowned. "Never known you to be attracted to a woman before, though."

I raised a brow and waited, knowing what was coming.

"Speculation is that you're gay," Coach added, under his breath.

I'd known that because I'd always rejected the whores who were brought to me. They thought I was gay because of it and would try to piss me off by talking about the whores not having the right equipment. I didn't give a shit what they thought.

"Hmm," Coach mumbled and ambled toward the bag.

I followed but not before I glanced at her. It was as though I had to know where she was at all times. Carter had her on the cross trainer, and the way her ass moved made my mouth water and my cock rock hard.

"What's her name?" The minute the words flew out of my mouth I wished them back when I saw the look on Coach's face.

Coach rubbed his brow, and quietly added, "Evangeline, but goes by Evie, and her friend is Millie. All I know is that they've been friends since they were kids. They're more like sisters." He glanced at them then back to me. "I'm not telling you, I'm begging you to keep your distance from her. I've heard that Patrick is a jealous prick, and you don't want to mess with him, or...never mind...hit the bag." He nodded toward it.

I watched Coach shuffle toward the bag, his shoulders slumped forward and he looked uncomfortable, which made me wonder what he'd been about to say when he switched direction to the bag.

But what the hell, my concentration had been shot to hell with talk of *Evie*. I now had a name to put with her beautiful face, and I'd give anything to be able to talk to her—to hear *my* own name on her lips.

As I steadied the bag in front of me, I cast one glance back at her and smiled to myself when I caught her eyes on me through the mirrored wall in front of where she worked out.

"*Stryker*," Coach growled. "Are you doing this to piss me off, or do you want Patrick involved because I'm telling you that will happen with his spies around here."

"Patrick won't do shit to me. He's a fucking pussy."

"The men who work for him won't have the same problem." Coach shook his head. "Get your mind back on training."

With one last glance at Evie, I froze. My dick hardened, pulsed, as she bent to pick up a bottle of water from the floor.

I squeezed my eyes closed to avoid the image of her on her hands and knees as I pounded into her. That didn't work because all it did was heighten my awareness of my woman.

Fuck!

Flexing my hands as much as the gloves allowed, I tried to breathe through my frustration, and hoped like hell the bag in front of me helped get rid of all the pent up need inside of me.

As my feet started to dance around the bag, I did small jabs with my fists to help loosen up my muscles that had become tense while my eyes had been focused elsewhere.

Shaking the image of Evie from my mind, for now, I started a fast and furious pace. The feel of the hard bag as my fist connected with it was familiar and sent me into the 'zone'. Everything was forgotten the more I pounded into the black leather. Eventually, my frustration disappeared and was replaced with loneliness.

It was my constant companion and, while in the gym, it allowed me to block every sound from my mind and concentrate on my task.

I needed to stay focused without anyone in my eyesight to cause a distraction.

Distraction for me would become a choice of life or death.

EVIE

AFTER MILLIE AND I had placed our food order with the server, I sat lost in my thoughts. They were filled with the fighter from the other night who I hadn't been able to take my eyes off at the gym. Stryker...and he had definitely struck not only that punching bag but something inside me. I tried to make a mental note of what I'd learned today but nothing came to mind. We'd been there so I could research my next book, but all I'd learned was how to work the cross trainer...and what fun it was to witness my friend melt into a puddle every time Carter had glanced her way. It had been cute.

"Instead of dreaming in silence," Millie nudged my arm, "please dream out loud so I get a thrill out of it as well."

I smirked, "I'd have thought you'd have your own dream to get a thrill out of."

Millie sighed, a sappy look on her face, which stayed until the server interrupted us with our drinks—water with ice and lemon for me, an orange juice for Millie.

"Did you notice his body?" Millie practically drooled into her drink. "I mean, he had me panting with just one glance in my direction. I'm sure he watched my ass when I was on the stepper thing."

"He did." With a straight face, I teased, "I'm sure I caught him adjusting himself when he turned away." I raised a brow and then started to laugh at the light blush that coated Millie's cheekbones.

My friend was all out there and no embarrassment, until you outright described how someone reacted to her.

Like now, she was flustered and had no clue how to handle my words. Instead of leaving her lost, I added, "Carter seemed really sweet, and I think you should try and talk to him more when we go back tomorrow."

"I don't know." Millie looked worried with a small frown across her brows. "I usually go for the classy suit guys, not someone as rough or hard as Carter." She sighed. After taking a long drink of her juice, she added, "He has an amazing body. I kept wanting to push his brown hair back from his forehead, which I'm sure he knew by the twinkle in his eyes."

"Oh, he twinkled." I let Millie ignore my comment while I remembered the other man to have a twinkle in his eyes. Even from across the gym I could see how focused on me he'd been. No one had ever looked at me the way that he did. It was as though he wanted to eat me for a snack and nothing or no one else would do.

His eyes had been so black; his large muscular body had been frozen in place while he'd watched me. His coach had tried to get his attention, but it had taken time. He'd glanced in my direction several times and I'd felt his gaze on me even when I didn't look. His slightly long dark hair was tousled from his workout and it stuck to his forehead as sweat coated his skin.

I'd felt a reaction to the man right down to the tip of my toes, and the more he'd stared, the more I'd felt a deep ache between my legs, which left my panties damp with desire for the stranger…or was he a stranger?

I took a long sip of my drink before I played with the straw, swirling it around the glass. Glancing up at Millie, I told her what I'd been thinking from the minute I met his gaze, "My reaction to having his eyes on me was the same as the night of the fight, and last night in the bar." I gave a mirthless laugh. "I'm going crazy, right?" I cast a glance at Millie and bit my lip. "Do you think the fighter and the bar guy are one and the same? That would explain my reaction. I don't want to think I've started getting aroused by every Tom, Dick, and Harry."

She laughed. "Tom, Dick, and Harry? Now you're just being weird. He could be the same guy. He's big and you said the bar guy was big." She snickered. "No pun intended."

Millie grasped my hand. "Look, I think he felt it too. Whatever is going on between the two of you, he couldn't take his eyes off you." She sounded worried, glanced around us, then confessed, "I mean his stare even turned me on and it wasn't directed at me."

The server interrupted to place our food on the table and after a quick glance at our joined hands, smirked, and left us alone.

Rolling her eyes, Millie chuckled, and started to eat while my stomach felt twisted in knots.

I picked my fork up and started to slowly eat, but my mind was in turmoil.

I'd always considered myself a one-man woman, so why couldn't I stop thinking about the fighter who'd looked isolated from the others in the gym. My mind should be on my fiancée, but now, when I thought about him, I felt nervous.

Since my first few dates with Patrick, I'd known that we were wrong for each other, or at least he was wrong for me. Except the more I tried to back away, the more he pushed forward. Dates had become long term commitments, which had become engagements and plans for the future.

It had just been easier to go along with what he wanted while I'd secretly been cursing him. That was wrong and I needed to get some balls and stand up for what I wanted for a change, which unfortunately wasn't Patrick.

"Get rid of Patrick."

Startled at Millie's words, I paused with my fork halfway to my mouth and stared at her. "What? Are you a mind reader now?"

She smirked and laughed. "Nope." Her fork waved through the air, salad flew across the table, which she ignored. "You get that look on your face when you're thinking about Pat*prick*…the screwed up look as though you've just bitten into a lemon."

"I don't—"

"Yes, you do."

I cast my eyes down to look at my plate. I'd hardly eaten anything while I was lost in my thoughts but I knew that she was probably right. "The engagement has been in the national newspapers because of my father. What will it do to his reputation if I break off the engagement? He won't be happy." I gave up trying to eat and placed my fork down onto the plate.

My father's career was important to him, to my mother, and to me. Maybe not completely but I'd been trained to think of the campaign and my dad's career before anything else. He loved his job as a state senator in Washington and he always had. At times, I think he loved it more than he loved his family. He was born to be a politician, after all. But any sign of scandal—like a failed engagement—was a sign of weakness and blood in the water drew sharks. My dad had gained some enemies along the way because he would always fight for the underdog and I knew they would use the scandal as a way to hurt his reelection.

I sighed. The last thing I wanted to do was disappoint him, which I'd do if I called everything off at such short notice. If I was honest though, Patrick's father, Declan, was the one I feared the most.

"You know what I think?" Millie started. "I think you need to visit your father in DC, tell him how unhappy you are and explain that you can't go through with the wedding. Tell him that you feel everyone has pressured you into it when it's not what you want. Admit to him that you don't love Patrick." She finished the last of her salad and before she'd finished chewing, pointed her fork at me. "You're daddy's girl and he'll understand more than your mother. I know all she wants is a baby in the family. Probably to bring your father into the headlines, again."

"I'll think about it." I smiled to reassure my friend and sighed when I'd succeeded as Millie buried her nose into the strawberries and cream that had been placed in front of her. I chuckled because we'd just worked out at the gym and she was eating fresh thick cream, and didn't bat an eye.

We both had good metabolisms, which was good considering we both loved our food. Apart from doing research at the gym, I wanted to get fit. I wasn't skinny and I had curves in the right place, but I wanted to be able to jog through the park, run up a flight of stairs, all without wanting to fall over in exhaustion once I'd reached the top.

Once I was finished at Patrick's family training gym,

I'd look into membership closer to where I lived, where I'd be given a personal trainer to kick my butt.

"So," Millie drawled.

I raised a brow and waited for her to continue.

"Stryker, huh?"

"What? You change direction so quickly that you leave me behind half the time."

"Sorry. My brain never stops. So, back to Stryker. What do you know about him?"

"Nothing." I shrugged, finishing my drink.

"I thought you'd researched the fighters before we arrived there."

She was right. "I did. The picture on their web site for Stryker is dark and you can't really make him out. But watching the fight, I would never have recognized him. The only information was his fight statistics. Nothing personal like the other fighters profiles. It's as though he didn't exist until he won his first fight. I was curious about him before I saw him today…" her voice trailed off as she thought of the puzzle that presented, "and now, I'm still curious, but I felt a connection with him, even though the way he watched me sent a mixture of fear and desire down my spine."

Millie rested her elbows on the table with her chin in her hands, deep in thought. "He really did affect you? I'll admit to being distracted most of the time with Carter, but, I'm worried about you."

When I started to protest, Millie held her hand out to keep me silent. "I'm worried because that fighter looked like he was ready to eat you alive, and you're, well, too innocent for the likes of him."

Surprised, I laughed. "Too innocent? Millie, I'm not a virgin."

When I heard a throat being cleared behind me, I turned and met the amused gaze of the man sitting at another table who was obviously eavesdropping on our conversation. He looked to be in his sixties with salt and pepper hair, and while he couldn't hide the laughter in his eyes, his dinner company looked sour, as though my words caused her to grimace.

I smiled, which he returned, and I very nearly laughed out loud at the surprise on the woman's face. "Have a nice day."

Turning back to Millie, I grabbed my purse and indicated that we should leave. I left money on the table to cover our bill before I followed Millie outside as she chuckled to herself.

"Evie strikes again." She nudged into me before pulling me into her arms for a hug. "Be careful, Evie…and please use the keycard to my apartment whenever you need an escape. I have a nice desk and chair set up in the window now so you can work there."

I needed to get away from her before she discovered just how upset I was with the whole mess I'd found myself in. I needed to learn to say 'no'.

I swallowed a few times, and finally said, "I promise, and the location of the desk sounds tempting. Very tempting."

She grinned. "Thought it might." She turned away to walk to her apartment a few blocks away. "I'll see you tomorrow unless you call around later."

"I need an early night, so it will be tomorrow at the gym."

Millie ran back and kissed me on the cheek before she hurried down the sidewalk.

The early night was the truth, but I wanted to spend time on my laptop and make notes about the gym first—the set up, the men that trained, and most of all, I wanted to do more research on Stryker. He intrigued me more than he should, but he'd made an impression on me that I had a feeling wouldn't be so easy to get rid of.

CHAPTER 4

STRYKER

FASTENING UP MY RUNNING shoes, I pulled my hoodie on and stepped outside onto the balcony where I breathed in the fresh air. My hands tightened around the railing as I took in the view of central park in front of the building. The high rise buildings across the park were far enough away to give me a sense of seclusion but close enough where I could still feel the city. Looking down, the early morning workers dashed past the building. I often wondered how it would feel to be kissed goodbye in the morning as I left for a normal day job, and to return in the evening to that same person—*my* redheaded beauty.

A pipe dream, I knew that, but I had a feeling my distraction with her would cause trouble. Not just for me, but for her as well.

Entering my line of sight below, a white horse drawn carriage trotted along the road gaining beeps from impatient drivers before it turned into the park. The couple in the carriage were well wrapped, and snuggled together under a blanket.

My mind drifted to Evie again. What would it be like to be that couple in the back of the carriage? Heaven came to mind. As usual though, I didn't have the luxury of doing something for enjoyment, especially with a woman. Even though I'd disappear and visit Julio, I didn't consider it enjoyment, I just considered it peace, and somewhere that I could go without a shadow hovering over me.

Inhaling once more, I exhaled slowly and pushed away, backing into my apartment, knowing my day of training was about to start. I'd be lying if I didn't admit to enjoying the training aspect of my life. It kept me going on the days that I'd thought about ending it all.

That would be the easiest way out, but I'd become a fighter and fighters didn't quit. I wasn't a quitter and now that I was older, I intended to figure out how to be free without causing consequences for anyone else. My main problem was to figure out a way to find the 'Irishman' and actual evidence to what they'd done to me, and maybe others. I was sure that more illegal stuff went on behind my back as well. I knew that the only way I'd be able to walk away was to sell the fuckers out by giving everything to law enforcement. I just hadn't worked out how I was going to do that, or how I was even going to make contact with them.

It would be dangerous, but it could work.

"You running first?" Jamie asked, which made me realize I'd been standing in the living room gazing into space. He'd been part of my security team for three years and was one of the more lenient guards. We had a kind of understanding. At least, the best we could under the circumstances. He'd turn a blind eye to me sneaking out alone, and I'd return within two hours of leaving. It amazed me that he trusted me to return, but he probably knew I had nowhere to go. No friends. No family. No means to support myself. They had everything. His trust in me had gradually grown, and now I had three hours to myself on occasion.

"How's Julie doing?" His wife was pregnant and had a bad case of morning sickness, which sometimes would have him looking a bit green when he'd arrive in the mornings.

Jamie smiled. "She's doing great and, even better, no sickness for four days, and counting." He chuckled. "She thinks she looks huge."

I raised a brow in question and hoped I hid my amusement. "Really?"

"No... She looks sexy as fuck." He grinned. "I keep having to show her." He coughed as a slight blush coated his neck.

"I guess you'll need to continue to show her, huh?" Turning my back so he wouldn't see my smirk, I headed through the apartment before I strode out the door and into the elevator.

"Do you ever miss that?"

"Miss what?" I asked, knowing what he meant but taken off guard by the question.

"Having a woman to keep you warm at night?"

I blocked Evie from my mind, and admitted, "You can't miss something that you've never had." Even as the words left my mouth, I wasn't all that sure I spoke the truth.

My eyes dipped so he wouldn't see the longing. Over

the years I'd become good at hiding my emotions behind a wall of indifference, but since I'd seen *her*, my emotions were so close to the surface that they scared the fuck out of me.

Outside, in the crispness of the morning, every breath we took could be seen in a trail of white mist. I wouldn't feel it soon though.

Jogging on the spot, I turned to face Jamie and nodded when he pointed toward the park with his head.

Then I was off at a run.

No one had ever been able to keep up with me when I decided that I wanted to run in the park instead of a treadmill at the gym. I was surprised as fuck that they actually allowed it.

Head down, my eyes searched out my usual route. Crossing the road, I jogged into the park as I allowed my body to warm up. My pace stayed steady. My feet knew this route and I could run it with my eyes closed.

The freedom caused my breath to come easier. My feet pounded on the path as I picked up speed now that my body had started to warm. I felt my muscles loosen as I ran past the pond, the grass covered in a light covering of morning frost. My heart pumped the more I ran, sweat beaded at my shoulders before it ran down my back but I felt exhilarated. My body was used to this treatment and my thighs wouldn't burn unless I ran miles, but I knew that I had to go to the gym because Coach would be waiting.

My five-mile run was coming to an end as I reached the area that would usually be filled with children. Today was no different. Except today, as I passed parents with kids feeding the ducks, I wondered about Evie, *again*. Would I see her today? My thoughts had run wild again during the night because every time I closed my eyes, I saw her glorious red hair. I couldn't escape her, but I had to try. The attraction that had been obvious to us both couldn't go anywhere. Not only was I basically held captive, but she was engaged to one of the fuckers who was involved with the 'Irishman'.

"Fuck."

Did she know about me? About what they'd done? Or was she totally innocent?

I wiped a hand down my face, tiredness suddenly hitting me at the thought that Evie could know about *them* —about me.

Walking out of the park, I pressed a hand to my chest and rubbed at the ache inside of me. She couldn't know. Could she? Either way, we were dangerous to each other, and that had to stop.

Inhaling, I moved my gaze from the sky to search out Jamie when a blonde caught my eye.

Evie's friend.

Where had she come from? She'd just exited the Starbucks with a large drink in her hand as she waved a taxi down. That meant she had to live around here. Why else would she be in the area?

I dashed across the road and raced toward the cab, but I was too late. I don't know what I'd planned on saying if I hadn't missed the cab, but my want had propelled me forward.

My breath caught at the back of my throat, as I dropped my hands to my thighs. I let my head drop.

"Stryker, what's going on?"

"Nothing." I shook my head.

"That wasn't nothing. Do you know that woman?"

I closed my eyes and stood to my full height, knowing that most people would be intimidated, but not Jamie. He didn't match my strength but he was close to my height of six foot five.

"Did you see where she came from?" I clarified, "Before Starbucks."

Jamie stared at me and backed away. "No." He met my gaze with a frown. "She was pretty?" Jamie commented, and waited.

"She was…that wasn't why I was curious." I didn't want to alienate him since he was one of the few that allowed me some freedom so I gave him something. "She's a friend of someone."

I watched his reaction from the corner of my eye and saw surprise flicker across his features before he frowned.

"We need to go. Coach is waiting." Jamie cleared his throat. "Please be careful," he muttered, following me to the car that he had waiting to take us to the gym.

EVIE

I WAS TIRED. LAST night I'd gone to sleep with images of Stryker in my head, and woken up pretty much the same. He'd been all I could think about so my disappointment at not seeing him at the gym when I arrived had taken the enjoyment out of being here.

"He'll be here. I bet he never misses a day," Millie tried to cheer me up with her words while her eyes caressed over the muscular form of Carter.

He was a handsome man and if I hadn't become obsessed with Stryker, I might have taken a second look. Carter was full of boyish charm around Millie. His light brown hair fell casually on his forehead, giving him a rakish look, but I had to laugh at their size difference. Carter looked to be around six-foot-three or so, close to Stryker's height, but Millie was only five-foot-two. At least I was a bit closer to Stryker's height at five-foot-eight.

Carter's hazel eyes followed Millie around the gym, and his tongue would wet his lips when Millie bent to grab her towel from the floor.

It was amusing and they were both as bad as the other. I wondered when Carter would make the first move. I knew that Millie wouldn't. She loved to be chased, and had often told me it made for hotter and sweatier sex once she'd been captured.

Leaving Millie to her thoughts and her flirting, I started the treadmill and built up to a fast walk. I'd no wish to run, but I could handle a brisk pace while watching the others in the gym through the mirrored wall. I was supposed to be making notes and talking to other fighters, but Patrick had told me that they'd been warned to keep their distance from Millie and me. I knew that he didn't take my writing seriously, but I sure as hell did. Even Carter had been evasive when I'd asked questions about routine and fighting.

It didn't make sense.

I was here to research and yet everyone had been told to keep their distance. Patrick was a jealous man and when he'd first told me, I'd thought it was because he didn't want me near other men, but I wasn't sure anymore. Who knew what he was up to. I'd rather not know.

My body started to warm along with my thirst for water. With a glance to my right, I spotted *his* coach standing next to the water dispenser. I grabbed the bars of the treadmill in surprise to keep on my feet. I slowed the speed until I started to cool down, quicker than usual, and stepped from the machine. Grabbing a towel, I walked toward him and smiled as I filled a plastic cup with the cool water.

He held my gaze as I took a long sip from the cup, and once it was empty, I tossed it into the trash.

Stryker's coach made me uncomfortable but I refused to move away because of it and refused to be the first to look away.

He smirked and held his wrinkled hand out to me. "Coach."

I returned his handshake. "Evie."

"It's nice to meet you, Evie."

"Likewise, Coach." Then the thought struck. "Would you be willing to answer some questions for me about the fighters?"

His gaze darkened. "Depends on who you're asking about?"

No sooner had the words left his mouth than the doors into the gym opened and silence descended.

My eyes flickered to the right, but I already knew who it would be. His eyes met mine and held for mere seconds before he glanced at Coach then back to me. My heart pounded and as he took a step in my direction, he glanced again at Coach before he halted mid-step. I made to go to him, but Coach grabbed my wrist.

"Don't…if anyone finds out about whatever is going on between you two, it will bring a lot of trouble down on him. Please keep to your side of the gym. I need to keep him safe."

Funny choice of words.

Coach let go of my wrist with my nod of acceptance, but his words didn't make sense.

Stryker looked to be in his twenties, and was undefeated in the ring or cage, so how could Coach keep him safe? He looked to be in his eighties and frail...as though a puff of wind would blow him over. I was surprised that he coached the fighters because he didn't seem like one.

I glanced at Stryker and realized he'd moved to his own designated space while I'd been watching Coach.

"You didn't answer my question?" I quickly asked as he started to move away.

He paused and glanced over his shoulder, his gaze flirting around the gym before he answered. "I'm not sure they'll allow it." He shrugged and moved over to Stryker who had been glaring at his coach while we talked.

I couldn't help the tears of frustration that hovered on my lashes. I was so sure that he'd agree; it was almost as though he was afraid. But of what?

Rapidly blinking to hide my distress, I couldn't stop myself from casting one last glance at Stryker. He looked angry and I realized he was still watching me. Coach said something to him and the look Stryker gave me was lethal, as though he blamed me for something.

With one final glance, I turned on my heel and smacked straight into Carter.

"What's the hurry?" He grabbed my arms to keep me on my feet, and frowned. "Are you okay?" He glanced over my head, his frown deepened as he quickly dropped his hands. "Let's go and I'll show you and Millie how to use the weights."

I pulled myself together, smiling at Carter. He hadn't

put the tears in my eyes and he'd only ever been nice to Millie and me, although I suspected that he had an ulterior motive with Millie.

Following him to the weight area, I chuckled at the mischievous look on Millie's face as Carter collected some weights from the stand. Her eyes were fixed on his nicely toned ass. Smirking, I nudged her. "I totally agree."

She grinned. "Mmm…I have a feeling that he's deliberately teasing me."

"He isn't the only one," I mumbled, sure that she was too distracted to even hear me.

Carter turned and caught her licking her lips, his eyes darkened so I took that as my cue to leave them to it.

"I'll be sitting over there." I pointed toward the wall where I'd left my notebook. "I need to take some notes." I wasn't sure my words were heard, but what the hell. I moved away and dropped to the floor, my notebook open at a blank page. In fact, the only information written between the pages were notes on Stryker. I hadn't been able to uncover anything that I'd really wanted to know—like his date of birth, his real name, or where he came from. So many questions were unanswered and my obsession with the dark and brooding man across the gym had only grown.

There was something about him, regardless of the fact that he made my belly quiver with fear…and so much more. I knew deep down he'd never hurt me and when he looked at me I felt like he could see straight through to the fraud I was.

No one other than Millie knew the real me. Sometimes, I wondered if my father did, but how could he…he spent most of his time in Washington these days and I rarely saw him. Sighing, I chewed on the end of my pen, and realized that I was going to have to call my mom to put a stop to whatever wedding arrangements she'd made. That wasn't something I looked forward to, but it had to be done the minute I spoke to Patrick. He'd been evasive these last few days. Maybe he had been before and I just hadn't noticed, but I'd started to notice now.

I knew that he was uncomfortable with me being inside his family's gym, but since he started wearing a suit to his father's office, he'd changed, and it wasn't for the best either.

Looking around me, most of the fighters ignored me, which didn't bother me. What bothered me, and shouldn't, was that Stryker was one of those fighters. Other than when he'd arrived, when I'd felt his look to the tip of my toes, he'd gone cold.

He was the only one who continued to draw my attention. No matter where I looked my eyes found their way back to him.

His muscular physique drew my gaze.

His strength made my heart race.

The loneliness in his eyes made me want to wrap my arms around him and not let go.

Most of all, when his gaze landed and held on me, a slither of fear would slowly slide down my spine to finally erupt in my belly as desire.

He knew that I watched him, wanted him, just like I knew how much he held himself together so that he didn't lose his concentration. Except today, I missed having his eyes on me. Yesterday he'd been fixated on me, like I him. I missed that even though I had no idea how to handle it…or him.

I finally glanced at Coach and realized he watched me, a deep frown on his face.

From what I had researched, the old coach had worked at the gym for sixteen years, but he'd spent at least forty years as a coach in the New York area; first as a boxing coach before he branched into kickboxing and several other martial arts and finally ending up coaching at the New York –East Coast Martial Arts Fighters Club. Coach would know everything that was going on in the gym even though I only wanted to know why me talking to Stryker would cause trouble for him. Patrick had told me to stay away from the fighters. At the time, I thought it was so I didn't distract them from their training, but now I wasn't too sure.

"He makes me tingle." Millie slid down the wall and sat beside me. "Lots of other things as well."

"Did I really need to know that?"

"You told me about your wet pantie reaction to Stryker and the guy at the bar." She raised a brow.

I opened my mouth to deny it, but closed it again remembering. However, now that she'd mentioned him, I wondered if my mind played tricks on me because when Stryker was frozen in place, I saw the guy at the bar as well.

"As you're ignoring me and watching the fine specimen across the room, I think you should let me read your notes. To make sure you haven't missed anything."

I laughed and smiled gratefully. "Nice try."

"Evie, you're annoying at times." Millie grinned as she bumped against me in mock frustration.

"To be honest, I don't have any notes. No one will talk to me." I shrugged at the frown on Millie's face as she turned to face me. "I introduced myself to his coach," I added as I nodded at the old man across the gym. "I asked him if I could ask him some questions about the gym. He replied that he wasn't sure if 'they'd allow it'."

"Why? I mean, I know we were told to stay away from the fighters. Carter seems to have made himself our keeper, which I'm not complaining about, but why wouldn't they allow Coach to talk to you? You're here for research."

"I know." I frowned as I glanced around at the fighters. They were all absorbed in their training and seemed to be ignoring me completely. It was like I didn't exist but I could sense a tension in the room…they were definitely uncomfortable with us being here. "Something is going on and I'm going to talk to Patrick about it."

"Do you think that's wise? His family own the gym, he might be behind the silence."

"I won't push, but I'll ask."

"Be careful, okay? And call me if you need me."

"Always, Millie." I rested my head on her shoulder, my eyes fixated on the way Stryker moved around the bag. The way his shoulders rolled with his strikes. The way his feet danced, which were so light for such a large man. The way his skin glistened, as the sweat beaded on it. I wondered what he'd taste like against my tongue; my hands twitched to touch him—to feel his hardness against my softness.

"Evie," Millie dislodged my head, which caused me to clonk it against the wall.

"Ouch." I rubbed the sore spot and glared at her.

"Stop daydreaming while staring at that fighter. He

keeps losing his concentration with your eyes on him." Millie smirked.

My head whipped back to him, and he'd stopped hitting the bag and stood glaring at me until Coach gripped his jaw and tugged him around to face away.

I closed my eyes knowing that I was in so much trouble.

CHAPTER 5

STRYKER

THE MEAL I ATE went down without any flavor hitting my taste buds, which was a sign to slow down. I needed to chew more instead of knocking it back, except I was too distracted with thoughts of a curvy redhead to concentrate.

I'd lost concentration at the gym once I'd caught the intense look on her face through the mirror in front of me. Her eyes had devoured me and all I could think about when she licked her lips was having her mouth on my skin. My dick had lengthened and throbbed in my shorts, which caused the slowness in my rhythm. Because no way in hell could I continue to dance around the bag when the ache between my legs nearly left me crippled.

Shoving my plate away, I breathed deeply to try and get my body's reaction to my thoughts under control before the security team got more than they bargained for.

Five minutes later, I moved into the bedroom to dress. Dropping the towel that I'd wrapped around my waist after the shower, I tossed it into the hamper and pulled on sweats. I was ready to crash in bed with a book. It was still early, just past seven, but I was tired as fuck for a change and wanted to get lost in the world of vampires and lycans.

That plan soon went on the back burner when I heard the apartment door open before it was slammed shut. It wouldn't be Jamie. He'd left after I'd returned home.

Curiosity, more than anything, had me moving to the door of the bedroom to see which of the security team had decided to invade my space. My heart sank as I found Patrick pacing in the living room. I crossed my arms and rested against the doorjamb

I should have asked Jamie that morning if he knew anything about Patrick. I always stopped myself from questioning him though. I didn't have friends. No one had the balls enough to even approach me. Jamie, however, was different than the others, and although I still kept my thoughts and fears to myself, sometimes I felt like he'd help me out of the situation I lived in. I'd never risk asking him because he was a family man with a wife, and a child on the way.

I'd hinted a few times that he needed to find a different job, so far though, he hadn't listened.

As my focus went back to the asshole who continued to pace, he'd yet to see me because he was riled up about something. He was here in my apartment so that meant it involved me. Had he found out about my distraction with his *fiancée*? Or was it something else?

I watched him silently for a few minutes before his pacing grated on my patience. Finally, I cleared my throat, which got his attention.

I waited and let the silence stretch while I observed him through narrowed eyes.

Outward appearance, he looked like any young businessman. Lawyer maybe. His dark blue pants were neatly pressed along with his dress shirt and blazer. He certainly didn't look like he'd come from the gym.

Finally, Patrick stood facing me—hands on his hips, and deep frown lines across his forehead.

"We need to talk about your upcoming fight."

I stiffened, my eyes filled with a hardened resolved as I focused more clearly on him. He'd definitely had my full attention. I waited silently…everything was a waiting game with these guys.

"It's not that long off," Patrick stated, not looking happy. "You should have had a sparring partner long before this, but it couldn't be helped. Coach is getting in touch with Carter. He's similar height and weight to your opponent. Just don't kill him."

"Who? Carter or my opponent?" I moved closer and dropped down onto the chair in front of him, feeling so damn tired but not willing to let Patrick know that. Anger clouded my face, which he would see along with the clenched fists resting on my thighs.

Patrick narrowed his eyes in annoyance. "Don't get *smart* with me. You know who the hell I mean. Carter is to be used for sparring only, your real opponent…anything goes."

I clenched my jaw tightly before I let fly what I really wanted to say. An anything goes fight meant no rules. It was underground, usually Russian organized—from past experience, and it wasn't legal.

"Who?"

"That doesn't matter."

I froze, my anger churned just under the surface and I knew that was a lot closer to the surface than *Patrick* would like. "Don't you want me to win this fight?" I growl. "Isn't your money going to be going on…ME?"

Patrick jumped in surprise at my anger and before he could cover it, I caught a brief glimpse of fear.

Yeah, fear me fucker!

"Calm down," he said calmly, before he offered a nervous laugh.

I smirked because I'd rattled him.

"I'll be calm once you leave."

He sat down opposite and glared. Obviously, courage and anger had replaced the fear that I'd seen. "My spies at the gym told me you haven't spoken to my fiancée or her friend. That's good. Very good. Let's keep it that way."

Leaning forward, I smiled, throwing him off balance. I rested my arms on my thighs as my hands hung loosely between my legs while I breathed deeply.

What would he do if he knew I hid my stiff cock because thoughts of Evie filled my mind? That I'd jerked off *hard* all over my stomach and chest with thoughts of her sucking me off. What would he do if he knew that I wondered how it would feel to sink inside her softness, to have her wetness surrounding my shaft that ached so badly for her touch? That she was the only woman I wanted, that my heart ached because I knew I could never have her. Even if my situation wasn't what it was, she was still too good for me.

"Evie is only going to be there one more day if I have my way…I've also heard that her little friend, Millie, has something going on with Carter. I want you to make sure he's too occupied tomorrow to even say hello to them." Patrick's nostrils flared in annoyance and I felt the same as I glared back at him.

I wasn't completely annoyed but the panic at the thought of not seeing her again made me want to hit something and he was close. Very close.

Don't do it...as much as you want to, don't...

Deep down I knew it would be safer for her to stay away from me. I wouldn't hurt her. All I wanted to do was cherish her. I just didn't trust the fuckers to not use her to remind me of who had the upper hand.

Even though I'd wondered if she knew what Patrick was involved in, and about me, deep down in my heart and gut, I knew she had no clue. She looked too sweet to know about anything that was going on. The fact that Patrick was happy to keep her away from the gym proved that she knew nothing and I should be happy that she wasn't going to be there too.

You still have the bar.

The bar!

I'd forgotten about that, in fact, I'd forgotten that Patrick had told me about the fight. I still had no idea who my opponent was.

"Tell me who my opponent is, and I'll keep Carter busy tomorrow."

"You're trying to bargain with me?" Patrick laughed. "Incredible." He shook his head.

"So I'm guessing that you're either planning on putting money on him, or nothing at all on anyone." I raised a brow and waited.

It didn't take long for the look on his face to switch

from amusement to pissed. He was angry. About damn time.

"You're fighting Lethal Black." His sneer said it all. He hated my fucking guts and wanted to see me bleed.

Fuck!

I held my shock and surprise back, and let him see the anger inside of me. I wondered if they really did want me dead. It would be so much easier for them to have someone else kill me, and what a better way than to do it in the cage. I wouldn't go down without causing some damage of my own, but *Lethal Black* was taller and more muscular than me. I knew my ability and if I'd been fighting in a professional fight, I wouldn't have worried, cage or ring. I knew the rules and how far the fighters could go. But there are no rules in the illegal underground.

"And, you're going to win a small fortune for us," Patrick continued. "Coach has been told what you need to concentrate on and he knows the Lethal Black's weaknesses. Listen to him." Patrick stood, brushing imaginary wrinkles from his pants.

He moved to the mirror beside the door and straightened his tie. His short blond hair was neatly styled.

When he turned, he grinned. "Think I'll do for my hot date with Evie. Dinner and sex. What more can a guy ask for?"

My gut clenched as my head screamed, *No, no, no; she's mine*!

He sneered before he turned and slid through the doorway like the snake he was. Part of me wanted to chase him down and pummel him into the ground.

Instead, I grabbed the coffee table and threw it straight

through the balcony doors in lieu of not being able to go after Patrick.

The glass doors splintered and shattered as the table hit. Luckily my balcony was large, otherwise, the table and glass would have ended up on the street below. That wasn't something I'd thought about when I'd let my anger out. I was damn lucky. The last thing I wanted was to hurt an innocent bystander.

The apartment doors flew open.

The security detail had arrived.

They met my gaze before moving toward the shattered doors. Their attention flitted between me, and the damage I'd caused.

My anger was still there, and the pain of knowing that he was going to my girl hurt more than anything. The jealousy was about to eat me alive.

I needed to get out of here.

I needed to be somewhere I felt close to her.

While security cleaned up my mess, I turned, disappeared into my room to quickly change into jeans. Once I'd accomplished that I managed to slip out while they were distracted.

EVIE

I STARED AT PATRICK in relief as he fiddled with his cell phone. He was clearly distracted with his messages and that was a lot better than he'd been since we'd arrived at the restaurant. He'd been abrupt, and almost cruel, since we'd sat down. I stared at the phone, silently thanking the thing, which was never far from his reach since we'd become engaged. Thinking about it, I'd never seen him use the thing before the engagement.

I studied him and could see what had originally caught my attention. Patrick was handsome in the blonde haired, boy next-door type of way. Comfortable like the sex was. No heat, no drive; just the basics that were over before it had really begun. I didn't see what the whole big deal about sex was. I certainly wasn't naïve with the birds and the bees, and had experimented with boyfriends while away at college. While some had been a little exciting; most of my sexual encounters were innocent and rather… boring. I'd known something had been missing from those experiences but they seemed hot when I compared them to what I had with Patrick.

I sighed and took a sip of water as I watched him smile at a text. It was obvious he had no wish to be here with me tonight. It was like sitting with a total stranger because there was no other place to sit. In fact, I'd probably get more conversation out of a stranger.

Patrick was angry because he hated the fact that I'd talked him into letting me hang out at the gym. I'd been underhanded and blown him to get the answer I'd wanted. It had worked out so I shouldn't complain, and this was the first time I'd seen him since I'd been to the gym with Millie.

Millie was the one who was urging me to end the farce of my life with Patrick tonight, but I couldn't. Not only was I nervous about how he'd react, which was why tonight at the restaurant would have been the ideal place, but if I did end it, my access to the gym would be instantly revoked. No more research for the novel. Oh, who was I kidding, there would be no more Stryker.

"Why the long face?" Patrick asked.

I glanced up from my plate of uneaten food and realized he'd put his cell away and focused on me. "We're on a date and you've been sitting there for about thirty minutes having more of a conversation with your phone than with me." I shrugged. I wasn't bothered about his lack of interest in me, but I couldn't let him know that.

Anger crossed his face before he'd schooled it to one of apology. He reached across the table and took my cold hands into his. His thumb rubbed along mine. "I'm sorry, Evie. You know that I've been busy since I started working for my father, and tonight just isn't a good night." He looked to the side and pulled away, taking a sip of his red wine.

He winced as the wine went down his throat, probably because he preferred beer. Sitting forward he ignored his food and held my steady gaze. "We have a temperamental fighter who causes trouble, and tonight I've been dealing with that." He sighed, which sounded a bit over the top, and continued, "Which is why I'd prefer for you and Millie to stay away from the gym."

I knew it!

"There was no trouble while we were there." I frowned and dipped my head, hoping I had time to hide my panic.

I had to go back to the gym. Perhaps I needed to ask myself why because I'd certainly never acted like I was before. No one had ever caught my eye to the point that he was all I could think even when I was with my fiancé.

"If you think it's for the best, I'm sure that Millie and I can find another gym." I gave a small smile. "I mean, the Club is big and we're in New York so there are tons of gyms filled with fighters that are available to use." My smile widened as if I'd just thought of the option and was really the best one. I just hoped he wouldn't see the lie. I didn't want another gym, I wanted the one Stryker went to.

"Mmm, you'd do it as well, wouldn't you?" Patrick leaned back in his chair, the stem of the wine glass in his fingers while he watched me.

I tried not to squirm and pump the air with my fists, when he said, "To the end of this week only. He's preparing for a fight and doesn't need any distraction. Although I think he's gay so you'll be okay."

My surprise wasn't hidden. "He's gay?"

Please tell me he wasn't talking about Stryker because no way was he gay? I couldn't believe that.

"The guys think so."

"How do they know?" I frowned. "Have they seen him with…guys."

"No. Which is why they speculate." Patrick started to eat the now cold food. He didn't seem to notice.

"Why?"

"Dammit Evie," he hissed, fighting back his anger. "He's a single guy and doesn't fuck the whores that are given to him after he's won a fight…happy now?" He glared and went back to his food before he shoved it away. "Too damn cold now."

I tried not to let the tears fall. He'd been harsh but I shouldn't have expected much else from him. This had become a common thing since we'd gotten engaged. I stopped myself from pointing out that if he'd eaten instead of messing on his cell then it wouldn't have been. We might have even been out of the restaurant as well.

"Why are you so angry?" I asked carefully. "I was curious and since you often ask me questions about my family that I answer." I waved my hand to end the sentence.

"That's true. Stryker isn't family though." He sighed and took my hand again. "I'm sorry, okay? It's just been a bad day. The best thing for you is to concentrate on the research for your book." He kissed my fingers, his hold tightening. "I'm just concerned about you. Stryker isn't someone to be messed with and with a fight coming up, he's going to start sparring with Carter. Please tell Millie to stay away from them."

A slither of fear ran down my back. He may have said that with a loving caress to my hand, and a smile on his face, but his eyes were filled with anger and it was clearly a warning.

"I hear you." I tugged my hand free and prayed his father would call and ask him to do something that involved leaving me here.

The thought of going back to my apartment for anything else turned my stomach. I'd started to dread it but was more resigned than any time before. Now though, the only thing I wanted from him was access to the gym…and my freedom, which I would get when I called off this engagement.

At the end of the week, I'd break things off with him and call my parents. I winced at the thought of talking to my mom about the wedding and cancelling everything. It would be a headache, one which I was going to have to deal with to save my mom the hassle. After all, it was my fault that I'd let the engagement go this far. Last minute as well.

"You're sulking like a five year old now, Evie. A fighting gym is for fighters whether they're male or female. I know my father's gym only caters to the male fighters because he discovered having women around too distracting for the men. But it isn't a place that I want you, or your little friend around."

Arrogant asshole!

"Okay," I mumbled as his cell started to ring.

I pretended to ignore his call as I stirred the ice in my glass of water but I listened to him the entire time…and noticed the tightness of his lips as he listed to the caller.

It was all I could do to keep the happiness from my face as he waved the server down for the bill. He stood, urging me to do the same while still in the middle of listening to his call.

Reaching for my purse, I realized that he'd want to drop me off at my apartment, even though it was only a few blocks away. So not wanting that to happen, I made my escape.

"You go. I'll get a cab right outside the door after I've used the restroom." I kissed him on the cheek and quickly dashed into the ladies' room.

I could breathe.

Finally.

He wouldn't follow me in here. Would he?

Holding my breath, I dashed into a stall and made sure it was locked before I dropped to the toilet. No one looking underneath would know that I was just sitting on it. Well, they might, as I didn't have my panties down, but heck.

After a few minutes of silence, I started to chuckle with how ridiculous I was being. Totally. Patrick had better things to do than search stalls in the restroom for me.

Shaking my head, I laughed as the automatic flush triggered and made me jump slightly. I moved out of the stall and over to the vanity table with a huge mirror in front. I searched out my lipstick and quickly applied the cherry red color, smacking my lips together. It was one of my favorites and, of course, Patrick didn't like it, which was probably why I'd worn a muted lip-gloss when I met him for dinner. Now that dinner was done, my lip-gloss was off, and my favorite color was on my lips…to hell with Patrick.

Stryker would like it.

Popping the lid back on the tube, I slipped it back into my purse and headed outside.

I knew where I was going and it wasn't home.

CHAPTER 6

STRYKER

AS SOON AS I arrived, Julio cleared my usual table, much to the grumble of the group of guys who occupied it. All it took had been one look at me and they moved. I hadn't even done anything but stand next to Julio. Unfortunately, there was no disguising my size and I looked threatening, if I wanted to that was.

An hour later, the crowd had thinned, which suited me just fine. I liked to be able to see who'd entered on the off chance I'd been found. My luck was still with me so far in that respect, but not in the other—no Evie.

Even though I wanted to run tonight at the thought of Patrick being with her, I still came here…hoping, even though I knew it was hopeless. She obviously loved the prick and he had so much more to offer than I ever would so this infatuation was stupid. It needed to stop before I made a fool of myself, or before anyone discovered she was constantly in my thoughts and could be used against me.

Hearing a throat being cleared, I watched Julio as he took the seat beside me. "Can I ask you something?" His voice had a huskiness to it after many years of smoking, or so he'd once told me.

I nodded.

"You always keep to yourself…and you're always alone. Never come in with anyone, or talk to anyone here. I have no idea what's going on, but I want you to know that I'm here to help you if you need it…I don't want trouble, but I want you to know that you don't have to be alone." Julio moved back to the bar as soon as the words had left his mouth.

Not only did my heart pound with fear for Julio because he couldn't know what my life was like, but the longing to accept his help caused a pain in my chest. I wanted to be free of them, but not at the expense of anyone else, especially not Julio who'd only ever shown me kindness.

My thoughts quickly changed direction when the door opened and in walked Evie. My breath caught at the back of my throat at her beauty. Tonight she wore a pale green dress that was fitted around her chest and flowed into lots of material around the skirt. I wasn't familiar with women's clothing so I had no fucking clue as to what it was called, but either way, she was stunningly beautiful.

Locks of hair bounced around her face as she moved and I ate up the sight of her. She wore low-heeled shoes but her soft, silky legs seemed to go on for miles, causing my fingers to twitch with the need to touch her. Through the people lingering around a subtle scent floated toward me, light and flowery, which I knew was Evie.

My senses had become attuned to her, and every move she made caused a reaction within me.

I wanted her to sit with me.

Talk to me.

Eat with me.

Sleep with me.

None of that would ever happen.

My head knew that, I just wished that my heart did.

Evie stopped at the bar and laughed with Julio while my eyes continued to caress her. I couldn't move them away even if I tried.

Desire rapidly warmed my body, and my dick hardened, lengthened, and pulsed.

As if she felt eyes on her, she slowly turned and stared. She wouldn't be able to see me because of the dark corner but I could certainly see her. Her gaze faltered when Julio drew her attention back to him and his eyes shifted in my direction.

He knew there was something going on with me. He'd seen me rush out to chase her down…and he'd watched me stare with longing at her. I hadn't told him anything, I knew that he trusted me, and that meant a lot.

She knew someone watched her from this corner, but she had no idea it was me. The connection we'd felt at the gym hadn't been a fluke. It had been powerful, and I wanted her to know that it was me sitting here. I didn't want her to think it was a creepy stalker. Perhaps if she did know who it was, then she'd come over. There was no one here watching us. No security keeping her away from me like at the gym where eyes followed me everywhere. A fact that surprised me with my reaction to her being in the gym. I'd expected to have my distraction pointed out, which was what I thought the visit from Patrick had been about. But no. I was off the hook…for now.

My attention back on *my* woman, I noticed her slipping down the side of the bar to the restrooms. I blinked and narrowed my gaze when two guys followed her.

Without thinking, I moved to follow them and caught the frown on Julio's face as I started to pass the bar.

"I'll come with you." Julio lifted the hatch, but I stopped him with a steady hand on his arm.

"No. I have this. Follow in a few minutes but stay back." I didn't wait to see if he listened, and quickly made my way down the hall.

I was just in time to catch the back exit as it closed with a clunk. Pausing, I listened and decided to check it out.

My fear of alleys had stayed with me all these years, but my fear that something bad was about to happen to Evie overrode everything. I had to protect her at all costs.

Shoving through the heavy door, my head snapped to the right at the sound of scuffling. My fear for Evie rose as I let the anger I'd felt take over when I saw the two men dragging her down the alley.

"Hey," I shouted as I jumped over the railing, bypassing the five or so steps down to the ground.

Startled, they glanced at each other, and straightened when I moved closer.

No way would I let them take Evie. I didn't look at her because I knew if I did it would be her I went to. My anger would snap like a twig so I kept my concentration on the assholes who'd chosen to take her.

I was bigger than they were, and I had years of training. I could easily take these guys. The one on the right looked to have more muscle than his partner, but they were both about to have a lesson they wouldn't forget.

"Give me the woman," I growled, my fists flexing at my side.

"Go back inside and mind your own business," the bigger of the two men spat the words out while the other guy looked between us and took a step back.

Yeah, that's right. Keep going.

"You really don't want to threaten me... This is the last time I'll ask nicely. Give me the woman."

"You ass—"

"Fuck no." The other guy grabbed his friend's arm, effectively cutting off his words. "That's Stryker."

His friend blinked and shoved Evie forward so abruptly that she flew down to the ground, crying out in pain. She lifted her face to look at me, and fear, stark and vivid, glittered in her eyes. Panic welled in my throat as I crouched down to help her.

The two guys took off down the alley and disappeared around the corner.

Fucking pussy assholes!

"Can you stand?"

"I don't know," her voice wobbled, and tears streaked her face.

"I won't hurt you. I only want to help." Before she could do anything, I had her up in my arms. She snuggled into me as my heart pounded with a mixture of fear and relief.

Evie rubbed her face into the curve of my neck and I nearly stumbled when she inhaled. Her arms slipped around my neck, her fingers threading through the hair at the nape.

"I won't hurt you," I repeated, my voice a whisper against her ear.

The tension was gone from her face when she met my gaze. Her arms tightened around my neck. "I know, Stryker." She offered a wry smile. "I had a feeling that you were one and the same."

I frowned as I carried her back inside the bar, wondering what she'd meant.

We didn't have more time to discuss what she'd meant as Julio was rushing down the hallway. When he saw that I carried Evie, his eyes widened before he ushered me into his office.

"Is she all right?" he asked, panicked.

"She's fine," Evie reassured him while I placed her on the desk, the only place where Julio hadn't stacked papers.

"I do things a bit backwards." Julio shrugged. "I have to get back. Busy again. There's a first aid bag in that cabinet." He closed the door on his way out.

I met her gaze before I did a once over to see where she was hurt. Her knees looked to have taken the brunt of her fall and, as she held her hands out, I realized she'd scraped the palms of her hands, as well.

My anger at those assholes was seething inside me and I wanted revenge against them. I would love to chase those fuckers down and let my fists tell them just how mad I was. But Evie was more important than my revenge so I tamped my anger down…I'd save it until I met them again.

She was a small thing, at least to me she was. Fragile.

Her wince caught my attention though, and brought my eyes up to hers. She was hurting.

Opening the cabinet, I grabbed the first aid kit and placed it beside her. I was familiar with a lot of the stuff inside, having had to be patched up plenty of times in the first few years of having a 'leash' around my neck.

I set a few things aside and moved in closer to her. My eyes unable to leave her face for long. "I know I promised not to hurt you, but I have a feeling I'm about to when I clean your knees."

"I trust you, Stryker."

I closed my eyes and had to swallow a few times to hold my emotions in check. She made me feel so much more than I knew what to do with.

The touch of her hand to my cheek had my eyes snapping open with surprise. She smiled and taking hold of my wrist, brought my hand closer to her knee. "Please. Let's just get this over with."

I nodded and started to clean one of her knees, my hand unsteady but after a deep inhale, and a slower exhale, I quickly cleaned both of her knees, and palms, while I tried not to hear her audible gasps of pain. I was as gentle as possible and I hated causing her more pain.

Her eyes stayed on mine the whole time, my face, my chest, my hands…and lower. I tried not to react to her gaze on my body, but I wasn't sure I succeed because my dick throbbed behind my zipper. All it would take was one more glance downwards and she'd see just what her closeness did to me.

Standing between her legs, I met her searching gaze and quickly looked away, feeling heated. "What did you mean?" I asked to hide my embarrassment. I'd never been this close to a woman before, and with how much I craved to really touch her, I was afraid that I might give in to that need.

She cupped my face in her palms and urged me to meet her gaze. "Mean about what?"

"One and the same."

She smiled and her whole face lit up. "I saw you fight, and the other day when I noticed a large man sitting in the bar… I wondered if you were one and the same. I'm so glad that you are."

"You are?"

Her fingers caressed along my flushed cheekbones not only with shyness, but arousal.

"Yes, I am…very glad." She smiled, moving her hands away, leaving me craving them back on my body.

She moved forward to slide off the desk, but, with me not moving, all she did was come up against my thighs, hers spreading wider. She tilted her head to look at me. I breathed in as I tried to fight the urge to sweep her up in my embrace. A few seconds later, I reluctantly moved to the door. Without looking at her, I told her, "I'll walk you home."

Her touch on the small of my back had me turning and I finally met her gaze again.

"I usually get a cab, but I'd love to walk with you."

EVIE

AT MY WORDS, A look so sad crossed his face before it was replaced with longing, his eyes sparkled, and then he hid them from me.

He guided me outside, a hand low on my back.

However, once outside, a shudder rippled down my spine at the thought of what would have happened if Stryker hadn't appeared.

I glanced at him from the corner of my eye, and the large man walked silently beside me. We moved in sync, thanks to him matching his pace to mine. As we walked, our hands brushed together until he hooked my thumb with his.

Butterflies took flight in my belly at the light touch and when our fingers intertwined, desire pooled low. Every slight movement caused the bodice of my dress to brush lightly against my pebbled nipples.

I wasn't sure he knew how much he affected me, but I'd certainly seen his reaction to me back in Julio's office. He'd been heavily aroused with just my tender touch, which had surprised me. Me being forward, making the first move was a change. Usually I'd be too shy, but with Stryker, I wasn't, and I realized that I wanted to touch him. I sensed affection was missing from his life. I didn't know why, considering I didn't know anything about him.

"Please talk to me," he asked gruffly, surprising me in the dark. Obviously I'd been too lost in my own thoughts.

I looked up and he turned his head to meet my gaze. He didn't smile but the longing in his eyes made me open my mouth.

"I'm not sure what to say."

He flexed his fingers around mine. "Tell me anything. No one talks to me unless they want something from me." He glanced away before meeting my gaze again, and this time my step faltered when he smiled.

A real smile that lit up his face.

My heart pounded knowing that this gorgeous man was

interested in me, and even though I shouldn't encourage his attraction, I wasn't going to do anything to stop it.

He raised a brow and I realized that, not only had I been staring, but that he'd been waiting for me to start talking. On impulse, I raised our joined hands and kissed his knuckles. I'd surprised him with the kiss because he stumbled forward, which made me smile all the more as I admitted, "My mom is a homemaker and my father is a state senator." He hesitated slightly, which was really subtle and I would have probably missed it if I hadn't expected it. "My mother wants me married; popping out grandbabies...my apartment is the fourth building up."

He growled, looked around, and pulled me into the alcove of my favorite Italian restaurant, which had now closed for the night.

"Not with him," he hissed through clenched teeth. "Please tell me it won't be with *him*." His forehead dropped to mine, his hands gripped my hips, and my hands reached up and stroked along his shoulders.

"It won't be with him, Stryker. The wedding is supposed to be soon, but at the end of the week, I'm going to call it off. If I do it now then I won't have access to the gym. I need access."

"Why?" he breathed the question.

Because of you...

"I haven't finished researching my book." I smiled, shyly. "I write even though I haven't published anything. I'm hoping my next book will be the one for me to give others to read."

"I'll read it," he whispered, brushing the hair back from my face. "Tell me more about your family, please. Something that *he* doesn't know."

"Okay, but only if you promise to tell me your name when I'm finished."

I'd caught him off guard, and knew it instantly. His body went tense beneath my hands, but as the tension drained from him as quickly as it had come, he nodded. "I promise, but my Christian name only."

That would have to do.

"At first, I hated that my father was running for senator because it meant he'd be away from home more than he already had been. I missed him and wanted him home. My mother was the social butterfly and still is. She told me that I was selfish and that my father needed and wanted the support of his only child." I sighed. "When he won, I got caught up with all the celebrations, and accepted that I'd become the daughter of a senator. The thing is, as I became older, I realized he was good at his job. He wasn't a pompous ass like some of the others I'd met, but he really was making a difference. Slowly, but he was. He always supported the underdog and would only support a cause if it were something he believed in regardless of how popular he thought it would be. I love him for that, and I'm proud of him."

Silence followed my words and then I almost missed his whispered word, "Jake." He licked his lips and swallowed, which told me that he was nervous at having shared his actual name.

My gaze caressed his face and I saw the trust that he had in me, regardless of my connection to Patrick, his boss.

"Thank you. I know that there is a lot of speculation about the 'real' you, so I promise I won't repeat it to anyone. You're secret is safe with me." I moved closer, knowing that I had to always call him Stryker so that I didn't slip up.

When our bodies brushed together, I pressed closer, still wanting his warmth surrounding me. His breath was warm and moist against my face, and my heart raced.

The heat on Stryker's face, high on his cheekbones, made my body tingle. I wanted to get closer still. My arms slipped under his and my hands against his back kept me snug against him. My heart jolted and my pulse pounded when I felt his erection twitch between us. His cock would feel so good as he slipped inside my soaked channel.

Slowly, his hands moved downward skimming either side of my body to my thighs. He grasped one thigh and started to lift it, then the other. Before I could get used to the new sensation, I found myself with my back against the door, my breasts crushed against the hardness of his chest, and his large jean-clad erection pressed, up close and personal, against my panties.

Stryker groaned and dropped his head into the curve of my shoulder. His breathing ragged, he admitted, "I want you, Evangeline…but I can't have you." He thrust against me, and my eyes rolled, so close to release.

He rocked his hips and I swore I saw stars as I grabbed his head blindly, wanting, needing more. Wedging me between the door and his taunt body, one of his hands slipped up and rubbed against my pebbled nipple.

I gasped, "Don't stop," hoping that he would hear me.

Instead of stopping, he licked my neck before his mouth covered mine hungrily. The kiss sent new spirals of ecstasy through me. When his hands flexed on my bottom, his hips started to thrust hard against the swollen nub between my thighs. His searching tongue slipped between my lips. My eyes closed as wave after wave of pleasure rippled through me.

Stryker gasped into my mouth before he grunted in what I presumed to be his own release. I caressed the strong tendons in the back of his neck to sooth the shudders wracking his large frame.

My trembling limbs clung to him while he held me so tightly against him that I could hardly breathe. I didn't care because I was in his arms after he'd given me a powerful release.

He slowly let me slide down his body and straightened my dress. His eyes looked everywhere, but at me.

Surely he didn't regret what we'd just done? We didn't know each other but the attraction, connection, between us was off the charts.

Instead of wondering, I reached for his jaw and when I brought his face around to mine, I realized that he didn't regret it, but he was embarrassed.

"I have loved every second of being with you tonight." I heard his sigh as he sunk into my caress. I continued, "What you make me feel is powerful, and no one has ever caused me to react the way I have with you. This is all new to me."

He kissed my palm. "This is a first for me too," he admitted, and blushed like a teenager.

The urge to feel his lips against mine again was so strong that I raised to my toes, and with pressure behind his head, pulled him down to meet my lips.

Stryker raised his mouth from mine and gazed into my eyes. "I'm not sure what to do about you. It would kill me to cause you harm."

I frowned at his choice of words, and watched as he

started pacing back and forth in front of me. Why would he cause me harm?

He suddenly stopped and gently shoved me back into the doorway.

"He's waiting for you," Stryker growled, his eyes full of sorrow. "Don't mention being with me tonight, or—"

"Your name?"

He cupped my face, his thumbs rubbing along my lips. "I wasn't going to say that, but yes. Don't mention that you know my name. Knowing me is dangerous… Go." He gave me a shove toward where Patrick stood waiting, and when I glanced back he'd disappeared down the alley.

I wanted to run after him, but after the trouble I'd gotten into earlier I thought better of it and moved toward my apartment.

Stryker's words made me wonder what was going on and why it was dangerous to know him. I'd wondered at the gym what was really going on there, and now my curiosity was more than piqued.

I couldn't ask Patrick because then he'd become suspicious, and I sure as hell didn't want him paying more interest to what I was doing than usual. It was then that I realized Patrick was indeed waiting for me at the door to my building. I glanced back. Had Patrick seen me with Stryker? I raised my chin. Maybe it was for the best if he had.

As I approached him, he glanced up from his phone and it was clear that he hadn't seen me. And he didn't look happy. In fact, he looked damn right angry. I glanced down at my dress and winced when I realized that it was dirty from when I'd hit the ground in the alley. That wasn't the end of the world, so I squared my shoulders ready to face him.

"What happened?" he drawled, as though I was a naughty child.

"I was attacked, rescued, patched up, and brought home."

His eyes widened and then narrowed. "Attacked? By whom?"

"Two men, and before you ask I've no idea what they wanted as they didn't tell me."

He watched me and tried to decide as to whether or not I was telling the truth. It didn't take long and then he let out a heavy sigh.

"Let's go inside." He took my arm and led me to the elevator, ignoring everyone else in the lobby.

I kept my eyes cast downwards, trying to think of a way to get him to leave. My heart sank. I had to remind myself that at the moment he was still my fiancé.

As he led me inside my apartment, I tried to move away, but he held firm to my arm. "You're pulling away from me, Evie."

"I'm not the only one," I snapped, trying to pull free but to no avail.

"You want to fight." I hadn't feared him before. But when I felt the hand to the back of my neck as he gently shoved me against the wall, I feared him now.

"Don't fight me, Evie... You won't like the consequences," he breathed into my neck, causing my stomach to roll with nerves.

My knees throbbed against the wall as he pressed into me from behind. Even though I was afraid of what he'd do next, I was relieved when I felt his trousers rub against my leg because it meant that he was still clothed.

I started to shake as silent tears ran down my face. "Please, don't do anything you'll regret," I begged, trying to escape his hold, but knowing I wouldn't be able to because he was too strong for me. "This isn't you, Patrick. Please don't hurt me."

"Shut the fuck up. You don't know a damn thing about me, or my life… *So shut up*," he yelled, slamming my head into the wall in his agitation.

Pain ricocheted through my skull as my vision dimmed. Tears continued to run down my face, but I refused to break down into sobs.

"Tell me why you're here," I spat out, "and go." I bucked into him. He was too strong and wouldn't budge, but seconds later his hands flexed in my hair as he grunted from pain when I managed to stomp on his foot.

"Fuck," he hissed. "You're a fucking hell cat. I'm only here to tell you that there will be a wedding regardless of your thoughts on the matter… Don't piss me off again, Evie."

I didn't answer, and seconds later the weight of him was removed, and then, silence.

Minutes more went by and then I hissed, "I hate you."

No response.

I chanced a glance behind me, but he'd gone and then I heard the click of the apartment door as it was closed.

The sob I'd held inside of me rose and I finally let it burst forth as I made my way to the bed. Grabbing a pillow, I hugged it close and cried. I wanted Stryker to be here holding me, loving me, keeping me safe. If he'd been here I know that he'd have killed Patrick to keep me safe.

My tears eventually gave way to anger. How dare Patrick come in here and threaten me. I suppose I should be grateful that he hadn't done a lot more.

That asshole!

Quickly jumping from the bed, I checked the apartment to make sure that I really was alone. Sliding the security bolt into place, I swiped at the tears brimming in my eyes. He wouldn't make me cry. He didn't get to do that to me but I knew that he had. I gagged on the nausea threatening to overwhelm me and raced into the bathroom.

Glancing in the mirror, I stared at the dark hollows under my eyes and the haunted woman that was staring back at me as fresh tears brimmed in my eyes.

Turning the shower to scalding hot, I climbed under the spray and collapsed down the wall of it. Tears flowed freely now and I gave into them as I allowed the hot water to wash away every memory of Patrick's anger, and touch. I was alone and a night that had been almost magical had taken on a horrid twist.

I wasn't sure how long I'd been in the shower but I stayed there until it ran cold. Sometime during it, I'd pulled myself to my feet and scrubbed my body until my skin was red. And then I'd planned. First I would pack a bag, then I'd move in with Millie while I ended things with Patrick. He didn't deserve me. He never had and all the guilt I'd been feeling was gone. I hated him enough now to walk away and what he did tonight would give me the leverage I needed to get him to leave me alone. If he thought I wouldn't carry out a threat of exposing him, he would be so wrong.

CHAPTER 7

HE JUST MADE IT to the alley before he lost the burger and fries he'd eaten in the car on his way over.

The image of what he'd just done ran through his mind, causing his stomach to lurch again.

"Here." His best friend, and lover, passed him a bottle of water.

He took it and greedily gulped the bottle down.

"You did it?" his lover asked, but the answer was obvious.

He nodded anyway.

"I wanted to explain…but, I can't and it's killing me." He tossed the bottle into the dumpster. "That in there," he pointed toward the apartment, "wasn't me…which she pointed out." Tears clouded his vision.

His lover gave a tug and embraced him. He was kept in the cocoon of his lover's arms, where he felt safe.

It was only temporary, but he'd take whatever he could get while trapped between family loyalties and doing the right thing.

CHAPTER 8

STRYKER

SWEAT RAN DOWN MY back and my feet danced around the bag as my fists connected with the old leather. I'd alternated between the bag and the ropes since I'd arrived a few hours before. It felt good, and helped me focus because I sure as hell was having a hard enough time at concentrating. *Hard* being the condition I'd been in since last night.

Having Evie in my arms, rubbing her sexy little body over mine, had been a dream come true. She'd felt perfect. The soft murmurs she'd made while I gave her pleasure had been enough to send me over with her. My first orgasm with a woman and I stayed zipped.

The mess I'd made had been washed away with a shower once I'd gotten back to the apartment, to questions of where I'd been and with whom. I ignored them all and had been surprised when Patrick wasn't there this morning to question me about the shattered door, and my whereabouts.

Everything went back to Evie though. Her smile, her scent, her small hands compared to my much larger ones. She was amazing, and I wanted her so much. I knew I could never have her. Her life meant too much to have her associated with me. She was too good. Her parents wouldn't even want me near her because they'd know that I wasn't good enough.

"That bag have a name?"

I stumbled when I heard Carter's voice behind me. I turned and glared at him, but the grin he offered nearly had my lips twitching.

"Maybe," I offered.

He chuckled. "You want to spar in the ring?" Carter nodded toward the empty one.

"They told you about the upcoming fight?" I asked, walking toward the ring.

Carter pulled his gloves on, making no move to get into the ring. "They did." He frowned, and turned to sit on the edge of the ring. "What's wrong with that picture?"

I rubbed at my forehead with my wrist and wondered whether Carter could be someone I trusted. He willingly kept to himself most of the time, unlike me who was forced to be alone. "I think they sense I've had enough, and want me to go out in a different way than I usually do after a fight."

His eyes widened at one of my assumptions.

"Wouldn't they lose a lot of money if you lost?"

"Or, they could believe that I'll win and by doing what they're doing, my odds could be set higher than usual, in which case, they'd make a hell of a lot more money than they would usually do."

Carter nodded but he didn't reply, so I climbed into the ring and waited for him to join me.

When he did, he moved closer and held his gloved hands out. My gaze met his and as my gloves met his, he whispered, "You ever need anything, I'm here."

Carter tapped my hands before backing up and into position to start the sparring session except my heart wasn't in this today. I needed it though.

Cameras were hidden throughout the gym and no one could do anything without security knowing about it. If it involved me, then management—whoever they might be—would be informed.

The only place without cameras was the locker room and showers. No windows large enough for me to fit through.

When Carter caught me on the jaw with a left hook, I blinked my surprise.

"Concentrate." He grinned.

I shook my head, my eyes narrowing.

My concentration was back, and although, when I had the opportunity to spar, I held back, Carter was going to hit the mat today. Something told me that he'd be pissed if I held too much back.

We hadn't been sparring long, when the doors opened and my head whipped around to watch as Evie walked in…pain exploded in my jaw as I hit the deck.

"Fuck." I laid there stunned for a minute, and then glared at a grinning Carter. "What the fuck?"

He laughed and offered a hand to help me up. "I told you to concentrate."

"I was."

"Like hell. The girls are back, and the redhead distracts you."

"She doesn't," I snapped and turned away.

"Oh yes, she does. I'm not blind…and neither are they." Carter moved his eyes to the camera, and back to me. "Be careful, Stryker. I don't know what's really going on here with you and them, but they're watching… Don't forget."

Carter jumped from the ring and made his way over to Evie and her friend. They smiled in greeting, but it was Evie that I couldn't stop looking at. My heart raced knowing she was so close. Her scent had been all over me last night. The sap that I was had slept with my T-shirt on the pillow to feel her close. I wasn't sure how wise that had been considering my dick had woken me, wanting Evie's touch.

EVIE

AFTER WHAT HAPPENED LAST night with Patrick, my nerves were all over the place. I'd snuck into Millie's apartment around two in the morning, telling her I'd explain later and that we both needed sleep.

I'd avoided her gaze since I'd appeared from the room that she'd designated mine, but I knew Millie and she wouldn't wait too much longer. I was surprised that we'd made it to the gym without her prying the information out of me.

While she spoke to Carter, I tried to edge away to the stepper before she could corner me for answers, but that didn't work. Her hand reached out and grabbed hold of my wrist. She laughed. "Oh, no you don't. Even Carter can't distract me from what I want to ask you." She smiled, her attention back on Carter. "Can you give us five minutes?"

He looked between us, a frown marred his brow. "I can."

Millie watched Carter walk away, her eyes trained on his ass.

"He's going to turn and catch you," I commented.

"I hope he does." She grinned.

I rolled my eyes, and finally admitted to her what happened last night from arriving at Julio's up to Stryker walking me home. I left out the part about what 'actually' happened with Stryker, and didn't want to think about what followed that, but…

"And the rest," Millie raised a brow. "I'm not stupid. You don't come knocking in the middle of the night when there's no reason." She didn't miss a beat. "What happened with Patrick?"

Hearing his name, my shoulders sagged and tears threatened to fall. Then one escaped, which I swiped from my cheek in a mixture of fear and anger. I was scared of Patrick and what he did and I was angry…at him…at myself for allowing him that close…for not fighting harder.

Millie moved to hug me, except before she could I was tugged around. Stryker's gloved hands cupped my face; his worried gaze met my startled one.

He cursed, tore his gloves free before he let them drop to the floor. Then he was cupping my face as his gentle fingers brushed my tears away. "Evangeline, talk to me," he whispered.

"I love hearing my full name on your lips, it sends

goose bumps through me," I whispered against his lips. "I'm fine," I mumbled, hoping they'd both accept that even though, deep down, I knew they wouldn't.

Stryker stepped closer, and the minute I placed my hands at each side of his waist I felt his body tremble and watched as his eyes dipped with pleasure.

"I really am, okay."

"No, you're not," Stryker insisted.

"I'm beginning to think that you left out a bit of information with regards to him walking you home," Millie mumbled.

Heat filled my face at Millie's deduction, and my heart threatened to beat out of my chest at the smirk on Stryker's handsome face.

"What happened with Patrick after I left?" Stryker guessed, correctly.

"I knew that bastard had something to do with this," Millie steamed and tried to get closer to me, but Stryker held steady.

"He...I thought..." I inhaled and dropped my eyes so Stryker wouldn't see the pain, "he wanted me." I shrugged and tried to move away but Stryker moved with me. "He didn't rape me, but he threatened me." Another tear escaped, which he caught with his thumb.

"Did he hurt you," Stryker growled, his eyes looked wild. "Did he, Evie?"

"Cameras, Stryker," Carter reminded him. From the look on his face, he didn't give a shit. "The fucker hurt her."

He dropped his forehead to mine, our eyes met, the look I felt right down to my toes.

"I don't want you to get in trouble with them because

of me. Please, Stryker. It would hurt me to know that." I licked my lips, an action he followed with his eyes.

"I'm afraid to let you go," he whispered, indecision clear on his face.

"I'll be fine. Don't worry about me. Worry about yourself."

"Stryker, let's go." Carter dragged him away while collecting his gloves from the floor.

Millie took my face in her hands and made me look at her. "I'm not sure what's going on with you and him…but it was intense."

I wrapped my arm around Millie and hugged her close. "Stryker has started to mean everything to me, and that fact alone scares me. I've only met him the once. Last night. There's just something about him that calls to me, something that wants to be constantly close to him. Touching. I really can't explain it." Pulling back, I met her gaze. "I know he feels it too."

After a few minutes of looking anywhere but at me, she answered, "I feel the connection between the two of you. It's powerful. It doesn't scare me, but it does make me long for someone to look at me the way Stryker does you."

I smiled through my tears. "Carter looks at you like he wants you for breakfast."

My friend started to blush to the roots of her hair. "He can have me…eventually." She smirked.

I laughed, which I didn't think I'd be doing today. Millie always had a way of making me smile when I really didn't want to.

"Come on. We're done here today." Millie wrapped her arm over my shoulders and tugged me toward the door.

My feet felt heavy, and my head was full of Stryker as I turned and met his gaze across the room. I couldn't look away, and didn't until Millie closed the door behind us.

He looked angry, disappointed, and so damn alone, even in a gym half full of men training.

"Evie, don't worry about him. He looks more than capable of taking care of himself."

I knew she was right and I followed her down the sidewalk, but I hesitated. Despite her words, I wanted to go back and wrap myself around him.

CHAPTER 9

THE MINUTE HE ENTERED the office, he knew by the anger on the other man's face that he wouldn't like the reason he'd been summoned.

He hated the man behind the big mahogany desk, the Irishman. At one time he'd loved him.

He'd always tried his best but it was never enough. Even now, he still wanted to please him, and he hated that about himself.

"Sit, and watch this."

He immediately dropped into the chair opposite him and glanced at the screen that the Irishman had turned to face him.

Oh, hell!

That wasn't good. He couldn't really care less, but now he knew why the Irishman was angry.

Not only did the Irishman's protégé have his hands on a woman for the first time, but it had to be *her*.

Just his fucking luck.

He didn't even have to imagine why she was upset, and that made his stomach lurch all over again.

Fuck!

"I want that," the Irishman fumed, "stopped now," he roared. "Do I make myself clear?"

Asshole!

CHAPTER 10

STRYKER

THE ANGER INSIDE OF me wanted out, and the only way that would happen was if I got the chance to use my fists on Patrick for what I knew he'd done to Evie. She had a very open face and it was easy to see her distress when she was pushed for more answers.

That bastard needed someone stronger to teach him a lesson that he wouldn't forget. Regardless of the hold he had over me, I was going to teach that fucker a lesson. One day soon. In fact, that might happen sooner rather than later after me being up close and personal to Evie at the gym today. There was no way that the cameras would have missed what happened between us. I should have thought about that before I interfered. The last thing I wanted was trouble to fall on Evie.

Stepping out of the shower, I wondered how Evie would feel if I turned up at her apartment. If I slipped out like usual, I could go to her. I'd have to keep watch for

Patrick or any of his friends. But I could do that. I needed to see her. To make sure she was really okay.

My heart felt lighter now that the decision had been made. So, stepping out of the shower, I quickly dried off before I pulled on a pair of jeans and long sleeved T-shirt. They were casual enough to not warrant questions about what I had planned. The trick tonight would be leaving without anyone following me.

If I wanted something enough then I could do it. I would do anything to just get five minutes alone with her. I needed to hold her in my arms and tell her everything would be okay. Would it be though? I wouldn't be around to protect her from that fucker, Patrick.

The feeling to protect had come out of the blue, more so, my feelings of rightfulness with Evie. Every time I thought about her, my heart would pound in my chest. Just wanting her hands on me, even if she only held my hand would sooth my soul. I looked away from the mirror, and brushed the hair back from my forehead as I walked barefoot into the living room.

What the fuck!
I wasn't alone.

"To what do I owe this visit?" I growled, trying to act as though finding them already in my apartment didn't piss me off.

I hadn't heard anyone enter. It was surprising and proof of how distracted I was. I always heard them, even if it was just a slight click of the front door.

Keeping my eye on Patrick and the man he'd brought with him, I moved to the wall and propped myself up against it. The last thing I wanted was to have my back vulnerable, or to be trapped in a corner.

My eyes snapped to Patrick, and the bastard looked to be boiling with rage, which made him the dangerous of the two right now.

My fists clenched with the need to pound into him for what he'd done to her, and he knew it.

The smug look on his face said it all.

I took a step toward him, but the man stepped in front, blocking my view of Patrick. The man was as tall as me, not as wide in the shoulders and I knew he wouldn't be trained as well as me to fight. He wouldn't have a chance and Patrick should know that. So why did he bring him?

"I can handle this, for now, Oliver." Patrick stepped around his *bodyguard* a hard look in his eyes. "Stryker is well aware of why I'm here…aren't you?"

Fuck you!

I clenched my jaw and waited for him to say more because I'd be damned if I volunteered anything. In fact, Patrick must be feeling brave because he stood directly in front of me, anger building by his stance.

I was angrier.

"I told you to stay away from Evie…I specifically said not to go near her, look at her, or talk to her. You completely ignored everything I said. We own you. So why would you risk making things more difficult for yourself?" His head tilted to the side as though he could pull out the answers.

This didn't just concern me, it concerned Evie as well so I had to tread very carefully so as not to be the cause of anymore pain for her.

I briefly glanced away to contain my anger and then looked back at the man who one day would feel the power behind my left hook. "She looked distressed." I met his gaze. "I may be controlled by you but I'm not a heartless bastard when there's a woman in tears. It was instinct to make sure she was okay." Now to cover for Evie. "She just kept saying she was okay. Wouldn't tell me anything, other than she had a bad nights sleep."

Patrick's eyes narrowed and it took everything I had not to reach up and tighten my hands around his neck. He deserved that and more for laying his hands on Evie in anger.

"Hmm." He turned away and walked toward the door. "In the future her tears have nothing to do with you. You stay away, and listen to my warning. Things won't go as smoothly next time you're anywhere near her. She's mine. She's going to be my wife."

He moved back in front of me and got in my face, which was a fucking brave move to make considering how badly I wanted to crush him. "My wife, Stryker. Stay the *fuck* away from her." He straightened his suit blazer and with a flick of his head left with his puppet close on his heels.

No way would I react to his words. At least where he could see or hear my reaction. The bastard would be knocked off his high horse one of these days.

Closing my eyes, I breathed deeply to calm down. It took a good few minutes, but once I was calm, I quickly pulled on socks and sneakers.

All I had to do was get out onto the sidewalk without anyone seeing me. Because I'd been angry when I'd returned home, I hadn't bothered to check which guard was on watch. A couple of them took their job more seriously than the others so I had to be more careful when slipping passed the apartment next door that they used to monitor me.

As long as I didn't lead them to Julio's then I wasn't bothered about what I had to go through to get away for a short time. One day I wouldn't come back, and they knew that. There was always relief in the guard's eyes when I reappeared.

So now, slipping out of the apartment door, I hoped Evie would be at her apartment. If she wasn't, and I didn't see her tonight, my disappointment would be huge.

EVIE

WHEN I'D WALKED INSIDE Julio's tonight, my eyes had immediately gone to the corner where Stryker would sit, and then my heart had sank at not seeing him there.

I'd managed to put a smile on my face while Julio had rushed around behind the bar, and his eyes had popped when I'd asked for a beer. I couldn't fool Julio though and somehow he knew why I was there that night. He knew, and guided me over to Stryker's table.

"Sit," Julio urged. "He doesn't usually come tonight," he raised a brow, "but neither do you." He smiled and left me alone to deal with his other customers.

Was I so obvious?

I sighed and leaned back while I watched what was going on in the bar. Tonight a two-man band had started to set up on the opposite side of the bar, their guitars strapped around their necks. I'd listened to them play before so at least the music wouldn't be too loud.

I'd love to be sitting here with Stryker, cuddled into him while the music swept over me. I'd never known what it was like to be in a man's arms who really wanted me to be there.

That thought shouldn't even enter my head, but it was the truth. Patrick always acted as though he couldn't wait to put me aside, and it often felt like he touched me for show. I'd known there was something wrong from the beginning, but had buried my thoughts on the subject for peace. I'd never doubted or hated anyone but Patrick had given me a reason.

With another heavy sigh, I dipped my head and started to peel the label from my bottle of beer when a shadow fell over the table.

My heart thudded in my chest when I glanced up and realized he was here. He'd come. Our eyes collided and I felt the heat of his stare to the tip of my toes.

I held his gaze and slipped out from the table. Stryker took my hand, and just his touch alone had heat pooling in my panties. He gathered me into his arms; his hand gently cupped my face as he pressed me into his chest.

His heart thundered loudly against my ear as my arms slipped around his back, and there was no mistaking the shudder that ran through him at my touch.

He rested his chin on top of my head, and whispered, "I've been looking for you." I smiled, hearing his words, but it soon turned to concern when he continued, "I went to your apartment."

"Patrick—"

"Wasn't there," he finished for me. Brushing his fingers through my hair, he continued, "I stayed outside once I'd found out which apartment was yours. No lights were on. So I took a chance that you'd be here."

"I'm glad." I finally raised my head, and let out a small sigh when he dropped his forehead to mine.

My heart knew that I wanted to be with him even if my head told me that being close to him would cause trouble.

"We need to sit." Others in the bar had started looking at us, and I hated being the center of attention, more so now that I wondered whether or not Patrick had had me followed.

He had, once before, and I'd let him know of my displeasure. He'd promised not to do it again, which was a promise that he hadn't kept. I knew that he watched my apartment. Not all the time, but occasionally.

No way did I want him to know that I was with Stryker. He'd flip because not only am I supposed to be his fiancée, but it was *Stryker*.

"I've lost you," Stryker whispered, pulling me down beside him at the table, a frown furrowed his brow.

I took his hand and held it between mine. "You didn't lose me. I was just hoping that I hadn't been followed." I shrugged when his frown deepened. "Patrick likes to keep tabs on me. He watched the apartment but I think, or rather hope, that's all he does."

He caressed my face. "I didn't see anyone lurking around when I was there. I hid and waited for about thirty minutes, watching…and nothing."

"Thank you."

"You can't feel anything for him when there's something between us." His face heated, but I knew that it must hurt him to think that I was with someone else. It would hurt me if the tables were turned.

I chuckled, leaned in and kissed his cheek. "I feel alive when I'm with you," I whispered into his ear, and smiled when he shuddered as my breath tickled his ear. "You liked that." He shuddered again.

"You need to stop teasing me." His eyes were hooded, but I sensed that he could still see me. In fact, all my senses were still alive and buzzed with awareness of him.

"I can't stop. The way you react to me is real, and it makes me feel good knowing that." I shrugged away the twinge of embarrassment that I felt. "I don't think anyone has reacted to me like you do."

Stryker paused, and then his hand cupped the back of my head as he moved me against his chest. His arm closed around my shoulders to keep me against him. I wouldn't want to move even if his arm wasn't like a band of steel.

I wrapped my arm around his waist and rubbed my nose against his chest, inhaling his musky scent into my lungs. He gave me peace and, considering my situation, that said just how much he affected me.

"You make me crave things I've never dared to before." I felt his fingers stroke through my hair. "I don't know what to do about it."

I raised my head to meet his gaze. "Would it be easier if I stayed away?"

His hands tightened around my shoulder. "No." He breathed deeply and exhaled. "It would make it easier for me at the gym, but I can't imagine not seeing you now. We just have to be careful. We were on video today at the gym. Patrick saw me with my hands on you. He wasn't happy."

I bet he wasn't.

I dipped my head so that he wouldn't see my pain. There was certainly no love lost between Patrick and me. It would be nice to have it all over with. I knew what I had to do, but deep down I knew Patrick would make it difficult for me to walk away, even after what he'd done.

"I'm going to talk to him." I sat up and curled into his side, so I could face him. "I'm not even sure why we're still engaged. The thing is, until I met you, I was more or less okay with my life." I smiled. "Now, I realize that for once, I need to take control and instead of hiding to keep the peace, I need to say what's in my heart even though I know he won't want to hear it." He should expect it after the other night because he had no excuse for what he did.

His fingers tightened in my hair. "Promise me that you'll make sure someone else is with you when you do talk to him, okay? I don't trust him."

"I will." I couldn't blame him for that after what I'd left unsaid about last night, but perhaps I did need to tell him. Regardless of how much Patrick frightened me the night before, it could have been worse.

"Don't think about it."

"What?" I blinked in surprise.

"You're easy to read." He frowned.

I whispered, "He didn't rape me, Stryker."

The change in him was instant. His fisted hands rested on top of the table and he breathed deeply like a bull ready to charge.

I thought my words would put his mind at rest over what he thought had happened, but I was wrong.

My hands slipped over both his fists in a gentle caress, and when his gaze met mine, I reached up and placed a sweet kiss to his lips. His eyes were hooded and his body shook so I did the only thing I could and wrapped my arms around his neck, my face buried in the curve of his neck.

He froze and, seconds later, I felt his arms wrap around

my waist as he held me against him. "I'm sorry," I mumbled. "I thought you'd feel better knowing that."

"I do." He exhaled, more like deflated. "He did something though."

"Yes. He didn't physically hurt me and I have no plans on being alone with him again."

Shuddering, I clung tighter and as I felt his hand slip to the top of my bottom, I was so tempted to climb astride him. What would he do if I did?

"Why are you still engaged to him?"

The question I should have expected, but while I was thinking about getting closer to him, he wanted to know that. The sad thing was, I should have told him when I talked about Patrick.

Lifting my head, I met his dark as midnight eyes and admitted, "I'm in a jumbled mess really." I shrugged. "The wedding is soon, and yet I've stayed silent. At first I had planned on being honest and admitting that it wasn't what I wanted, but then I had access to the gym because of Patrick. If I spoke out, then all that would have been taken away and I wouldn't get to see you. I know it's stupid, but that's my reasoning."

He cupped my face and kissed me. His lips hovered over mine while he kissed me again. "I know where you live, Evie. I can come to you."

I shook my head. "No. I don't want any trouble for you because of me... I could call you. We could arrange to meet."

"I don't have a cell phone." He seemed almost ashamed at that confession. Perhaps I was naïve because I thought everyone had a cell these days.

"We need to get you one."

Now it was his turn to shake his head. "I'm not sure." He looked away and then back to me. "Let's get out of here. I want you to myself and there's too many people in here now."

I wanted that as well. I wanted a lot more.

"Yes."

My one word had him tugging me out of the booth with him, and with a quick goodbye to Julio I found myself outside the bar with his arm tightly around my waist. It felt good walking down the sidewalk with him holding me close. Feeling his side pressed up against mine caused my blood to thrum with more desire than I've ever experienced before.

His own desire looked hard and uncomfortable against his zipper, which caused a moan to escape my lips.

That was all it took to find myself shoved up against a wall, my legs around his waist and his hands on my bottom while his mouth hovered above mine.

I wanted this man with everything I had, but not in an alley again. I wanted and needed to see him. To be able to touch him where I wanted to as opposed to where I could reach. Where though? Where could we go?

Millie's apartment.

"My friends apartment. No one knows she has a new place. We can go there."

Even though I'd spoken the words, I wasn't sure he'd heard because he didn't move and stayed frozen against me.

"I want you. Badly," he whispered against my lips.

"I know." I pressed my hips against his and felt the pulsing length of him twitch. He was long and thick and, with another wiggle of my hips against him, his hands clamped on my bottom real tight so that I couldn't move.

"I don't want to come again in my jeans, which I will do if you keep doing that." He blushed and wouldn't meet my gaze.

All too soon he let my feet drop to the ground and stepped back, raking a hand through his hair in obvious frustration. His bulge, if anything, had grown and the thought of having all of him inside me caused my sex to clench with excitement.

He chuckled, groaned, and then mumbled, "Stop looking," before he took my hand and tugged me down the sidewalk again.

"I've no idea where your friend lives, but it's near the park, right?"

"Yes. It's in the Regents building."

Stryker pulled to a sudden stop. "Fuck."

I frowned. "What's wrong?"

He looked at me as though I had two heads. "I'm in the same building. Corner unit on the twenty-first floor."

Stunned was an understatement. "Millie is on the nineteenth, 1908."

"I'm 2110…we have to be careful, and enter separately. They watch me." He looked away and although it felt like minutes had passed, in reality, it was probably seconds before he got us moving again. "When we get there," he looked around us, the frown not leaving his brows, "you go in the front door as I presume you usually do, and I'll find my own way up to you. Leave Millie's door on catch so I can quickly enter before the camera picks me up."

All the cloak and dagger stuff worried me, but I

guessed we both had to stay off Patrick's radar for now. But what would happen to Stryker once my engagement was no more? Would he lose access to the gym as well? Or would he be kept on because he makes them more money than any of the other fighters?

It was all a mess and I had a feeling that Patrick's father might be the one to want the marriage between his son and me. He always seemed to have control, icily so. I couldn't help but wonder if that was the reason Stryker was so isolated.

Ask...

She could. Quickly as well before she chickened out. "Stryker, can I ask you something?"

He looked wary, but agreed with a nod of his head. "Anything."

"About Patrick, do you ever see his father?"

He pulled to a stop and frowned down at me, his fingers intertwined with mine.

"No."

"So Declan has never been down to the gym or spoken to you?"

He frowned. "I don't know the names of everyone who appears, but I get the feeling that Patrick is controlled by someone else so that's possibly his father. The gym is family owned so it all makes sense." We started walking again, about a block away from the apartment building, he asked, "Tell me about Declan...please."

I blew out a breath because what the hell could I say about the man. I ended up saying the first thing that came into my head. "He scares me."

Stryker flexed his fingers around mine. "Go on."

"There's something about him that makes me feel sick

whenever I'm in his presence, which I have to say isn't that often. He asks someone to do something, they do it without question. Even Patrick jumps when his father gives a command. It's just a vibe I get. I mean he's never done or said anything to me; it's just the way he looks at me. Gives me a sick feeling." I shrugged. "He actually terrifies me a lot more than Patrick, so I'll be relieved to be free of their family."

We continued to walk until the entrance of the building was visible, when Stryker tugged me into the doorway of another.

"I don't like what they make you feel, and I sure as hell don't want you alone with either of them…but right now you need to quickly get up to Millie's apartment and wait for me." He gave me a shove.

My legs carried me inside the Regents building and up to the nineteenth floor. At my friend's apartment door, I used my own keycard and security number to enter.

The smile on Millie's face as she turned to look at me made me feel better after the conversation about Declan and Patrick.

"You know, I'm waiting for you to move in with me," Millie laughed. "And I'm serious about that. You already have a room here." She came toward me, her arms wrapping me in a warm embrace.

"I know and I love you even more for that." I bit my lip. "But, um, right now I need you to show me how to stop your door from locking so that Stryker can get in."

Her mouth hung open before she swallowed hard as a light appeared in her eyes. "Stryker? As in the hot piece of fighter from the gym Stryker? He's coming here? To my apartment?"

I rolled my eyes. "Yes to everything. Now hurry."

"Yes, Mom." She strolled to the door and did something with the locks and closed the door. "That's it, and you better explain before he gets here."

"That's what I planned to do." I took a deep breath and quickly glanced at the clock on her microwave. I doubted that I had much time before he slipped inside and I wanted to be alone with him. "We discovered that he lives in the same building. The twenty-first floor. That's why we didn't come here together. Neither of us wanted Patrick to know that we entered together, but I just want to be alone with him. To talk. He appears so lonely, Millie."

"I get that. There's certainly something between you both. That became apparent earlier at the gym, even Carter noticed." She brushed the hair back from my face. "I'll give you some space."

"Thank you, but this is your apartment. We'll go into the other room when he gets here."

"Your bedroom you mean."

I smiled. "My bedroom."

No sooner had the words left my mouth than I was shoved from behind when the door opened. I turned and grinned like an idiot when Stryker entered, closing the door behind him.

CHAPTER 11

STRYKER

I'D USED THE BACK entrance to the building, and even though my card would have come up on the system as being used, they wouldn't be able to find me. The camera in the service elevator worked but was easily covered. So I'd pressed lots of different floors and sent the elevator up, down, up, and then back down once I'd gotten off on the nineteenth floor. The cameras on the floors had a narrow view, and moved slowly from side to side. Luckily for me, Millie's apartment was close to where I was.

The minute the camera changed direction, I ran to the door and shoved inside, quickly closing the door behind me. With a bit of luck, hopefully, I hadn't been caught on the closed circuit video.

It made it all worthwhile though, when I came face to face with my beautiful Evie. I'd been so hard since the minute she'd touched me that I hadn't been sure that I'd be able to walk back to the apartment, but through gritted teeth, I had.

Even as I stared at her, my eyes moving briefly to greet her best friend, my dick had stayed hard as a rock. I blushed slightly at the fact that it was evident for all to see.

Her friend looked between Evie and me, her eyes alight with mischief, but before she could do or say anything, Evie led me to a bedroom. Closing the door, she sat on the bed, her back against the headboard before giving me a shy smile and patting the space beside her.

I sure as hell didn't need telling twice.

Especially when she snuggled against my chest, and I wrapped my arm around her shoulders. My fingers tangled in her beautiful hair as a sigh of contentment escaped my mouth.

I kissed her forehead. "What I'm going to tell you, I'm trusting you to keep to yourself."

"You can trust me, Stryker." She kissed my chest and my heart swelled with longing.

"My real name is…Jake Rivers and I'm twenty-four years old. I want you to know that. I've trained to fight since the night my life was taken from me when I was fourteen. It's all I know how to do. How to live." My voice broke, but I continued because it was important that she knew the real me, "I'm not educated, Evie. I'm no good for y—"

"Don't say that." She covered my mouth with her small fingers. "Don't ever put yourself down. You're perfect for me. We fit together just fine, and," she straddled my waist; I nearly swallowed my tongue as her pussy rubbed against my cock, "I'm sure we'll fit together when we venture into *other* positions." She smirked.

I closed my eyes but that made it worse. All I could see and feel was Evie against me. All I could imagine was making love to her in the bed we currently laid on. She'd be my first, my last…my only, woman.

My hands slid up her thighs and kept her against me. I ignored the pain of being hard and swollen, trapped behind my zipper because having her so close made my heart lighter.

"Stryker," she whispered, her breath tickled along my lips.

Opening my eyes, my whole body tensed with the heat I saw in hers. My breath stuck in my lungs and shards of pleasure teased beneath my skin, making me twitch and tingle…lengthen. It wouldn't be long before I spilled my release.

She reached up and, gripping my shoulders, wiggled on my lap as she moaned.

"Fuck," I hissed, pushing her away from my dick. "I need distracting."

Evie smirked. "I know just how to distract you."

"Although I'm certainly up for that kind of distraction, we still need to talk."

"I know." She wiggled against my groin and got comfortable. "That's better. I want to be close to you." Her arms went around my shoulders and her head rested against my neck.

My body still ached, but it was more manageable as I continued, "My life isn't easy, Evie. It's difficult than most. I'm under…contract…" I winced at the lie but I couldn't tell her the truth or I was sure she would involve herself regardless. "Which means that I have to do what they say. They hold me tight to their chest and, right now, there isn't anything I can do about it except warn you to get away from Patrick. I don't trust him with you, and if word should get out about us spending time together, I'd hate to think of what he'd do."

"He'd go crazy, Stryker." She kissed my neck. "I need to continue to think of you as Stryker so that I don't slip up, but you've no idea how much I want to call you by your real name."

"I look forward to the day when you can."

I arched up and moved us down the bed, rolling Evie from her straddled position. I kept her tucked into my side, and caressed her thigh when she straddled it over my hip. "I've never laid in bed with a woman before."

Her eyes widened and met mine. "Never?"

"Never."

"So, I'm the first."

"The first with everything."

I gently tugged her head to my chest and rubbed soothing circles on her back. It wasn't long before she slept wrapped in my arms. I wasn't sure how I was supposed to walk away from her. To do so would leave her vulnerable, but if I didn't, I knew the men wouldn't just let me leave and she'd then be caught in the crossfire.

EVIE

WAKING, I REALIZED THAT I'd slept on Stryker. Used him as a bed and my smile couldn't get any wider. I loved being so close to him, and the fact that he'd held me without pushing for more said a lot to me.

His confession of the night before raised questions that I didn't know how to ask. I mean, what exactly did he mean 'the first with everything'? Surely such a strong, handsome man would have some experience. Wouldn't he? Trying to chase the thoughts away, I glanced toward the curtains, but couldn't see anything with the light being off.

How long had we slept?

I frowned and slowly moved my head to the clock and realized I'd slept until four in the morning. I'd had about six hours of much needed sleep. The movement had woken Stryker and he caressed the hair down my back. "I love this," he whispered, his voice husky with need.

How much he loved having my body against his was obvious with the constant erection that he couldn't hide. I wanted to see him, pleasure him, to know what it was like to have him pleasure me.

Sitting up, I wiggled in his lap, knowing it made him harder. Cupping his face with my hands, I brought our lips together. I deepened the kiss, learning the shape of his mouth, his taste as our tongues slipped together. Before long, Stryker growled and flipped me to my back. Following me down, his jean-clad erection pressed against my wet panties with my skirt hiked around my waist.

He used his arms so that he didn't crush me, but as he dipped his head to continue teasing my mouth, I wanted his weight covering me. My breasts ached to be touched. To be pressed tightly against his chest.

The moan that had been lodged in my throat burst forth, and Stryker finally lost control. His chest came down to mine, his hands held my head while he devoured my mouth. It was a kiss so wet and carnal that I seriously thought I'd come.

It was over too soon.

Stryker pulled his mouth away, cursed, and rolled to

his back. His heavy breathing could be heard in the quiet of the night, and I felt his fist clench beside me.

Rolling to my side, I came face to face with his impressive erection. With a quick glance up to his hooded eyes, I took a chance.

I reached out and made quick work of his fly. Once I'd got that over with, I inhaled and kneeled between his spread thighs. His eyes glittered, his jaw clenched tightly together, but he didn't stop me.

Taking hold of the top of his jeans, I tugged and, with his help, got them to his thighs where I stopped.

I swallowed and moaned.

He was long, thick, and so hard that I'd have been able to use him as a hammer. The more I looked, the more he twitched, and the crown leaked precum. Arching up, Stryker fisted the cover under him, but his eyes never left mine.

"I'm so close," he growled. "You need to know something."

"What?"

I bent my head and seconds from licking his balls, he admitted, "I've never been with anyone before. Ever. Sex. Blowjob. Nothing."

My mind spun and I'd think about that later, but for now, I wanted him on my tongue. My mouth.

At the first swipe of my tongue, his body jerked as though he'd stuck his dick in an electrical socket. I didn't want him coming before I got my mouth around him, but I wanted him to know what my tongue felt like.

I licked again, massaging his balls in my mouth. Out of the corner of my eye, I caught his hand moving to his dick so I reached out and held both of his arms down at his side while his hips strained. My tongue licked up along his length, circling around the bulging head, which was soaked with excitement.

I released one of his arms and used my hand to hold his erection straight up. As I held his gaze, I slid my mouth down his length. Withdrew to the tip. Sucked him back into the wet warmth. He trembled. I used my hand to cup and gently squeeze his balls, as I took more inside me. He tensed seconds before he started to spill down my throat. I sucked and swallowed. He came so hard that I nearly choked on the amount he'd released.

I didn't though.

As soon as he relaxed, I licked him clean and grinned when he started to enlarge again. Stryker had other ideas, and I was suddenly hauled up his body with his lips sealed to mine. He held my head down to his mouth and ravaged me. That was the only word for it. He consumed me with his passion and the intensity of his kiss told me more than words ever could.

I was his.

He rolled me to my back, my skirt wedged around my thighs, and his hardness rocked against my wet panties. No matter how much I ached to be filled by him, I didn't want that to happen tonight. My eyes stung with tears. He'd never been with anyone before me and I felt the excitement of being his first. I just struggled to get my mind around that fact.

"You're thinking too hard." He pressed against me while watching my reaction. "I want to have you naked against me. To be able to touch you, make you feel what you just made me feel." He frowned a look of uncertainty crossing his features. "It's just as good for a woman, right?"

I smiled, and reaching up, cupped his face. "Oh, yes," I reassured. "But tonight isn't going to be about me. It's about you. I can wait."

"Let me take your panties off."

My eyes snapped to his and although 'yes' was on the tip of my tongue, I honestly wanted tonight for him.

"I promise I won't shove my cock inside you. I just want to see you." I followed his gaze to my crotch and knew what he wanted, even if I hadn't twigged with his words.

I reached down, started to tug them down when Stryker knocked my hands away and pulled the scrap of material the rest of the way off, tossing them over his shoulder.

His eyes heated and arousal pooled between my thighs, which he felt when he ran his finger between the lips of my pussy.

"You're really wet," he moaned, taking his cock in hand. "Is it normal?"

"Yes," I panted. His finger didn't stop stroking and when the tip entered my sex the muscles clenched as nerve endings sizzled. "It's because of you. You arouse me and make my sex wet, swollen, and achy to be filled."

"Touching you like this makes my cock rock hard and there's a sensation that keeps running along the length. It pools at the head." His breathing uneven, his eyes were still fused to what he was doing between my legs, and then all of a sudden he dropped to his belly and kissed me.

He opened me up with his fingers and licked with quick swipes of his tongue. While his mouth and tongue loved me, his heated eyes lifted to mine.

The pleasure became too much as my gaze roamed over his body and fell on his erection. It twitched and throbbed and I ached to feel it again. I quickly yanked off my dress, followed with my bra, and tossed it across the room.

Stryker's, "Oh, fuck," was the only warning I had. The next thing he hovered over me, his gaze on my breasts, the nipples calling to him with how hard and erect they were.

"I'm going to come again, too soon." He dipped his head and lapped at a nipple.

I couldn't help but squirm with the arousal rushing through me, and when I felt the base of his shaft against my naked pussy, I froze. So did Stryker. He lifted his eyes to mine and rubbed.

My eyes rolled and I knew I'd let him do anything he wanted to me. Except the more he ground against me, and lapped at my nipples, I knew I'd be coming before he even got inside me. From Stryker's breathing, I knew he was close as well.

And then he stopped.

He raised his head, and asked, "What do you want me to do?"

My confident man was asking me even though he looked as though he was losing control.

Without words, I pulled him down on top of me, wrapped my legs around his waist, and kissed him. While we were locked in the tender kiss, he rocked against me, seconds later I convulsed in pleasure before I felt his wet release between us.

Sliding my fingers through his hair, I held him in place so that he knew exactly where I wanted him to stay.

"I want so much with you Stryker," I admitted, hoping my words didn't scare him away.

But as his forehead rested against mine, I knew there had been no need to worry. "You need to be safe, Evie. That's my priority. But my heart wants what you do."

"That makes me happy…" I sighed and then said, "I need to get you a cell phone."

He blinked at my rapid change of subject. "As much as I'd love to be able to get hold of you anywhere. I'm not sure that's such a good idea. I'd have to keep it hidden as they couldn't know I had one."

I hoped that I hid my question well, because there was real fear in his eyes talking about a cell.

"Leave the cell for now," he added, but then his worry turned to a smile on his lips. "I need to clean you up." His grinned widened.

I chuckled. "You like me being covered with your release, don't you?"

"Hell, yeah." He quickly kissed me on the nose and climbed off the bed, holding his jeans up. "I'll grab a washcloth from the bathroom."

As I watched him saunter to grab a washcloth, I realized that he'd have to leave me soon to go back to his apartment. I wondered if Patrick knew that I wasn't home. Knew that Stryker wasn't either. Would he put two and two together and come up with the correct answer?

CHAPTER 12

STRYKER

SHOWERING AT THE GYM with a hard dick was something that hadn't happened to me before. Normally, after working out, I'd be ready for sleep, or wired for more, instead of some action. But after lying with Evie last night and being close to her, my body had been constantly hard.

Even when I'd snuck out of the apartment to head back to mine, my body had cried out for her. So had my heart. It was the thought of bringing trouble to her door that had me moving my ass regardless.

Coach had noticed my distraction even though he'd kept his mouth shut. All I'd have done anyway was deny it.

As the heat of the water came down on my tense muscle, I heard someone enter the showers. A quick glance over my shoulder told me it was Carter. He was the only other man in the gym that I'd considered asking for help. But the question in my mind was what would happen if I trusted the wrong person. Since my father, I hadn't trusted anyone. Coach needed his salary so I hadn't risked trusting him to that extent before, but Evie. Evie I trusted. I wasn't ready to trust her with the full story of my life, but I trusted her to keep anything I told her to herself. Now though, I was tempted to trust Carter.

"You want to do some sparring tomorrow?" he asked, out of the blue.

Checking my erection had shrunk, I knocked off the shower, grabbed a towel and wrapped it around my hips as I turned to face his back.

He was covered in tattoos, tasteful ones at that, and when he turned and saw my gaze on his back, he smirked. "At least you weren't looking at my ass."

My surprise was evident, but then I laughed.

He grinned.

"You heard the rumors, huh?"

"I did. Thought there might have been some truth in them until I saw you watching Evie."

I frowned.

"Hey, it was only an observation. But you do need to step back when she's around before others notice. You hear me?"

Nodding, I headed for my locker.

It had been on the tip of my tongue to ask him a favor. Just the thought of asking sent my heart into overdrive. I could trust him, couldn't I?

Only one way to find out.

Quickly dressing in sweats, T-shirt and sneakers, I went over to his locker and only had to wait seconds before he appeared with a towel wrapped around his waist and another around his neck.

He stopped when he saw me, a look of wariness on his face.

I closed my eyes and asked, "I need a favor." I moved closer and while my heart went frantic, my palms sweated, I asked him, "Can you get me a cell phone without anyone finding out?"

His eyes widened with surprise but he agreed. "Prepaid will be better for you. I'll load it up."

Fuck.

I hadn't thought about money.

"Don't worry about it. I'm not as clueless as they think and I'm happy to help you." Carter reached for his shoulder and rubbed before turning to his locker. "I'll get it later today."

"Thank you."

I didn't know what else to say or do, so I turned and headed out of the gym only to freeze when I spotted the black car at the curb. Tinted windows and a chauffeur meant one thing only to me.

I had to get in.

I felt like running, but instead I did what was expected and climbed into the back seat.

Patrick awaited me.

A very angry, but controlled, Patrick.

"I'm going to get right to it. The keycard says you entered the building at ten-forty-three, yet you didn't appear in the apartment until close to five am. Want to tell me where you went?"

Fuck.

"I didn't go anywhere. The time must be wrong."

His jaw tightened. "Someone spotted Evie entering the front of the building around ten-thirty but he has no idea where she went after that. So, I'll ask you again. Where did you go? And a new question, was Evie with you?"

I clenched my fists at my side praying for control because I really wanted to knock the smug bastard out of the car. I could do it as well.

Inhaling before I slowly exhaled, I let him see that I was pissed. He moved into the corner and watched me, his face showed concern for his own safety, finally.

"Evie was not with me. The only time I've been close to her was yesterday morning when she was upset. As for the time-lapse, I've no idea what's going on with that. You know that I have no clue about anything to do with technology. But we weren't together, and I came straight in and to my apartment."

He couldn't decide whether or not I told him the truth, it was in his eyes.

"Regardless, Evie *will* be my wife very soon. In fact, I'm on my way to pick her up for a visit to her parents' house for the weekend." He smirked. "So go...make my family more money this weekend and I'll try and forget the lapse in time."

My first thought was to pound into him, or warn him of what would happen if he so much as laid a hand on Evie again.

Seconds from doing what I wanted, I jumped out of the car and walked.

They'd follow me.

Right now I didn't give a fuck what they did.

She wouldn't be here for the fight.

Until that moment, I hadn't realized how much I wanted her there. I wanted her in my corner, my name on her lips. Not Stryker...Jake.

That couldn't happen.

Didn't stop me from wanting it...wanting it so badly that I was that close to telling them to have her there or there'd be no fight.

I gave a mirthless laugh. I wouldn't do that because then they'd realize that she meant something to me. They'd use that against me, and maybe harm Evie. I wouldn't allow that, or be responsible.

Reaching the park, I took off. I needed to run. And I needed to run fast.

So what if I knew they couldn't keep up to me.

EVIE

I WAS NERVOUS AS hell that Patrick was picking me up, and had been surprised that he wanted to travel together for an unplanned party at my parents' house. The only thing keeping my fear at bay was the fact that we'd be in the car and then at my parents' house. He'd only be able to use words to get at me, instead of his strength.

Closing my eyes, I tried to center myself and calm my nerves.

I could do this.

I had to do this.

I had to end whatever this was over the weekend.

Sighing, I met my gaze in the mirror and carefully applied my plum-colored lip-gloss while I tried to get my mind focused. Being distracted would be noticeable, and my father never missed anything. How could I focus when I knew Stryker was fighting over the weekend? I wouldn't be there to watch him. To wrap my arms around him and ease his aching muscles.

But I could let him know I might not be there for him at the fight but my heart was.

He didn't have a cell though, but Millie was finally seeing Carter tonight, so maybe…

Spying my cell lying next to my purse, I turned it over in my hands, dropped to the sofa in my living room and went for it.

Waiting for Millie to pick up, my foot tapped against the floor with impatience, more so when I noticed the time. Patrick would be here soon. Ten minutes. He'd be five minutes early like always.

"Evie, is everything okay?" My breathless friend sounded worried.

"I guess."

I let the silence hang while I tried to figure out what to say, but in the end, straightforward would work best. "I need you to ask Carter to get a message to Stryker for me. Can you do that?"

"Evie, you don't need to ask. I'll do anything to help. You know that. Tell me the message?"

"I need him to know that…that I might not be at the fight, but that my heart is with him. I need him to know how I feel Millie."

"He'll know. I promise."

The tightness in my chest released as I sagged against the back of the sofa. "Thank you."

"You're welcome. I'm worried about you."

"I'm fine, really, and it's not like Patrick can get up to anything in the car. He's a very private man so at least I'm reassured by that. He's in his usual room at my parents' house because you know they don't condone sharing unless there is a wedding band on a finger. I'll be fine."

There was silence. "Who are you trying to convince?" she asked, her voice a concerned whisper.

I smiled, sadly. "Please don't worry about me. My father won't let anything happen to me. You just enjoy yourself with Carter while I'm away."

"I will on the condition that you call and let me know how you are. I also want to know when you plan on moving in with me?"

Chuckling, my face lit with happiness. "We'll talk about it when I get back."

"Good! Because the security is much better here than where you live. Anyone can knock on your door."

That wasn't quite true, but I wasn't going to argue. The thought of living with her gave me something to look forward to. But for Patrick we would have lived together after college, but there again, I let him talk me into this place.

"I need to go, Millie. Please don't worry and we'll talk soon. Don't forget my message."

"I won't. Love you."

"Love you." I hung up, but stayed seated, my cell going back and forth in my hand.

Minutes went by before I heard a car pull up outside, which was what I needed to get myself moving.

Patrick would frown when he saw me because I had jeans and boots on. I figured that I needed to dress my outfit up a bit so I'd paired the jeans with a cream tank, and a cream silk blouse on top.

Hearing the knock on my door, I breathed deeply through my nose before answering because the nerves were back in my stomach again.

He stood before me in his usual navy blue trouser and

blazer with a pale blue shirt. He was a handsome man but there was no spark between us. There had been a small one when we'd first met…the reason why I was in this mess… but that spark had died a long time ago and any hope that it would reignite had died after what he'd done to me. My skin crawled at the thought of being alone with him.

"We need to talk." He stepped around me, waiting for my attention to be on him.

Sighing, wondering whether I could trust him, I slowly let the door close behind me and leaned against it. "I'm listening."

He cleared his throat. "I want to apologize for the other night." He impatiently brushed the hair from his forehead. He had a cowl at the front that constantly got in his way. But what did he expect with a head full of blond hair. "I don't know what happened. I just lost it and didn't think. I'm sorry, Evie. Can you forgive me?"

Stunned.

I wondered whether his words felt as alien coming out of his mouth as they did to me hearing them. He never apologized for anything, even when he was wrong so the fact that he did now made me nervous. It was as though he wanted something from me. Or he wanted me to be more complacent over the weekend at my parents' house. There was something more to this than an apology.

"Please say something," he requested with impatience, taking a step closer.

It took a lot not to cringe, but I stood my ground. "I don't know what to say." *Because I can't forgive you.*

"I want you to stop moving away when I come close. I want you to say you'll try and forget what happened so we can move on. I don't want your family, especially your father, getting wind of anything wrong between us."

My father? I should have known.

"I can act." *For now!*

Slipping around him, I grabbed my overnight bag and purse. "Let's go."

He cursed and removed the bag from my hands. "You're damn stubborn."

I watched him walk off down the stairs while I made sure my apartment was locked tight, wondering what was really going on with him. Stryker was also in my thoughts but for a different reason entirely. I wanted to be with him, and the fact that I had to spend time until I'd talked to Patrick being nice to him in front of my parents made me feel nauseous.

If only I'd have been able to talk to him before this weekend trip so that I'd be making it on my own instead. But for the other night I probably would have gotten it out of the way by now, but he'd scared me to the point that I didn't want to be alone with him again. Not only had he scared me, he'd surprised the hell out of me. By his half-assed apology and he knew it too.

Patrick was on his cell when I walked out of my building, pacing as though agitated. He completely ignored me as I slipped into the car. Once settled with still no sign of Patrick joining me, I slipped my sunglasses on. He always said my thoughts were clear in my eyes so that was the last thing I wanted him to see.

Once we arrived at my parents' house, we'd have to find somewhere quiet to talk, but close to where others could hear if he pounced again.

I hated feeling afraid in his presence.

CHAPTER 13

STRYKER

"YOU KNOW HOW TO work it, right?" Carter frowned at my puzzlement over the alien object in my hand.

A cell phone.

I'd seen plenty, but never held one in my hand before so of course I'd never used one either.

"Here." Carter took it back and started pressing buttons. "Look, it's a basic one, okay? To make a call press this button, select the name of the person you want to call or punch in the number. At the minute, you only have Evie, Millie, and my number programmed in. After you've made a call, I'll show you how to clear the call logs just in case."

That seemed simple enough.

The excitement at being able to talk to Evie must have shown on my face because in the next breath, Carter was shoving me into the bathroom. "Call your girl. We have ten minutes before I'm called to take you downstairs."

He slammed the door behind me.

What should I say to her? It's been so long since I used a phone that the thing really did feel alien in my hand, but for Evie…and Carter, I wouldn't have one now.

I paced in the bathroom of my hotel room that I shared with Carter. I'd been surprised that we'd been assigned the same room because usually I'd have a guard in with me, or I'd share with Coach.

The fight was happening tonight, and I'd received a message from Evie via Millie and Carter, which had made my heart clench with *something* for Evie.

Love was the first thing to come to mind, but how could I be in love with her after only knowing her a few days? There was something about her that made me crave to have her close. To want her in my sight at all times. To be able to touch her when I wanted to. To not have to worry about anyone seeing us talk, or exchange a small caress. My fingers constantly twitched to touch her when I'd be at the gym, in fact, that hadn't been the only thing that twitched.

Time was getting on and if I wanted to hear her voice before I went out there, I had to do it now. The small black cell wouldn't dial itself. So, I finally took a deep inhale and pressed Evie's name. My chest tightened with fear, as the cell showed it was trying to connect to her.

My palms felt sweaty and my stomach was in knots while I waited to hear her voice, and then her soft voice was in my ear.

"Hello?"

My mouth felt dry.

My brain shut down, stalled.

"Stryker? Is that you?" Just hearing my name on her lips sent shards of pleasure straight to my heart...and other places.

"Yeah," I whispered and cleared my throat. "It's me." I closed my eyes and imagined her. She was breathtaking and I remembered the way she'd felt. Her breasts, large and firm, in the palms of my hands. Between her legs, wet and silky, ready for us to join. We hadn't yet, but we would soon. Hopefully I'd be able to stay loaded long enough to pleasure her. Because being inside her, warm wet sex, would be out of this world and not just because it would be my first time inside anyone.

It was all Evie.

She did things to me.

"Are you still there?"

"Yeah. Sorry. I was thinking about the other night."

She groaned, and my dick went rock hard. "Did you get my message?"

"I did."

"Wait? You have a cell phone?"

I smiled at her excitement. "Carter got me one."

"I'll save your number when we're finished talking... Are you all right?" she asked, her tone tender.

"I'm hard as rock just listening to you."

My blunt statement was followed by silence and then she giggled. "I wasn't expecting that, but I like that I affect you with just my voice."

"Everything about you affects me." I closed my eyes and dropped my head to the wall in front of me, one hand held the cell and the other fisted on the wall. "Are you all right, Evie?"

"I am now."

"You're crying."

The tears in her voice were easy to hear as her voice shook.

"I'm okay, really. It's just everything's getting to me. I keep trying to pin Patrick down, but it's as though he has a sixth sense and knows what I'm going to say. I just don't understand why he'd avoid the issue though. He doesn't love me and I don't love him. I never have." She sniffled again, and added, "I just want to be with you, especially tonight."

No matter how much I wanted her there, I couldn't tell her that. Not while she was upset, but what should I tell her? I've never had a crying woman over the phone before.

At least now I felt as though I'd had a bucket of cold water tipped over me with things shriveled.

She continued to sob softly while I acted like an idiot.

"Evangeline, babe. Please stop. You're killing me with your tears when I can't hold you."

"I'm okay."

I actually smiled at that comment because she was anything but. "Who are you trying to convince, me or you, babe? C'mon, I need to hear your voice, knowing that the tears have stopped before I head down to the ring."

"You're fighting in a ring again? I thought you usually fought in the cage."

More often than not they shoved me in the cage when it was a 'no rules' fight.

"Not here. When are you back?"

"Tomorrow."

"You stopped crying?"

I could hear the smile in her voice as she said, "Yes," then she sniffled, chuckled, "A bit."

"Evie, if you need me, you call and tell me, okay? I'll work out a way to get to you."

"I don't want you to be in any trouble because of me, which will happen if Patrick finds out about us. His father's arrived not long ago, but luckily I was in the kitchen with my mom, so Dad distracted him. He always tries to talk to me. He's more of a creep than Patrick, and I can't believe that I never noticed how alike they were until recently."

Warning bells rang in my head and I was worried as I turned and paced in the small area. "Just promise me you'll call if you need me. Promise me, Evie."

"I promise."

"What—"

Bang. Bang. "Stryker, we gotta go." *Carter.*

"Evie, babe. I have to go. I think they're waiting for me."

"Be careful...please."

"Evangeline," I moaned, wanting to say more, knowing I didn't have time.

"I know, *Jake*," she whispered. "I wanted you to hear your name on my lips before you went into the ring."

She hung up and I found myself fighting tears. I held my finger and thumb into the corner of my eyes hoping that they wouldn't fall. I wanted her here in front of me, not miles away with that bastard.

"Stryker, hurry. They're coming off the elevator. I need to clear your cell."

I quickly opened the door and passed him the cell. It

took all of a few seconds to sort it out before it was back in my hands. Looking around, I glanced up.

I'd found the hiding place.

EVIE

SLIPPING MY FEET INTO my black-heeled shoes, I realized that I still clutched my cell to my chest. I'd rather be clutching Stryker to it instead.

"That's a heavy sigh." Patrick came up behind me, and reached out just in time to prevent me from falling in surprise. "Steady, now."

"What are you doing in here?" I moved out of his hold, turning to face him.

"Your mother sent me to escort you downstairs." Patrick tugged on the cuffs of his dress shirt while heading for the door.

My mother…ugh!

"We need to talk." I'd finally found the courage to start the conversation that we needed to have. We were alone and even though I knew we didn't have long, it was better than leaving it any longer.

"Later…your mother is waiting." Patrick opened my door and waited.

Tears of frustration hovered on my lashes, which I quickly blinked away.

Patrick pretended that he hadn't noticed and stepped out of my room, offering me his arm.

But for not wanting to embarrass my parents, I'd have left the ass to follow behind me. Instead, I took his arm and plastered a smile to my lips.

My father gave me a questioning look once we joined

the cocktail party and my mother looked unsure, which she hid seconds later.

"Evie, you look beautiful."

My body chilled at the words coming out of Declan's mouth as he joined us.

"Declan, nice to see you again."

No, it wasn't.

I plastered another fake smile to my lips and held my hand out.

He looked at my hand, ignored it, and leaned in to kiss my cheek. It took everything in me not to wipe my cheek. My skin crawled in revulsion.

"I need to speak to my son." Declan looked at Patrick, made his excuses and walked to the opened doors that led outside with Patrick on his heels.

"Don't worry honey, he'll be back." My mother came over and patted my hand reassuringly and I wanted to scream at her. I didn't need consoling, I needed Stryker.

I bit back the truth that was on the tip of my tongue and kissed both of my parents on the cheek. "I'm going to get a drink." Without giving them time to waylay me, I turned on my heels and disappeared into the kitchen.

At least I could stay out of view while I was in here, but it wouldn't be long before my mother found me. She'd watched me come in here so she'd be chasing me out soon with words like, "Please mingle, Evangeline." I'd get my full name because she'd be pissed underneath her cool exterior.

I loved her, and she had always been there for me when I really needed a mom, but we had our moments. She was always about the public image and how we had to be happy and strong in front of others. But when we were alone, she was there, she would let me cry and let me vent. But she wouldn't do that right now.

She had no idea what was really going on, and our arguments had grown more common since she only had eyes for the wedding that she was arranging. I think somewhere along the way she'd forgotten that real people were involved, especially her daughter.

Sighing heavily, I grabbed a couple bottles of beer from the fridge and snuck out the backdoor. I had no clue as to where Patrick and his father had disappeared to, so I needed to be careful that I didn't bump into them. The last thing I wanted while outside in the dark, alone.

It didn't take me long until I crept into the boathouse by the lake. It would always be the boathouse to me regardless of my mother's change in name to the glasshouse.

I kept the lights off and moved upstairs to the balcony above the boat. It had been made into a living room and was a quiet area away from the main house.

Except as I moved toward the window I saw shadows along the small dock leading out into the water, as though someone was there. I quickly moved away to stand behind the curtain and peered through the gap at the side. I didn't think that I would be seen but I was curious as to who was out there.

Patrick and his father came to mind as they'd disappeared not long before I'd made my own escape.

I shook my head. It probably wouldn't be them; perhaps a couple of guests who'd wandered away from the party for some time alone.

Smiling, and not wanting to be a voyeur, I came away from the window and sat on the sofa.

Unable to settle with worry for Stryker in my mind, and wondering when I was going to be able to stop the farce of a wedding, I snapped the cap on one of the beers and took a long drink, hoping it would help me to relax.

I quickly drained one bottle and lay down on the sofa. I'd stay here for a while.

CHAPTER 14

HE SHOULDN'T BE HAPPY that the Irishman had been pissed over that night's fight, but he found that he was. The man had brought it on himself.

After his meeting with the Irishman, he'd stayed outside in the dark. The silence of the night by the lake, and his lover by his side, calmed his racing heart with what he was about to do.

Growing up, he never thought he would ever betray his family, but he couldn't let it go on any longer. He hated being part of it. As long as his mother and lover were protected, then anything else didn't matter.

"Patrick?" His lover pressed a hand to his lower back, and moved in close to his side.

"I'm okay." He turned to face his lover. "Are you?"

His lover swallowed and met his gaze. "I'm worried about you, constantly… This thing you're about to do is dangerous if the Irishman finds out."

Their fingers intertwined and he briefly leaned in to kiss his lover. "I don't plan for him to find out."

The low hum of a boat approached and had them stepping apart.

He turned to his lover, "No matter what happens, what I have to do, to end him, I need you to know that I love you." He audibly swallowed, having never said those words to another soul, other than his mother, before.

His lover looked choked with emotion. "I love you, too. I always have."

Silence followed as they watched the men who he planned to help bring the Irishman to justice, slowly approach.

CHAPTER 15

STRYKER

STANDING IN THE CENTER of the cage while the referee held my arm in the air as tonight's winner, I felt nothing.

The fight hadn't only changed venue, but I'd been told the cage would be dropped. That had given me a few hours to prepare for the kind of fight that had then been expected of me. Before I'd met Evie those fights never bothered me, but now...now I hated them.

As I looked out at the crowd cheering at my victory, all I could think about was how much money had they'd made because of me.

That's all I was to them—money.

Looking around the arena now, I stared into a pair of eyes that I hadn't seen in ten years. I was too stunned to move, and by the time I'd snapped out of my shock, he was gone. I tugged my wrist free and looked, searched, but he really was gone—if he'd been there at all.

The cage slowly started to move upwards, and the minute it cleared the ground, Carter got in my face. "Tell me?" He turned to look out at the crowd, the same direction that had held my gaze.

"I thought I saw…it doesn't matter. Just get me out of here."

Carter paused, knowing that there was something wrong, but didn't press me. "Okay, let's go."

I followed him from the arena, reeling from the sight of my father. From the brief glance I had of him, he looked the same, just older and with a trimmed beard.

Ignoring Coach, I followed Carter into the locker room and, as soon as the door closed behind us, I held my gloved hands out.

Without asking any questions, Carter watched me closely while he removed the gloves, tossing them to the floor…and waited.

Unsettled, I dropped my ass to the bench and dipped my head. I squeezed my eyes closed not knowing how to handle seeing him. Even though I always looked for him, I'd given up hope that I'd ever see him again and the shock still rocked through me.

"My father," I whispered so quietly that I wasn't sure Carter heard me.

"I take it he doesn't usually show up at your fights?" Carter sat next to me and, for once, I felt like I had a real friend. Someone who wouldn't betray me to the boss.

"No…I haven't seen him in ten years." I shook my head. "I'm glad I didn't spot him until the end because the sight of him knocked me on my ass."

Other than shock I still didn't know how I felt. I thought when I'd see him again that I'd feel anger, but that hadn't even appeared. Instead, wave after wave of shock hit me in the gut.

"I think—"

Coach slamming into the locker room cut off Carter words. "Stupid fuckers," he mumbled, as he came to stand in front of us.

We both looked up as Coach glanced between the two of us. "We're leaving straight from here." He held up a wrinkled hand when I opened my mouth to question him. "Don't ask questions because I don't have the answers. They said we're to head straight back and that's what we have to do. Bags are already in the car from the rooms... fuckers." Coach stomped off as quickly as he'd appeared.

I groaned. "Fuck! I left the cell above the ceiling tiles in the bathroom."

"I'm curious as to why we're clearing out instead of staying the night." Carter frowned. "Don't you think it's strange?"

I sighed heavily, grabbed my shower stuff, and turned to face Carter. "Nothing surprises me anymore."

In the shower, I stripped and let the heat of the water pound down over my aching body.

Jaws had been a good opponent and we'd gone more rounds than some of my more recent fights. He'd gotten some good kicks and punches in before I'd taken him down.

Even though it had only been a warm up fight for when I faced Lethal Black, Jaws had made me work for tonight's win, which filled me with respect for the other fighter.

Now that it was all over and I felt the adrenalin gradually start to leave me, all I wanted was Evie. I couldn't even call her now that my cell was lost to me.

EVIE

I'D WORRIED ABOUT STRYKER all night. I'd tried calling him on the number that he'd called from, numerous times, and nothing. It was like he'd just up and disappeared. My agitation over not being able to get hold of him was showing with my temper. I'd been short with my parents at breakfast and had decided it was best to keep my mouth shut than open.

Patrick had disappeared for most of yesterday and had only shown up at the cocktail party last night, briefly. Now the asshole had gone back to the city so his 'later' hadn't happened.

One more day, and if he hadn't let me have my say by then, he'd find out over the phone, or in the newspaper, that our wedding wasn't going ahead. There was certainly no love lost between us, something that I'm sure my father already suspected.

My father had always let my mother follow her own direction with me. He was good though because he'd suggest things and eventually my mother would go along with his suggestion, and think it was her own idea. It had been like that for years, and now my dad had been hinting that he wanted to talk to me privately. I was afraid he'd see straight though me, but with the wedding a week away, I knew I had to tell them the truth. I couldn't leave it one more day, like I'd planned with Patrick.

The garden room that I currently hid inside was like a greenhouse, or even a sauna when the rays of the sun pierced through the glass. It was also where I was guaranteed some peace and quiet. It was always my sanctuary when I was at home. Just perfect.

My iPad was in my lap, as I bumped my cell phone against my chin in pure agitation at not knowing how Stryker was. Did he win the fight? Was he left in pain? Was he being cared for? It drove me crazy not having any of the answers.

I'd asked Patrick about the fight, but he'd been evasive. It had felt like he'd patted the little woman on the head.

Grinding my teeth, I held both my iPad and cell as I moved out of the room to find my parents who I knew would be drinking coffee in the kitchen.

Creatures of habit.

They turned to me as I entered, a frown on both of their brows, and it was all the clue I needed to know that they'd been talking about me.

"Come sit," my mom patted the chair beside her with a quick glance at Dad. It was as though she'd asked permission, except my father's gaze stayed unwavering on me.

"I'm heading back soon, and I need to say something that I don't think you're going to like?" I dropped into the seat offered, my heart heavy.

I glanced between my parents, sighed, and admitted, "I'm not marrying Patrick."

As expected, my mom gasped and grabbed hold of my father's wrist, her eyes were wide. She opened her mouth as though to argue and then closed it, completely stunned by my confession. My father met my gaze as my eyes filled with tears. I was positive they'd be disappointed in me. All that money, all those months of planning. The problem it would cause having to send back gifts, phone guests and cancel all the arrangements. I hated myself a little for waiting so long and I was so worried that they would hate me too. My dad nodded, silently telling me to go ahead and explain.

My nerves jumped but I'd started so there was no reason why I couldn't get through this. "I've tried to get Patrick alone all weekend to break it all off, but he's been evasive. It's as though he knows what I'm going to say, and doesn't want to hear it. The thing is I know he doesn't love me so I don't know why he'd want to go ahead with the wedding."

"Oh, honey." Mom patted my hand. "I know what's wrong with you." She looked cheerful all of a sudden, which didn't bode well. "You're having pre-wedding jitters. That's all it is. A case of cold feet but it will pass. I know it did for me. Go back to the city and carry on as normal and then we'll see you on the weekend." She hugged me and left the room, whistling of all things.

I turned to my father, bewildered. He wore a frown as his gaze followed my mother from the room. Almost wearily he turned back to me. "It's more than pre-wedding jitters, isn't it?"

"Yes."

"You need to talk to Patrick as soon as you get back and tell him. I'll talk to your mother and help her sort everything out. But today or tomorrow, Evie because we'll need to put the announcement out as soon as he knows."

I jumped up and wrapped my arms around my father's neck, crying. "Thank you."

He patted my shoulders in an awkward manner, which had me laughing out loud. As I pulled away, he looked puzzled at my sudden change in emotion. So I explained, "I was upset about disappointing you and Mom. I guess

Mom still thinks the weddings going ahead until you've spoken to her, but it's such a relief having told you."

"I bet it is, honey. It's Sunday today, so we'll wait until tomorrow to start cancelling everything. We'll start with the venues and our family but you need to tell Patrick so he isn't suddenly surprised. Just call and let us know when you've spoken to him."

"I will. Thank you." I hugged him again, and grabbing my iPad and cell, headed to the front door where my bags waited.

I'd quickly get home, change, and head to the gym to find out what happened last night. I wasn't sure if Stryker would be around the day after a fight, but at least I'd hopefully find out what had happened and how he was, even if I had to use *research* as an excuse.

CHAPTER 16

STRYKER

I HAD NOTHING BETTER to do on a Sunday afternoon so I headed to the gym and did what I knew best. Beating out my frustration with the bag. The only thing about last night that I was pissed about was leaving the hotel without the cell. Okay, maybe not the only thing because I hadn't been able to stop wondering about my father. I'd wanted to talk to Evie about him, but, of course, no cell. I'd had it for hardly five minutes when I'd had to leave it hidden in the ceiling tiles. Stupid. At the time, it was the only place I could think of that wouldn't be searched the minute I left the room.

Now though, I was back to square one with no way of contacting Evie. Even Carter had stayed out of my way since we came back, which I was glad about. I sensed that we'd established some sort of friendship, and with the mood that I was in, I didn't want to damage something that I hadn't had before because I liked it. I liked being able to talk to someone else who wasn't involved with the men responsible for me.

Everything I'd ever had had been taken away from me so I only prayed that somehow, someway, I'd be able to keep hold of Evie, and my friendship with Carter.

Only time would tell.

Nearly every five minutes I'd been glancing at the clock wondering what Evie was doing. Wondering whom she was with. Hating the fact that she'd gone away with another man; a man I knew she was afraid of.

The more I let that rile me up, the more I pounded the bag in front of me. My muscles flexed, my hands clenched together tight in the gloves, and my feet danced around the bag…but, it wasn't enough.

I wanted Patrick in front of me, but more than anything I wanted his father. At least from what Evie had said, I thought the 'Irishman' was his father. I'd have my minute of revenge one day. I lived for that.

But then *she* walked in and my concentration went straight to hell, so much so that the bag bounced back and banged into me. I caught it and leaned against it as though I was having a rest, and watched her.

The minute our eyes met, hers did a quick once over of me, and then a more leisurely one. A frown appeared on her brow as though she was worried about me.

She looked beautiful in her sandals and little summers dress. Her hair flowed in shiny locks down her back. There was a lot of leg on display, which made my mouth water. Beautiful. Sexy.

When she moved to walk toward me, Carter stepped in her way. Her frown deepened.

I knew that I couldn't stay and watch her because if I

did she'd be in my arms. The place that I needed her the most.

Turning, I headed toward the showers and kept my head down. There was only one way in and out of the locker room so it had become one of my favorite places.

No cameras.

My gloves came off at my locker; I tossed my sneakers, socks and shorts inside and grabbed a towel.

Naked as a jailbird, I stepped into the showers. Straightaway the hot stream of water beat down on me; soaking my hair, running down my body in rivulets, but my mind was still on Evie. Was she still in the gym? Would she stay and wait to talk to me? Ask me to meet her later?

She'd looked so lovely out there that the thought of having those long legs of hers wrapped around my waist while I sucked on her nipples had me rock hard and aching.

Growling, I dropped my forehead against the wall, my hands above my head. I looked down and hoped like hell that Carter wouldn't follow me in here right now with how obscene my dick was. I needed to take care of this before I couldn't walk out of here. I spread my legs, the throb in my balls and cock driving me insane. My breathing deepened and got stuck at the back of my throat as I felt a hand wrap around me.

My eyes snapped to the side and met the *very* naked Evie.

The other night hadn't prepared me for seeing her completely naked, and knowing that it was her hand touching me sent shock waves of delight straight to my balls. I needed to come with a desperation I hadn't known before. She changed hands, and slipped between the wall, and me. Her hand moved back and forth along my hard quivering flesh and when her lips suckled over a nipple, I came. Hard. I pulsed and jerked in her hand, but she didn't stop. Her thumb rubbed over the slit, and more release spilled onto her fingers. Her moan against my chest told me that she was just as affected as I was at our closeness. Her lips traveled to my other nipple and with the swipe of her tongue over the hard nub, I spilled again.

This woman brought me to my knees, and if she didn't stop, she'd take me down to the floor on my ass.

Until now, I'd kept my hands and mouth to myself, but no more. I needed her on my palms. Up against me. Writhing on my cock. The latter was still fucking hard and in need.

I grabbed her up in my arms. "Wrap your legs around me."

She did and I swear I saw stars when her pussy rubbed against me. So good.

I held her gaze and descended. Her taste on my lips drove me insane. Her hands in my hair, holding me in place, sent goose bumps down my spine, hardening my dick to bursting. The deeper I delved in her mouth the quicker my release approached. This time I wasn't going to come on either of us, but I planned on coming inside her, and when the tip of my dick entered her, my legs quivered. My dick entered another inch, my eyes nearly crossed with the feel of her heat. Her wetness surrounded me as she tried to pull me deeper.

"Jake, please," she whispered.

My name on her lips was my undoing, and I found myself fully seated inside her. I froze and held her against me while I tried to breathe, except all sensation was centered to where we joined and I couldn't catch my breath.

The hard buds of her nipples pressed against my chest and her inner muscles contracted around my shaft, bringing me close to orgasm.

"I'm on the pill, Jake." She wiggled, and when my hands held her bottom, her eyes darkened. "Make love to me. Slide in and out of me slowly."

I buried my face in her neck as her hands gripped my head. I prayed for strength because the first time at being inside of a woman felt so fucking amazing that I wasn't sure I'd be able to last to even pull out once.

But, above everything else, I wanted to make our first time together good for Evie. I wanted her to know how much she meant to me regardless of the fear that rode me when I realized that she was in my heart.

I could do this.

I could.

Slowly moving my hips, I slipped to her opening and then just as slowly slipped back inside. I did that over and over again, my jaw clenched and my muscles tensed with the effort of holding back.

"Oh," Evie gasped, and moaned, her hands clenched. "Don't stop."

I raised my head and held her gaze as I watched her climax on my cock. Her eyes fluttered, and her channel quivered around my flesh. While she whimpered in pleasure, I followed her into completion, groaning, "Evangeline." I jerked and filled her up with my release, her body still pulsed against mine as my legs trembled, struggling to hold us both up against the wall.

One more taste, though.

As my body started to relax, I leaned forward and, just before I captured her lips with mine, she whispered, "Jake."

Our kiss was slow and tender, and full of love. I only had to look into her eyes to know that she felt the same as I did. At least, I hoped it wasn't the sex that put that look on her face.

Slowly lifting her off me, I let her legs drop from around my waist and saw her frown at my frown. She cupped my jaw in the palm of her hand. "I love you, Jake. Only you." She smiled and everything righted itself.

With a cheeky smirk on her face, she turned to face the wall in front of me, spread her legs, and her arms over her head on the wall. "I need washing."

I gulped and looked down at my body which should be sated, but I found it was on the rise again as I looked at her in that position.

She looked over her shoulder and winked, her ass wiggled.

Groaning, I soaped my hands and caressed the cheeks of her bottom. The globes were firm and as I moved up to her gorgeous breasts, my cock wedged between her ass cheeks. She moaned when my thumbs rubbed over her nipples as my hips twitched.

"You need to hurry it up in there," Carter shouted, breaking into the heat that surrounded us. "I'm not sure how long before someone comes down here." Silence followed and then he laughed. "Just hurry."

I grinned. "Someone certainly has *come* down here." Kissing her neck, I continued, "One day I'm going to take you like this. Spill all over your ass or these." I fisted her glorious breasts, not wanting to let her go, but I knew that Carter was right. I kissed her neck again. "We need to get dressed."

"Um, I know. I wish we could stay together all day. All night. Just like this but at Millie's place, or yours." She turned and kissed my chest. "Let's dry and dress, and then we really need to talk." She grabbed a towel and quickly dried herself while my eyes ate her up. Her curves were made for my hands, and as I watched her fasten her bra, I smiled because her breasts were certainly made for my hands.

She caught my gaze and rolled her eyes. "Stryker." Her blush coated along her cheekbones, but the small smile on her lips had my heart turning over with the feelings inside of me for *my* Evie.

EVIE

STRYKER HAD TURNED ALL the showers on, and then beckoned Carter and me to follow him just inside. Not enough to get wet, but enough so we wouldn't be heard. Neither of them thought the room was bugged, but he didn't want to take any chances. Some explaining was about to happen and I was more than curious. For one, I wanted to know why they thought that the locker room would be bugged?

I stood beside Carter while Stryker paced back and forth, his hands tugging at his wet hair. When he finally stopped in front of us, my heart broke for him. His face showed his tiredness, but also, longing and despair.

What had happened to him?

"Stryker?" I stepped toward him and he took a step back. I tried not to be hurt by his action, but I hurt anyway.

He looked torn as he closed the gap and cupped my face in his hands. "I'm sorry, Evangeline." His forehead dropped to mine. "I've been alone since I was fourteen, which wasn't by choice." He laughed without mirth.

I wrapped my fingers around his wrists and held on. "What happened to you?" The concern on my face appeared to be too much for him to handle so he pulled me into his arms and held me snug against his chest.

"Peter, my father, had a large debt to someone known as the 'Irishman' and I ended up becoming the repayment." I quivered against him and watched as Carter's brows rose to his hairline, when Stryker continued, "My father gave me to them and got his debt wiped clean providing he stayed away from the arena. He left me to them. For ten years, all I've known is this life. I can't do anything without them knowing about it. I can't leave because I know if I do, they'll go after someone else. I can't be responsible for that, knowing what happens."

He cupped my chin, and tugged my face up to meet his searching gaze. "But Evie, I'm terrified that they'll hurt you if they know about us, but I can't let you go."

I reached up and placed a sweet kiss to his lips before wrapping my arms around his neck. "I love you," I whispered as his arms held me tight.

"How the hell do I get out of this life Carter?"

Carter had stayed silent and looked deep in thought. "Do you have any money to buy yourself out?"

Stryker shook his head.

"That would have been a long shot anyway because I don't think they'd allow that as you make far too much money for them to willingly let you go. There has to be someway without anyone getting hurt...all this time, Stryker?" Carter shook his head. "I can't get my head around this, but I will help you."

"I never wanted to involve anyone and, until Evie stepped into my life, I wasn't happy but I wasn't so torn either. No matter what happens Carter, I want you to make sure Evie is okay. I can't always be with her, but you can."

"Don't worry I have her back...and yours. Just don't go and do something stupid."

"I could go to my father for help. He's a state senator so he'll know people who can help because it's illegal what they did to you. What they're still doing."

"No." Stryker growled and it pissed me off so I pushed away from him.

"Don't you dare say no to me." I poked him in the chest. "I can help, and I want to. I love you, you big idiot, and if it means we get to be together in the end, then that's all that matters, right?"

Before he could answer, the outer door started to open. Stryker grabbed my hand and shoved me behind him as Carter moved in beside him.

"Friends stand together," Carter hissed at the surprise on Stryker's face.

Tears ran down my face as it really did hit me that he'd never had anyone to be on his side. No one to hold him when he hurt so badly. No one to be his friend and stand by him like Carter did now.

"Well, what do we have here?"

Patrick!

Stryker's hands flexed on my hips and my forehead dropped to rest against his back. I'm a coward for hiding behind him because Patrick would see me. There wasn't anyway that he wouldn't, especially when I watched around Stryker's arm.

"Carter, you need to leave," Patrick's voice hardened while he glared at Stryker, but the fighter refused to budge.

A tick started at the side of Patrick's mouth, which told me he was about to lose his patience. The two other men with him were large, and strangers. I had no idea what Patrick had become, but I knew it was someone I hated.

"Little Evie, you might as well come out of hiding and face the music."

Stryker's grip went hard, but I managed to slip out and stand between him and Carter.

"I'm actually curious, Evie, as to why you asked your parents' to cancel the wedding without telling me first." He raised a brow and my temper rose.

"You've avoided me and made sure there was always someone else around. I had no chance to tell you."

"Hmm."

Stryker wrapped his arm around my shoulders and tugged me against him. Patrick's eyes followed the movement, his jaw clamped tightly together.

"How touching," Patrick sneered. "*My* fiancée."

I felt fear the night he'd attacked me, but nothing like what I felt now when I knew he could cause harm to Stryker and Carter.

"Why?" I asked, my voice letting me down with how weak I sounded.

"Why what?" His eyes narrowed.

He knew what I asked and had decided to be a bigger prick than he already was.

"Why are you marrying me when there isn't any love between us?"

If I hadn't been watching him closely, I'd have probably missed the flick of something in his eyes. He wasn't as immune as he wanted me to think.

"What I want doesn't come in to it." He clenched his fists, and looked away before he narrowed his eyes on me. "We are getting married on the weekend regardless of what your parents think. Your mother has been instructed to continue to get everything ready." He looked at Stryker. "And you, are going to get to fight on the evening of my wedding. Lethal Black will be there, and so will you."

Stryker tensed seconds before he passed me to Carter, who put me behind him. "I'm with you, but there's no way to get Evie out of here if we fight," he hissed.

I wished Carter hadn't been so logical because his words brought Stryker's eyes to mine before he seemed to have a private conversation with Carter.

"We need to talk Patrick, but I want Evie and Carter to leave."

"What? No way. I'm staying with you," I begged.

Stryker grabbed my chin and brought my face so close to his. "I can't do what I have to do while I'm worrying about you. I need you safe." He kissed my cheek and whispered, "I love you, Evangeline. My *Evie*."

I started to cry at hearing his whispered confession, and didn't put up any kind of fight when Carter led me out of the locker rooms to the front of the gym.

The cold air hit me as soon as we exited. I turned to Carter. He silenced me with just one look.

"I need you to go to the café close to Millie's apartment. It's her favorite."

I nodded.

"Wait there for me. I'm going to try and bring Stryker there as well, but that might be more difficult."

"Where are you going now?"

"To help my friend..."

He gave me a shove in the right direction. I stumbled a couple of times so I stopped and fished out a Kleenex from my purse to mop my face up with.

I hated Patrick and his family for what they'd done to Stryker, and I hated that I was his weakness. But, as I ran along the sidewalk to Rose's Café, I thought about involving my father regardless of what Stryker wanted. I needed Stryker to be free to choose the life that he lived. I wanted him to have the life that was taken away from him. And most of all, I wanted him to have all of that with me.

CHAPTER 17

STRYKER

RUNNING TOWARD ROSE'S CAFÉ with Carter, I hoped that my head would clear. But so far it hadn't. For the first time in years, I had someone on my side who didn't want anything from me in return. I had no clue how to deal with it either, other than to go with the flow. Those words my father used to say when I'd moan about school or some other crap that was going on in my teenage life. Not that I'd had much of one.

My father was someone I had tried not to think about because the pain of his betrayal hurt more than anything. Since spotting him, I couldn't stop thinking about him. A physical ache that had simmered for years, just like the promise to get even with those slimy bastards who'd kept me close.

"Look out." Carter pulled me back before I slammed into a group of girls that I hadn't seen.

"Sorry," I mumbled as I ran around them and then stopped.

The most beautiful girl stood waiting for me outside the café. My feet carried me closer until she was in my arms, her head on my chest and her arms wrapped around my waist. She held me so tightly that her arms quivered and my body trembled with need.

I rested my chin on the top of her head and met Carter's gaze. "We need to head inside." I looked around. "They let me leave but that doesn't mean someone isn't watching."

Evie lifted her head, cupped my jaw and reaching up kissed me. It started out as an innocent peck, her lips to mine, but the minute she was close, my hands tangled in her hair. I nibbled on her lips until she opened for me and then I couldn't stop and devoured her mouth. The small moan she gave, I felt right in my balls and when she moved up against me, I dropped my hands to her bottom and pressed. My cock throbbed, and the urge to thrust was strong.

The throat being cleared reminded me of where we were so I softened the kiss and pulled slightly away, no matter how much my body screamed at me to continue—to not let go of her.

"I messaged Millie while you two were getting it on," Carter grinned, "and she's going to meet us at the back entrance to the apartment building. She'll use her keycard to get us in."

I frowned. "I don't like the idea of her being on their radar."

Carter shook his head. "She's already on it because of her association with Evie, but her apartment isn't listed under Millie Green. They also won't be looking for you under their nose so hopefully this will work."

The thought of why she hadn't registered the apartment under her name would have to wait as Carter started to move toward the apartment building. Evie slipped her hand into mine, intertwined our fingers, and walked beside me.

Her smile lit up her face and when she kissed my knuckles, I wanted to tackle her down to the ground and take her. My body was tense with arousal, and need thrummed through my blood. Her eyes darkened with answering need.

I wanted to have my cock inside her, and remembering what it felt like to feel the warmth, the wetness, the heat of her surrounding me in the locker room had me rock hard and tingling with precum. All it would take would be one touch from her on my shaft and I'd come. That was how close she had me while I tried to walk with her to the apartment.

When we finally arrived, my hood pulled low over my head and face, I wrapped my arms around her stomach and pulled her against me. While Carter talked to Millie as she opened the door, I quickly shoved the band of my sweats over the head of my dick so that I wouldn't be sticking out for all to see.

Evie knew though as there was no way she wouldn't after I'd poked her in the ass when I'd wrapped my arms around her.

Millie took one look at us and a frown crossed her face. She raised a brow at Evie and tried to smile but it was clear she was worried. Carter wrapped an arm around her neck and tugged her close, placing a kiss to the side of her head. He whispered something. Millie nodded and then started to lead the way upstairs.

I kept Evie close and hissed when she deliberately pressed against my erection. Her smirk told me that she knew exactly what she was doing. "I want you," she whispered. "On a bed."

I hissed between my teeth and tried to loosen the grip that I had on her hand, but nothing worked to clear the lust from my brain. Certainly not with the teasing woman beside me.

Finally, on Millie's floor, we walked along the hallway and into her apartment without any hiding from the cameras. Why? I know my brain was lost on memories of Evie naked, but we should have been careful. Now they'll know where we were.

"Relax, Stryker." Millie grinned, wrapping herself up in Carter's embrace. "I called in a favor and got the cameras in the building to play on a loop so if anyone is watching they won't have seen us."

"I dread to think about what favor," Evie drawled.

"We're going to my room for a bit." Evie gave me a tug, and I had no objection in following her anywhere.

"Wait up. We need to talk and come up with a plan on what we're going to do," Carter said.

"We'll talk later," Millie said, pulling Carter into the kitchen as I let Evie lead me to her room.

"We do need to talk, Evie." My eyes met hers and, seconds later, she'd toed off her sandals, kicked her panties across the room, and sent her dress and bra following.

"We will. Right now I want you inside me." She lay back on the bed, opened her legs, and held her arms out to me.

"Fuck." My T-shirt went sailing through the air as I pounced on her.

My hands went to her breasts and the swollen hard nubs while my mouth claimed hers. She scratched along my back, arched, rubbed, and moaned. "Now." Her hands started to shove my sweats down so I helped and the minute my dick was free, I entered her in one long thrust.

Evie arched beneath me, her pussy clamped around my length in one tight spasm, and then she convulsed. Her long shuddering groan of release was my undoing. I pulled out and thrust back inside her quivering sex and spilled. My release was just as powerful as hers and it took everything out of me.

Light flutters of sensation inside Evie surrounded my dick and caused small jerks of more release to spill from my sensitive organ until I collapsed on top of her. I tried to roll to my side so that I didn't squash her, but Evie wouldn't have it.

"Stay like this."

I really didn't have the strength to move anywhere.

While I caught my breath, the feel of her breasts against my chest caused my body to stir with arousal. I had a feeling that now that I'd sampled what sex was like with a partner, no, with Evie, that I wouldn't be able to get enough. In fact, the thought of doing that with anyone else made me want to puke.

Raising my head, I held Evie's gaze and gently sealed my lips over hers. It was a kiss telling her how much she meant to me without words, and I hoped she realized that.

I pulled away and, after a moment of surprise at her tears, kissed each one away. "You're so beautiful," I whispered, kissing down her chin, her neck, along her collarbone to her gorgeous voluptuous breasts.

The weight of them in my hands fit perfectly, and when I lapped at a nipple with my tongue, I felt her response against my dick, which was still inside her, and had already hardened with want.

After switching to her other breast, I buried my face between them. "I love these." I pinched each nipple. "They're perfect."

"Mmm." She arched up, her arms going over her head and the tightening of her pussy around me had my eyes rolling back.

She moaned.

"Straddle my stomach."

"What?"

She offered a shy smile, shoved a pillow beneath her head and repeated, "Straddle my stomach."

My breathing heavy, I had an idea as to what she wanted, but I was reluctant to pull out of her.

"Please, Stryker. I want to do something to you that I've only ever read about. Please."

Slowly withdrawing, I removed my sweat pants from around my thighs and straddled her. My hands shook and my legs quivered with the excitement that raced through me at the sight of my cock, cushioned between her magnificent breasts.

Evie smiled, and, taking hold of my dick, tugged me closer to her waiting mouth. I already leaked with precum and had to grind my teeth together when I watched her tongue sneak out and lick me clean. It was only seconds before I was covered again, my excitement beyond anything.

She pressed my dick between her great breasts and used one hand to show me what she wanted. I had to close my eyes and clench my jaw together so that I wouldn't come, but I would soon as my release was already gathered in my balls.

The tip of my cock was sucked into her mouth while I slowly started to fuck her breasts. I couldn't catch my breath as my body became overwhelmed with sensation, but as I watched her take my cock between her lips, it became too much and I started to spill into her mouth. Seconds later, I pulled out and held myself to each of her breasts in turn. I coated her with my release, and when I was left spent, I rubbed my fingers through it.

"I've marked you," I said feeling so damn happy. "You're mine now. Mine to take. Mine to protect, and mine to fucking love."

"Yes." She cried, wrapping her arms around my neck, tugging me down to her waiting mouth.

I settled between her legs and felt her wetness against my cock.

EVIE

THE MINUTE OUR LIPS sealed together, I came, convulsing against the length of his cock that had settled between my legs.

Stryker buried his face into my neck and panted, grinding against my pussy, which kept me high. I didn't want to come back down but when I did he was smiling above me, as he caught me against him.

"I'm so fucking exhausted I'm not sure I could move if my life depended on it," he growled.

Rolling to his side, he took me with him and kept me wrapped up tightly in his arms. It was almost as though he was afraid to let me go.

I hated knowing that we couldn't stay in this bed and that we had to go and talk with Carter and Millie. If something could be worked out, then it was worth it.

"We need to go out there," Stryker mumbled.

"I know. I'm too tired to shower, but we need to talk."

He groaned. "No way. We get in a shower then we won't be getting out for a while. You, naked and slippery in my arms… Mmm." He nuzzled along my neck, his hand clutching my bottom, pulling me closer. "Fuck." He pulled away and flopped to his back.

I couldn't help but smirk at the sight of his *large* cock. He was hard and proud, sticking straight up in the air.

All it would take was for me to straddle him to take a ride. My thighs clenched at the thought as tingles of arousal raced through me, and then I thought, what the hell.

Before he had any idea of what I planned, I was on my knees above him, sliding down his hard shaft. He gasped and grabbed my hips, but instead of pushing me away he tugged me down as his hips arched up. The sensation of being completely filled by him was an aphrodisiac all on its own.

"I'll shower later, so we have time for this." I slowly rocked on him, biting my lip when I felt the first flutters of climax rushing through me.

Stryker felt my reaction because he shot to a sitting position, rearranged my legs and sealed our lips together. His hands pressed me down on his cock, and as he ground into me, he caught my scream of release in his mouth as I caught his.

He pulsed when spilling his seed, which prolonged the electrical pulses that ran through my sex.

"I feel well and truly loved…and wet," I wiggled on him and laughed when his eyes rolled. "We really do need to get dressed now."

"If you say so."

He lay back on the bed so I teased him by lifting my arms and piling my hair on the top of my head. My entire torso was on display, especially my large breasts that I knew he loved.

He closed his eyes, breathing deeply. "Evie," he groaned, arching up.

My eyes widened at how hard he was, again. I raised a brow and he laughed when he opened his eyes. "I'm always ready for you. I also have a lot of years to catch up on."

I laughed. "Not in one day you don't."

Resting my hands on his delicious chest, I rose up and caught my breath at the sensation of him leaving my body. Goose bumps coated my skin, puckering my nipples, which Stryker's gaze landed on, and stayed.

"Oh no." I moved out of his reach and ran to the bathroom.

I quickly wiped myself down and wet another washcloth for Stryker. Back in the bedroom, he looked to be asleep and although I wanted him to rest, I knew that we had things to discuss, so I tossed the wet cloth onto his stomach.

He sucked in a breath and jerked up.

"I'd wipe your cock for you, but then we'd be in here even longer."

"Mmm."

I watched him wipe his cock and balls while he watched me dress, except the more his eyes followed my movements the harder, and longer he became until he tossed the cloth back to the bathroom and wrapped his hand around his shaft.

I stumbled, unable to take my eyes from him, but he stood, releasing himself and stretched. He had an amazing body, but seeing him naked with arousal running through him made me want to throw caution away and take.

He caught my gaze. "More of that later." He smirked.

Grinning, I quickly pulled the rest of my clothes on and waited for Stryker to get his T-shirt on.

My hand was wrapped with his as we left the room Millie had given me.

Stryker would have to go back to his apartment for now until a way out had been decided, which I hated. I wanted him to stay with me. I wanted to know what it would be like to sleep all night wrapped up in his strong arms. I wanted to know how it felt to be woken in the dark with his body already inside mine, making sweet love. I wanted everything with this man.

"Evie," he whispered, a hand lifted and cupped the side of my face. His forehead rested against mine. "Are you all right?"

I met his searching gaze, smiled, and reached up to kiss his lips. "I'm okay as long as I'm with you." I smiled and let him see everything I was feeling. It was written so clearly on my face.

Stryker didn't look all that reassured, and I knew why.

He'd have to leave me soon. He dropped into a chair opposite Millie and Carter, and pulled me down onto his lap, his arms like bands of steel around my waist.

It only took me a minute to get comfortable and when I was, Stryker sighed into my neck, his face buried. I wanted to stay like we were, and pretend that we were alone in the room. When I caught the smirk on my best friends face, I couldn't help the grin that split my face and then I laughed.

Carter rolled his eyes, muttering, and to my surprise Millie cupped his jaw and slapped a kiss to his lips. That certainly shut his muttering up.

My surprise must have shown because Millie grinned and shrugged. "He's a fast worker."

Carter raised a brow. "Fast, babe? I thought I'd be an old man before you agreed to go out with me."

Ignoring Carter, Millie turned to us, a frown clear across her brow. "What are we going to do? We have to make sure Stryker can walk free…and I'm thinking that maybe my father could help."

Millie's father would get involved without question if he knew that it was for me. I just wasn't sure if I wanted him to. He skirted the law more than anyone that I knew, which was why my parents had never wanted me to be friends with Millie.

Carter frowned, and shook his head. "Let's not involve parents unless we have to." He took Millie's hand to soften his words, which made me wonder just what he knew about her father. "I think I know how." Carter paused. "Give me a day or two to work some things out." He went silent while we waited for him to give us more, which he didn't. He shook his head. "I'm not saying anything for now."

Stryker nuzzled into my neck, and whispered, "I've been gone too long." He kissed my ear and rested his forehead against the side of my head. "I don't want to leave you, but, for now, I have to."

My arms wrapped around his shoulders as I turned by body into him. "I know."

CHAPTER 18

STRYKER

AFTER SNEAKING DOWN THE stairs of the apartment building, I ran through the back alley and came around to the street two blocks over. I continued jogging until I entered through the main doors of the building. With a quick wave to Andrea at the concierge desk, I kept my head down and entered the elevator. Using my keycard, I punched in my floor and knew that all hell was about to be unleashed when I entered my apartment.

My mind was constantly on Evie and what she made me feel. Crave. The attachment I had to her wasn't going to go away, and I just wanted to be with her. Right now my hope was solely placed on Carter. I believed him when he said that he might have a way out even though it filled my stomach with nerves.

I wasn't used to living outside of the wall that they'd built around me and had no idea about the technology around today. I remembered the old cell phone that my father had once given me. It was a flip cell and did nothing fancy other than to make calls or send text messages.

Money would be a problem because, walking away, I'd have nothing but the clothes on my back. The biggest prize of all would be Evie and she was worth everything.

The doors slid open and there, waiting for me was Roger and Earl, two of the regular security guards. Roger was okay and, on his own would always appear intimidated by me. Earl was different altogether and I knew he'd love to be in the ring with me.

"Let's go. The *boss* is waiting for you. He's already pissed as fuck that you disappeared." Earl went to grab my arm when I didn't budge, but for once, one look from me had him taking a step back.

I smirked, which angered him more. "I'm going, and I wasn't exactly stopped from leaving the gym."

Moving forward, I felt them right on my heels, but decided to behave for now, considering I had no idea who was in my apartment, and what they knew.

Patrick would be there especially after word got out that I'd left with Evie…and the bastard was with his bodyguard, Oliver.

My heart thundered in my chest, the blood pounded through my ears, partly with fear of not being in the position to defend Evie. I didn't fear for me because I knew what I was capable of. I had a whole lot of fear for Evie if these bastards chose to go after her. Carter had promised to protect her when I'd left them in Millie's apartment and I'd hold him to that.

The end of this life would soon be over and I only prayed as I walked toward Patrick that I'd survive to spend a new life with my woman.

"The wanderer returns, I see." Patrick sneered, his anger close to the surface. "Where is *my* fiancée?"

My fists clenched of their own accord at my side while my jaw clenched together in anger, and jealousy. He didn't have the right to use that title when discussing Evie. The only person I intended to use that was me. "She isn't your fiancée anymore," I ground out. "No wedding."

A muscle twitched in Patrick's cheek. "You don't have any say in it, and from now on, you'll stay away from her."

"He'll be kept away. Don't worry, son."

My body froze and all my senses went on alert.

That voice.

From that night.

My gut clenched as I slowly turned and found him standing in front of me, the man I presumed was the Irishman.

"You," I hissed through clenched teeth, part in anger and part in total surprise.

I'd hoped to see him again. I had so many things planned in my head, but now having him standing in front of me, I couldn't think of one.

"It's been a long time, *Jake*. I think it's about time that I introduced myself." He sat on the sofa and directed me to do the same. "Declan Fitzwilliam, the Irishman." He waited for something from me, but I guess he was disappointed. His jaw clenched before he visibly tried to relax. "You're screwing things up for Patrick and, indirectly, me."

I dropped onto the opposite sofa and tried not to let him see how rattled I was at seeing him.

"Why now? Why are you letting me know who you are?"

"Evie is going to marry Patrick, and you're going to stay well out of it. I thought you might need a reminder of who owns you. For the past decade, you've been mine and you've behaved. Beautiful women have been given to you time and time again and you haven't played…until now. Evie is special, and on the weekend she's going to be a beautiful bride for my son."

I bit back the growl that rose up my throat and kept my lips clamped together. For now, I wanted him to talk while it gave me a chance to work out just what was going on.

No way would Evie go ahead with the wedding. That I knew for certain. I also knew her father was a senator and, surely, he had ways to help his daughter get away from Patrick and his father.

"Still not got anything to say?" Declan glanced at Patrick who'd moved to stand over his father's shoulder. "My son wants to know where his *fiancée* has disappeared to. Apparently she isn't at her apartment, and her best friend gave up her last lease. So, where is she?"

Shock had worn off and anger thrummed through my blood again. He sat there and honestly believed I'd tell him where my girl was.

No way in hell.

Earl moved to Declan's other shoulder, whispering in his ear. Declan's face whipped around to stare at the man, and by the tightening of Declan's face, it wasn't good news.

I used his distraction to weigh my escape if things went sour. Earl was big, bigger than me, but I doubted he'd been trained as well as I had. He thought he could take me, but I knew that he couldn't. I wasn't sure I'd get past them all though. One on one yes, not all of them together.

"You're going nowhere, *Jake*... Earl, call Greg and ask him to take two others to apartment 1908 and to bring the inhabitants up here."

My heart dropped now that our place had been discovered, but Evie and the others were safe, thanks to Carter. They'd all left the building together and Carter had them with him.

"Will do." Earl turned and made the call.

Patrick frowned. "Who's in 1908?"

"Millie Michaels." Declan sneered, anger behind his words.

Patrick hesitated, his eyes widened in surprised. "Millie Michaels? I thought she was Green. The same person right?"

"Whoever checked the lease for the apartments in this building didn't do a very good job. Apparently, your fiancée's best friend is Millie Cora Michaels, the daughter of Jordan Michaels. Her new apartment is under the name of CM Michaels. She switched her initials around." Declan clenched his fists and stood to face his son. "You told me that a search had been done on anyone associated with Evie. Why didn't I know this about Miss Michaels?" He growled. "Jordan Michaels isn't anyone to piss with."

Patrick looked like a fish out of water, his complexion a hell of a lot paler than it had been.

He was saved from answering his father when Greg walked in, alone.

"Spit it out," Declan demanded.

Greg hesitated, and then found the balls from somewhere. "Empty. We used the passkey, and found nothing, but this." He passed the note to Declan who scanned it.

"Fuck." Declan turned back to me, his face was filled with fury and it was clear he struggled to control his temper. "They've ran to Jordan *fucking* Michaels," he spat.

My surprise at his words was kept hidden, I hoped anyway. I knew they hadn't gone to Millie's father, but either way, where they had gone they'd be protected for as long as they didn't discover Carter's involvement. I sure as hell had no intention of telling them anything different.

Declan glared at me while I could see the wheels turning in his head. "The fight with Lethal Black will be this weekend, so we'll get him to Chicago early. Make it happen, Patrick. I want everyone involved in this fight to be on the road by tomorrow morning." He tapped his chin with his fingers and appeared to look through me. "Earl, in the morning," he paused, "I want you to get Carter Stone when he turns up at the gym, and take him to Chicago with you."

"Are you sure you just want to drag him off the street? Won't it complicate things?" Patrick surprised the hell out of me with his question. Moments before, he'd seemed to cower when his father spoke.

Declan gave Patrick a glare of promised retribution before he turned to Earl. "I want you and Greg to stay inside until everyone leaves for Chicago."

"Understood."

Everyone just kissed the bastard's ass, but I'd finally had enough of listening to his, "Bullshit."

Yeah, I called it and had their attention.

"There are so many flaws with that plan." I stood and breathed through the anger and the inner voice telling me to fight. "I'll go to Chicago and fight, but there is no way that you'll get Evie to go ahead with the wedding. Her father didn't get to be a senator by being walked all over. And I've watched Carter at the gym. He'll have friends outside of the gym. How are you going to explain his sudden disappearance?"

"He's right about Carter," Patrick backed me up. "Carter stood beside him when I cornered him in the gym earlier today…we need Carter's address. The girls might be there with him. I've seen how he looks at Millie and she's just as bad."

Declan smiled and my heart fucking sank to my toes. "They went to Millie's family." I hoped they'd take the bait.

"Hmm. Maybe. Maybe not. Check out Carter's place, and Patrick you try and get hold of Evie and tell her what we've planned."

"What?"

What the hell were they talking about? Planned? Evie wouldn't do anything they wanted. The only way she'd go through with it would be if she were forced. Blackmailed. My eyes snapped to his. No fucking way.

"I think Mr. Rivers has just realized how we plan to bring Evie to our way of thinking." Declan smirked and moved toward the door. "No one leaves or enters until the morning when everyone does."

Silence followed Declan and Patrick's departure.

I seethed wanting to go after them. I needed to warn Carter but had no way of doing so, unless he realized once we'd partied ways that they might look at his place. I could only hope.

Not wanting the fuckers who were left behind to know

how rattled I was, I went into the kitchen area. Opening the fridge, I grabbed my prepped meal along with some milk, water and fruit before heading into my bedroom where I slammed the door closed.

There was nowhere for me to go, but I knew that I wouldn't get to go anywhere tonight. I was well and truly fucked.

I didn't give a shit about me, but I'd give anything to protect Evie.

If Carter came to Chicago with us, then who the hell would be left to look after the girls? I prayed they'd go to Millie's father who I now knew worried Declan.

I was angry.

Angry that they'd planned on getting to Carter my one and only friend.

Angry that I had no way of protecting Evie.

The only way I actually knew how to protect her was to stay away no matter how much it killed me, but I had a feeling that wasn't an option now. Nothing I did while I was with them would help her. They'd use blackmail so that the wedding would go ahead, but who would they blackmail? Evie or her senator father?

I'd go with the senator, but I had a really bad feeling.

EVIE

I HID MY TEARS from Stryker when we went our separate ways, but they flowed freely as Carter led Millie and me to his car. I also hadn't missed the way he held onto Millie. My friend seemed hooked, which was a change. I just hoped it lasted because Carter seemed like a really nice guy, and I trusted him to help Stryker and, indirectly, me.

But as we raced through town to an apartment belonging to a friend of Carter's, my brain worked overtime as to how I could help Stryker. I needed to be doing something instead of sitting on my bottom doing nothing. I also needed to be kept busy so that I wasn't worrying about how he was being treated now that they knew the truth.

"I can hear you thinking from here, Evie." Carter glanced into the backseat, briefly meeting my gaze before he turned back to watch the traffic. "You have to promise me that you'll stay out of trouble and let me help Stryker."

"I can't promise you that. Not when I need to be doing something."

"Why don't we go to your parents' place," Millie suggested. "At least, that way, we won't have to worry about cooking."

Surprised, I chuckled. "You don't fancy burnt pasta?" I replied, my voice full of amusement.

"Well, I can't even make toast." Millie fluttered her lashes at Carter. "But, if you're going to be staying with us then I guess we could live on your omelets and other things."

Shaking his head, Carter laughed. "You'd soon get sick of eating omelet."

"I'd rather live on that than burnt pasta and toast," Millie grumbled.

About to add more to the conversation, I had a sudden thought and shot up in my seat. Quickly scrabbling for my purse, I pulled out my laptop.

"What are you doing?" Millie turned in her seat to watch me.

"Peter Rivers is Stryker's father. What if we managed to find him? I don't know if it's the right thing to do or even if he could do anything to help us. I'm clutching at straws but it has to be worth a try."

I looked between them and sighed in relief that they were both on board with my idea.

"I have a wireless card in my computer so I can at least try to find something on Google."

"Wait." Carter pulled to the side of the road and left the engine idling. "Pass me your computer. I can get the information you want a lot quicker than you."

He didn't give me chance to pass it over as he took it.

"Right then."

"Evie, I have access to places you don't." Carter turned the computer on his lap so neither Millie or me could see what he was doing. "Anyone have an idea as to how old his father is?"

"No. But Stryker's twenty-four, so if he was born when his father was, I don't know, around twenty maybe, then he'd be at least forty-four."

"Okay. I have eight under fifty in the New York area. He could have moved, let his driving license laps or completely dropped off grid." Carter watched me over the top of the computer screen.

"I know. Don't get my hopes up. I don't even know what to say or how he can help if we do find the right Peter." I sat back and saw nothing but Stryker as I looked through the window.

"I think he'd help." Carter focused on me. "At the last

fight, he thought he saw his father in the crowd. It shook him up."

"He didn't say anything." I bit my lip wondering why he hadn't mentioned anything to me.

"A lot's happened in the last twenty-four hours, Evie. Don't think things that aren't there please."

"I won't."

He looked like he didn't believe me.

"I promise, Carter. I love him."

"I know." He looked back to the computer. "I've narrowed it down to three. Let me cross check them with something else."

I stayed silent and stared at Millie who watched me closely.

She grabbed my knee. "Are you really okay?"

Tears gathered on my lashes, but I was determined to keep them from falling. "I will be." I covered her hand with mine.

"Well, one has been in prison for four years so it can't be him if he was at the fight. Another one lives miles outside of town, but the one remaining lives in a nice neighborhood, about fifteen minutes from here and he's forty-seven. Let me check if anything was ever filed for Jake Rivers, and we have…a missing person report." Carter read and did a few more clicks, and then, "Bingo," burst from his lips. "The date of birth that Peter Rivers gave as his when he filled the missing person report for Jake matches the guy who lives close…in the end Jake was filed as a runaway."

"Wow. That's sad." I sat back stunned. "How'd you find all that out?"

"I'm not just a pretty face." Carter gave us both a smug

look, and laughed before he pulled out into traffic. "Let's go and visit Peter Rivers and find out how he can help his son." He clenched his teeth in anger.

Millie glanced at me before concentrating on her man. She rested her hand on his thigh, and I smiled when he intertwined his fingers through hers.

They stayed like that until we entered the residential neighborhood that Carter had found. My nerves got the better of me and I chewed on my bottom lip wondering whether or not it was Stryker's father that he'd found.

The houses that I looked at from the car window would have a nice price tag to them, which begged the question as to why would he have sold his son if he owned such a large house. I knew a lot could change in ten years, but still.

A well-maintained lawn with a large SUV parked alongside the house. Carter navigated their car onto the driveway beside the SUV, bringing it to a stop. The engine idled while we looked at the impressive house.

It was built of red brick with a dark wooden front door and matching window frames. Flower planters covered the bottom of the windowsills, which gave the property a welcoming feel. While I admired the outside a curtain twitched to the left of the front door. I couldn't make anyone out, but I knew we were being watched.

"What's the plan?" Millie asked, breaking the silence having focused on the twitching curtain.

"Let's just see what happens." I opened the door and jumped out.

I needed to do this for Stryker.

He wouldn't talk about his father, but my heart wanted to believe that there was something more going on back then because the thought of his father just handing him over to Declan was wrong on so many levels, and it hurt.

"Show time?" Carter fell into line beside me.

"This has to work out. It has to, Carter." I watched as he rang the bell, followed by a couple of raps of his knuckles against the hardwood door.

"Just remember you're not alone, Evie." Millie put her arm around my waist.

The door opened a fraction, the security chain still up, and all we could see was a tanned face behind a trimmed beard. "Can I help you?"

My voice wouldn't come to me but Carter had no trouble. "We're looking for a Peter Rivers who filed a missing person report ten years ago."

Surprise crossed his features. "Why do you want him?"

"Is it you?" I stepped forward and asked. "Please…"

His eyes looked resigned, as he whispered, "Yes."

"We're friends of Jake."

His eyes widened in surprise.

"Mr. Rivers, I don't know why we're here other than Stryker needs our help." I paused. "My name is Evie, and I'm in love with your son. These are my friends, Millie and Carter. We know what you did to him ten years ago."

Peter Rivers flinched, looked from one to the other before he closed the door in our faces. Seconds later, the door opened wide and he ushered us inside. He looked outside and slammed the door closed, the security lock going back on.

He was a tall man, not as broad in the shoulders as Jake, but even for forty-seven he was a handsome man. His trousers and shirt looked good quality, which gave the feel of money. He had lots. I wasn't sure what I'd expected but he was a surprise.

"I wondered if he'd ever get friends to help him. I've hoped. Longed. But no one has ever showed up here before."

"Mr. Rivers, please help me, us, understand what happened back then and maybe we'll be able to help him now. I want to have a chance at something with him. But even if things don't work out, I want him to have a life."

"Let's go through to the kitchen and I'll put some coffee on, and then, I'll tell you about back then as well as how I've come to have this." His arms spread wide and his meaning was clear. He'd tell us how he has such an amazing house.

He led us through the foyer of his large home, which made my head hurt. Why would he sell his son when he had this? I couldn't get that thought out of my mind. Why? Why? Why?

And then I caught a glimpse inside of another room and became rooted to the spot.

Stryker was everywhere.

As if in slow motion, I moved into the room, not knowing where to look first. Each wall had an assortment of pictures in different sizes and they were all of Stryker. No one else, just the man who held my heart.

Before I'd even considered moving closer, I stood in front of a large framed picture of Stryker as a young boy of maybe eleven or twelve with his father. There was no doubt in my mind as I looked at Peter's face that he loved Jake very much. The same expression was reflected on Stryker's face.

"I love my son, Evie," Peter whispered, unable to hide

the emotion behind his words. "I've loved him since the day he was born, and through the struggle of being a single man with a baby. My girlfriend left when he was two weeks old… I've always loved him, and all that I have now I've done so that he'd have something when I managed to buy him back."

I wiped at my cheeks and took the offered Kleenex from Carter. "I don't understand."

"I know." Peter dropped his eyes and slowly made his way out of the room. "Come. I can't talk in here."

I glanced at Millie and Carter, who stood silently beside the door before they followed us into the kitchen.

Even this room had a picture of who I presumed to be Stryker on the wall as a baby.

"That was taken when he was eight months old." Peter smiled. "A handsome boy, even back then."

We sat at the kitchen table as Peter placed mugs of coffee in front of us.

My mom would love this kitchen with the country feel to it. Displayed on the walls alongside the family pictures were dried herbs. Wicker bowls sat on the dresser to the side of the room and the very large range cooker took up a good space on the opposite wall. It made a person feel welcome, but right now I needed answers.

"Please tell us what happened to Stryker?" I asked, my hands cupped the coffee for warmth because I felt chilled.

"Why do you call him Stryker if you love him?" Peter asked puzzled.

"So I don't slip up when there are others around. No one can know that I know he's Jake."

Peter looked at me carefully and nodded. "I've always

loved my son, Evie. So much that it's a physical pain knowing how he lives."

"Then why—"

"Please let me talk." He smiled to take the sting from his words. "I've held my tongue for so long that I need to tell you everything."

I nodded and took hold of Carter's offered hand to keep me grounded because I felt like I was going to lose my composure with the nerves playing hell in my stomach.

"Ten years ago, I was pretty bad off. I loved the ring… or rather, what happened in the ring. I gambled on the fighters, and not just a bit either. I had an addiction and, in the end, I lost the one thing that mattered the most—Jake. I owed a lot of money and Declan Fitzwilliam gave me an ultimatum… I either handed over Jake to them to raise as their prime fighter, or they'd make sure he spent the rest of his life in a wheelchair." Peter paused and tried to take a sip of his mug of coffee, but his hand shook too badly to get it to his lips. He gave up.

"Declan was feared, and not just by me. People whispered that he had death on his hands, and it was more widely known that he was a thug. I don't think he did his own dirty work because he had a lot of men working for him. But I was scared for Jake. It killed me handing Jake over to them, but I loved him too much to have him beaten so badly that he'd never walk again." He paused to catch his breath.

"Even as a child he loved to run track, and he was always pretending to spar with someone as he ran." Peter smiled at the obvious memory. "He didn't know that I watched him, and I didn't know at the time that others watched him as well. In the end, I realized that Declan wanted Jake. Even if I hadn't owed him money, he'd have somehow gotten his claws into him." He wiped at a tear.

"That night I promised to never go to a fight again, or bet on a fighter. I didn't for a long time because I drowned the pain of what I'd done at the bottom of a bottle, until I met Alice, who is now my wife. The night I met her, I was drunk and she called me on it. A total stranger, huh." He smiled and it was clear how much he loved the woman called Alice. "I blurted out everything. She basically saved me, and helped me. Her whole family did."

Peter offered us a wry smile, and continued, "Alice has six brothers who would go to the fights and bet what little money I had, and eventually, I started building my savings up. I used it to go to college and get a degree in computer science. That led to a very well paid job, the house, and everything. Her brothers then started betting on Stryker and he won us lots of money."

My shock must have shown because Peter paused and glanced between us before he continued, "It's not what you're all thinking. Yes, in the beginning I used the winnings to create a better life for myself. You see, I realized that if I had any chance of helping Jake, that that was what I needed to do. Now, because of my job, every dime I made through betting on Stryker is in a separate account to the one I use daily. That money is there for him and has been for a few years. I add to it when he fights, but it's his money. Not mine."

"I've heard everything you've said," Carter frowned, "but I haven't heard you say once that you've tried to help him. Get him back."

Peter shook his head. "I have. It took awhile for me to get enough money to even try to buy Jake his freedom.

Every year for the past four years, I've gone to Declan and asked to buy Jake back. And each time he laughs in my face. Why wouldn't he though? Jake makes him a rich man. I can't compete with him and I doubt I'll ever be able to."

"What about the police. Why did you never go to them?"

I was glad that Carter could think because my mind couldn't form any questions. It was obvious that his father loved him, which was why I couldn't get there with my anger. I wanted to be angry at his father, and to shout and blame him. But I couldn't after listening to the broken man before me.

"I was afraid, and I guess I still am. I know that Jake lives in a nice apartment building. I've caught glimpses of him running through the park. He does that every Tuesday at around seven-thirty in the morning."

I frowned, and then it clicked. "You make sure you're there, and watch him."

Peter nodded. "I needed to see him and make sure he looked okay. He always moved well as though he was injury free. He didn't appear to have been…beaten. I know he hates me for what I did, and I don't blame him." Peter wiped at his damp eyes, and, reaching out, clasped my hand with his. "He saw me the other night, at least, I think he did, but before that he seemed down, more so than usual."

Carter admitted, "He saw you after the fight and just the sight of you nearly knocked him on his ass."

"If you know any way of helping my son, then please help him," Peter begged, accepting what Carter said.

"We came here hoping you'd be able to help us in

some way." Carter rested his arms on the table. "But all I know right now is that it isn't safe for Millie and Evie to be anywhere where they can find them."

"And you," Millie whispered and grasped hold of Carter's hand. "You can't go back. They'll know."

"I have to go back, Millie. I can't leave him alone."

"Then let me call my dad. I know he'll help."

Carter shook his head. "I wish I could say yes, but if you do and something goes wrong, then it might fall back on you and I won't allow that. You have to be safe in order for me to do this. Do you understand me?"

I certainly did as I looked at my stunned friend who just nodded in response.

"I can't just sit here and do nothing."

"You won't be doing nothing, Evie. You'll be staying safe for Stryker. And that is everything to him." Carter tried to comfort me, but I wasn't sure anything could unless I watched Stryker walk into the room, right now.

"Let me check my cell, it's been buzzing in my pocket since we arrived." I pulled it free, and froze. My eyes met Carter's. "It's from Patrick." My hands shook. "He say's he wants to meet later today. He wants to talk about Stryker. I have sixteen missed calls from him."

"Don't panic. If he calls again, answer and listen to what he has to say. Just don't stay on too long. We don't want him to track you."

My eyes widened because I hadn't even given thought to being tracked. "Okay." I tried to smile but I think it came off more as a wince. "He knows me, and he'll know that I'll meet him because he mentioned Stryker."

"I'll go with you," Millie offered.

"No way," Carter stated. "Millie, you are going

nowhere near Declan or Patrick. I can't help if I'm worried about you."

"Evie is my best friend so of course I'm going to go with her for back up."

Carter growled. "Like hell."

"You can't stop me."

"Children," I shouted. "You're both being ridiculous. Millie, when and if I meet Patrick, I will go alone, but I'll make sure it's a public area. Carter, please just concentrate on helping Stryker."

"I don't like any of this." Carter ran his hands through his hair in frustration.

"Everyone is welcome to stay here for as long as you need to," Peter offered. "My wife will be home soon and I know she'll be happy to help you in anyway that she can."

"Thank you. I'm going to leave the girls here." Carter stood and shoved his chair under the table. "Millie, walk me out." Carter bent and whispered, "Stay safe," into my ear.

I watched them leave the kitchen and turned back to Peter who watched me. "You really do love my son."

It wasn't a question, more of an observation so I stayed silent.

"You don't like me, do you?"

I sighed. "I came here not expecting to, but you're a surprise. I believe what you said and I still want to be angry with you because of Stryker, but I can't get there. It's obvious that you still love your son, and I want him to be here. I want him to see that room, this house. I want him to have a life with me."

My tears came quicker than I could wipe them away.

Peter moved and crouched down beside me with a handful of Kleenex shoved toward me.

"Thank you," I mumbled.

"All the other times he had no idea that I was here or even trying to help get him free. Now he knows that you're here waiting for him, he'll try as well."

"I know." I smiled through my tears. "I'm just afraid that he'll try too hard to get to me and something bad will happen to him." I shrugged and wiped my face.

"Let's try and be positive." He stood. "Now, are you hungry because I know that I am."

I chuckled. "I'm not sure you want to let me loose in your kitchen."

He grinned. "I'll cook and you can wash the vegetables."

"Okay."

"I'm still going with you," Millie stated the minute she reappeared.

"Does Carter know just how full his hands are with you?"

Her eyes narrowed. "You're my best friend, the sister I never had. I'm going with you."

"Let's not argue, otherwise, no one will want to eat, and I hate wasting food." Peter passed us both aprons, shoved a large chopping board onto the countertop before placing an assortment of vegetables in front of us. "I'm sure you both can chop just fine."

"We can do that," I agreed.

"I'm still going with you," Millie mumbled.

I laughed and ignored her for now.

CHAPTER 19

STRYKER

THUMP. THUMP. THUMP. KICK.

The thumping sounded good in my ears. It meant that I could shut everyone else in the gym out and concentrate on my fists hitting the bag. Sweat ran down my body as I danced back and forth in front of my hard, leather, sparring partner.

I kept my back to the others because I wanted and needed to believe that I was alone. No longer watched. No longer on a fucking leash.

Coach stood to the side and watched in the gym in Chicago, having arrived a few hours before. He counted, watched, and finally gave up the counting as usual. I worked out harder than anyone else, although Carter was a close second. Half the time I was sure he only persevered so that he'd be picked to match me in the ring as a sparring partner. I wasn't about to complain because I now considered him a friend. My only friend.

That wasn't true.

Evie was more than a friend. A hell of a lot more. She was the girl I loved, and the reason why I was more determined than ever to be free of them so that I could be with her.

My hands flexed as I remembered the feel of her skin beneath my fingers. My cock started to rise as I remembered how it felt when she rode me. How it felt to spill my seed deep inside her.

Fuck!

I growled and breathed through the pain of arousal, knowing that I had to shove my need for her to the back of my mind. It only needed to stay there until I could be with her where I knew it would be safe. That she would be safe.

"Concentrate," Coach hissed between his teeth.

Without breaking from the jabs to the bag, I slid my eyes to him and nearly stumbled. He'd never shown me sympathy or anything other than that of a trainer. His expression was worried. For me.

"Just get through these next couple of days, and then you'll be back home to your girl…just do what they want." He grabbed my arm. "Don't believe everything that you've heard about your father."

I did stumble then.

Wrapping my arms around the bag, I breathed heavily and stared at him. "What do you know?"

"Enough to know that what Declan wants, Declan gets. Your father didn't have a choice when he traded you. Declan led your father to believe he'd traded you for his debt. His debt was wiped clean, but he only got into that debt because Declan wanted *you*."

I couldn't believe what I was hearing, and I didn't

know whether or not to believe what was coming out of his mouth. So I asked, "How long have you known?"

Coach closed his eyes and all the color drained from his wrinkled face. "I've known a while."

"How long is a while?" I ground out through my teeth.

All this time I'd thought Coach was oblivious to most of what had happened to me. I shoved the bag out of the way and got in his face. "How long, Coach?"

"Don't draw attention to us," Coach hissed. "I've known, okay." He became agitated. "My niece is married to him."

"What?" I snarled, stunned.

"You heard me. I haven't done or said anything because I love my niece, and regardless of what Declan has done in the past, he really does love her."

I paced back and forth in front of him, not giving a shit who watched. "Does she know what he does? And why hasn't she helped you?" It felt surreal that Coach would allow his niece to be with Declan or that his niece would allow Coach to live the way he did.

"I doubt very much that she knows a lot of what he does, and I can see the wheels turning. My niece has tried to get me to leave the gym over the years. This is all I know, Stryker. I can't survive doing anything else, and, I feel that if I spend all my time alone at home that I'd just shrivel up and die. I'm not ready for that yet. I just don't want Declan's wrath coming down on me if I go to her and tell her about you and the real situation. I don't want him major pissed at me for telling Nina…or you."

"So you'll just let them carry on doing this until someone else puts a stop to it."

Coach stepped back as he looked over my shoulder, his eyes wide before he masked his surprise.

"Well," Lethal Black gloated.

I clenched my jaw and turned to face my opponent.

"If it isn't Stryker and his Coach having a mother's meeting," he continued. "I always knew you needed a wet nurse."

Asshole.

I threw my head back and laughed. Coach gave me a strange look while Lethal Black grew angry because I hadn't reacted how he probably wanted.

"Nice try." I laughed and walked away.

He let me go, but only because his coach stepped in front of him, and shook his head.

Since I turned eighteen and started to fight for them, I'd never let my opponents antagonize me into a before fight confrontation. I was good at walking away from them, probably because I didn't want to be forced to do that shit. I'd wanted to be a fighter for me, and so that my dad would come to watch me. Be proud of me. I never wanted to be owned.

"Stryker, you baffle me sometimes," Coach mumbled when he fell into step alongside me.

"Why's that?"

"You're angry, and always have been. Yet you've never fought outside of the ring."

"As long as they have control, I'm fighting for them. So why waste my time fighting when I don't have to."

"That makes sense. I think."

Grabbing a clean towel, I wrapped it around my neck and moved over to the mats to do some rope work. My head had started to pound with everything running around inside.

Coach shoved the ropes into my hands, and whispered, "Carter's here, but he's being watched so he's staying away from you for now."

My eyes shot to his.

"Ropes."

EVIE

ALTHOUGH IT WAS ONLY a day since I'd last seen Stryker, I missed him like crazy. I worried about him and Carter as well.

Carter sensed trouble when he'd left Peter's house last night, and so far today, Millie hadn't heard anything from him. So we both wondered what was happening.

Millie would be annoyed with me once she realized that I'd snuck out of Peter's house to meet Patrick especially after I'd promised Carter that I'd stay inside and wouldn't leave.

I'd promised Peter as well, but he'd had to go into work, and expected to find me at his house when he returned. I felt a small twinge of regret for sneaking out, but I had to know what Patrick wanted to talk to me about. I wished I could have ignored him, but I couldn't. Or rather I could until he told me it had something to do with Stryker. I'd do anything to protect him.

I wasn't stupid though, which was why I waited sitting on a bench on the East side of the pond in central park. I loved the park, the wide-open space, and just plain people watching. It usually made me happy, but today my nerves jumped in my belly and I felt nauseous.

It wasn't too warm yet but my temperature rose as I stood and watched him approach. I wasn't the only one to notice him either. Patrick was well groomed as always, and his suit, perfectly tailored. He was a good-looking man, and but for his recent change in personality, an easy man to get along with.

"Surely I'm not so unpleasant to warrant a frown on that beautiful face." Patrick reached up and ran a finger across my brow. It took everything in me not to flinch at his touch though.

He watched me carefully, and I felt that he was on his guard with me. Why, I wasn't going to waste my time trying to figure out. There wasn't anything I could do to him, other than bring his father's shady dealings into the light.

"Let's sit."

It didn't take much considering my legs had gone weak with apprehension.

I looked ahead at the pond and felt his eyes on my face so I turned, and asked, "What's really going on Patrick? Why are you doing this for your father?"

He sat forward, elbows on his knees and dipped his head. Seconds later, he met my gaze. "He's my father, Evie."

He looked back at the lake and I couldn't decide whether or not he was working at getting my defenses down. That made me wonder why? And then he continued, "You wouldn't know what it's like to always want your father's approval, but never to get it. Living in the shadow of having Declan Fitzwilliam as your father isn't what people presume."

Stunned. "Patrick, you know my father. You know

what he's like. I love him, and I know he loves me, but he's been absent more than he's been present. As a child, I lost count how many times I would call him to tell him of an award that I'd won at school, or that I got all my spellings correct at the Friday test, only to know that when he was saying well done, that he was distracted and hadn't really heard a word I said. I know what you're saying isn't the same, but even though he told me 'well done' it wasn't what I needed to hear."

I cleared my throat and still felt that something wasn't quite right. We'd never talked about our parents or our upbringing before and hearing Patrick say about his father, made me feel sorry for the little boy that he once was.

"I didn't mean to say that." He sat up and lifted his face to the sun that had appeared from behind a cloud. "I hate how this thing between us has gone off track. I hate how we're both being pushed and forced to do things that neither of us want."

"I don't understand. You texted me asking to meet you to discuss Stryker." I hesitated and bit my lip as I searched the area for some type of answer. "You've never talked to me like this before so I'm confused after the way you've treated me."

"I'm a bastard, Evie, and I'm so fucking tired." His eyes slid to my face before he continued to stare ahead. "I treated you the way that I did in hope you'd go to your father and get him to step in to stop the whole wedding." He sighed. "What my father wants, he gets. I've never gone against him, Evie, until…" He shook his head. "Even when I know what he wants is wrong. It just isn't done."

She wondered what he'd been about to say, but let it go

for now, and asked, "So it was your father who wanted the wedding?" I questioned, the frown back on my brow.

"You're father is a senator, he thinks," he paused, "it doesn't matter what he thinks. We have to get married to keep him off our backs and Stryker safe."

Goose bumps raced across my skin. "Safe?"

"He'll get rid of Stryker for good if the wedding doesn't go ahead. That's why I'm here. He wants the wedding on the weekend to go ahead, and he's promised if it does, he'll let Stryker…live."

My blood chilled listening to him and although I wanted to believe him, it all seemed farfetched. Stupid even. Which was why a chuckle escaped my lips that I covered with my hand.

The look of surprise Patrick gave me caused me to laugh harder.

"I don't see what there is to laugh about," he grumbled and proceeded to ignore me for a few more seconds. He then stood in front of me. "Evie, for God's sake! Pull yourself together."

Hiccupping to a stop, I wiped at the tears that had now appeared on my lashes. I had to will them away because I refused to cry in front of him.

"I need your agreement before I leave."

"Agreement to what?" I asked, confused and hurting. A headache was building at the back of my eyes.

"I need to tell my father that the wedding is going ahead on the weekend. I also need you to confirm with your parents, while I'm here, that we still need the minister on Saturday. It doesn't matter if the rest has been cancelled."

I opened and closed my mouth before I could get any

words out. "I can't marry you, Patrick...I'm in love with Stryker."

Patrick got in my space and pulled me up from the bench. "You haven't been listening. Stryker's health depends on the weekend. That's the only choice you get. Stryker's health. It's all in your hands."

My heartbeat raced as a wave of dizziness hit me. Patrick slid his arm around my waist, holding me against him as my legs went weak.

I pushed free and dropped back down to the bench. My fists clenched at my sides and my instinct was to punch him in the face, which I thought he sensed when he covered my fists with his hands.

"Don't hit out at me, Evie. You know it's my father who is pulling the strings. All I'm doing here is passing on his message."

"Doing his dirty work you mean."

Patrick flinched.

"Think what you will. It doesn't change the outcome... only you can do that."

There was only one option available and that was to go through with the wedding. But could I change the deal? Could I do it on my terms?

I inhaled deeply and met Patrick's gaze. "I'll marry you on one condition."

"My father was specific, Evie," Patrick replied, sounding tired, as though he'd had enough of everything.

He certainly wasn't the only one and I couldn't help the brief twinge of sympathy I felt for him. But then I remembered how he'd treated me, especially the time he took what he wanted.

It could have been worse though . . .

"I'll go through with the wedding as long as Stryker is given back to his father. A clean slate. Stryker and his father owe your family nothing. From the minute we say 'I do', your father and his friends never have any contact with Stryker or his family again. Ever. He's left alone to have a life."

Patrick stared at me with surprise. He should have expected me to counter his deal, but he hadn't. It wouldn't surprise me if his father had expected me to, though.

"Let me make a call." Patrick stood and moved out of hearing.

Oliver, the man with Patrick stared at me, and when I caught his eye, he looked through me. He was big. Not as large as Stryker, who was over six feet tall, but his dress shirt showed the muscular definition in his arms and torso. For some reason I didn't feel threatened, which confused me considering that I now had a better understanding of the business that the Fitzwilliam's ran.

"It's a deal," Patrick announced but wouldn't meet my gaze. "Make your call to your parents."

Something wasn't right.

"What did your father say?"

"Yes."

"Can I trust him?"

His eyes flicked to mine before he turned to watch across the pond. "You don't really have much choice."

He was right, and I didn't trust his father. I wasn't even sure I trusted Patrick.

With hands that were unsteady, I took my cell from my pocket and called my parents.

CHAPTER 20

STRYKER

THE MINUTE THE DOOR to the hotel suite closed, I dropped my bag and just stood and looked out of the floor to ceiling windows that lined the outer wall.

Married.

I was hurt and eaten up with jealousy that she was with another man. I wanted my anger to fuel me. Not on this occasion though. I didn't have it in me because the hurt went too deep. I tried to believe what the guards had told me was pure fiction, but I didn't think it was. She was going to marry Patrick tomorrow and there wasn't a damn thing I could do about it.

Stuck in Chicago with guards at every damn turn, and she was back in New York with *him*.

If only I could talk to her. Hear her tell me that everything between us meant nothing. Even as though words ran through my mind, I knew they weren't true. She'd wanted me just as much as I wanted her, which I never thought would be possible.

Clenching my fists, I turned to the desk where the phone rang and rang. It stopped and started up again. I wanted to knock the thing off the desk, but on the third round I grabbed the annoying thing.

"What?" I growled.

"Stryker? It's Carter. You alone in there?"

I blinked in surprise. I knew he was around because I'd seen him downstairs in the gym once Coach had pointed him out, but I was surprised to hear him on the phone.

"I'm alone right now," I replied, so damn tired that I wanted it all over with.

"I'm downstairs and we need to get you out of here and back to New York."

"I can't go anywhere. I can't risk Evie."

"Dammit, Stryker. You're both as bad as the other. Evie is only going ahead with the wedding because Declan promised her to let you go after the fight. She bargained the marriage for you. She thinks he's going to let you walk away and go back to your father. But that's a lie. Declan won't let you go and the fight tomorrow isn't officially sanctioned, which means anything goes. They make their own rules. You hear what I'm saying? You know what that means."

I'd never fought in an unsanctioned fight, but I'd heard about them. It was one way for Declan to end things with an enemy or someone who'd crossed him. Lots of blood would be spilled.

"I hear you. What do you want me to do, Carter?"

"I want to get you out of there, and I need for you to

trust me. If not for yourself, then trust me because Evie needs our help."

My hand clenched around the phone. "I'll do anything I can to protect her."

"Okay, I'm going to come up for you. Be ready." The phone went dead. I let it drop back to the desk.

Be ready. Ready for what?

Seconds later, I dashed into the bedroom and quickly changed into jeans, and a clean T-shirt. I fastened my sneakers, pulled a sweatshirt on, grabbed my cap and went to wait in the room.

A knock at the door had me looking through the security hole before I yanked it open to admit Carter.

"We need to go before one of them gets ahold of Patrick or Declan." Carter looked up and down the corridor. "Let's go."

I followed behind him and found that I wasn't surprised when he shoved me into the elevator.

"I got them to the lobby. Told them Declan was checking in and had sent me up to watch you while they went and helped him. It won't take long for them to realize it was bullshit."

He stopped the elevator on four.

Again, I followed him. This time we ran up two floors and got in the elevator again.

Carter grinned, and watched something on his cell. "Look." He turned it to me and I saw the lobby. "I planted a small camera down there so I could make sure the coast was clear." He grinned. "It worked."

As the doors opened, Carter looked out and then indicated we were still in the clear. "We're going to walk straight out of here and into the black SUV that's sitting directly outside."

I nodded.

My heart beat rapidly as I placed one foot in front of the other toward the exit. The doors loomed closer and tempted me to run, which Carter obviously sensed.

"Hold on. We're good."

I didn't know where his confidence came from because I was so fucking scared that I'd be caught and taken back to hell.

Outside, I breathed in the smell of freedom and followed Carter into the SUV. The minute the door closed, we were being driven away from the hotel.

Yanking my cap off, I wiped the sweat from my forehead and sat back breathing heavily while I watched Carter chat to the guy driving the SUV.

I presumed he was a friend of Carter's and that I hadn't jumped into more hell.

As we left the city behind us, Carter settled back and watched me. "Whatever you're thinking, stop. You're safe now and Evie will be soon. I have something to tell you about me and the private jet we have waiting to get us back to New York." He turned away and faced the way we travelled. "You, more than anyone, are aware that sometimes things aren't as they seem, and neither are people. Me included. My real name is Carter Thompson, and I have a story to tell you…

EVIE

MY MOTHER DROVE ME crazy with her constant chatter about the wedding that was happening tomorrow. My father had looked sad when I'd arrived, and after a tight hug, he'd kissed my forehead and left the house.

I sensed that he knew something wasn't right, but my mom certainly didn't. At least, her actions said she was clueless.

She'd wanted me married for a while now because she thought a marriage and then a baby would be good for my father's political career. Sometimes I wondered what planet she lived on. Although my marriage would make the local news, I'd be surprised if it made national news. I wasn't all that important. My mother was delusional.

Millie had travelled with me and had made it known how stupid I was being, and that Declan wouldn't keep his part of the deal.

I wanted to believe that he would though. I needed to believe that Stryker would be free to have a life even if it wasn't with me. I loved him so much that I wanted that for him. It would break my heart knowing he was with someone else, but wasn't that how he'd feel knowing that I was married to Patrick. It would kill him.

Tears ran down my face as I huddled on a chair in my mother's glasshouse. For years, I'd called it the boathouse, and still did, because that's what it held and it was on the bank of the lake. But, my mother had made the upstairs into a lounge where she'd entertain her lady friends while their husbands went out on the lake fishing in the boat. It was too frilly for my liking really, but the white furniture in here was comfortable.

I'd used it as a hideaway since I was about fifteen because on rainy days my mother thought it was too far from the house so I knew that she wouldn't bother me.

Having a Kleenex shoved in my face, I took it from Millie and watched her sit at the end of the sofa that I currently cuddled up on.

I sniffled some more until Millie broke the silence. "I'm worried about Carter. He isn't answering his cell or replying to my messages."

Wallowing in my own sorrow, I'd forgotten about my best friend's feelings for Carter. "I'm a terrible friend."

"No, you're not." She shook her head. "You have more to deal with. I'm sure Carter's okay." Millie bit her lip. "At least, I hope he is."

I moved and wrapped my arm around my friend, our heads together. "We're a right pair, huh?"

"I've been thinking that I want to ask my father for help. He knows that you've always been here for me, which means he'd do anything for you."

"Millie, please don't take this the wrong way, but I don't want more trouble and you know as well as I do that your father isn't very diplomatic."

She chuckled. "No, he isn't. But he'd be able to get Stryker free of Declan without the wedding going ahead. And I trust my father. I can't say the same for Declan."

I so wished I could agree, but I'd heard things about Millie's father and he sounded a slightly meaner version of Declan, not that I'd ever voice that. He'd mean well, but the way he'd go about it wasn't something I'd probably be able to live with.

We'd both be free though.

"Leave it for now, Millie. Let me try and do it this way

before your father gets involved. I need to believe that Declan will let Stryker go free." I grabbed hold of her hands. "I have to believe that because it's the only thing keeping me going."

Millie nodded.

"What about your father then? He knows this isn't what you want. I saw his face when we arrived. It was full of sorrow. I bet that's why he hasn't been around."

My father may have been absent a lot, but he'd know everything that happened at the house when he wasn't there. No one could get anything past him. So why had he left and stayed silent?

"I don't know. I'm just so tired and I've had enough. I feel if someone said boo to me I'll burst into tears. I hate feeling this way."

"Patrick's at the house."

"What?"

"I'm sorry to just blurt that out. It's why I came to find you because I was trying to give you some alone time. If it's any consolation, he looks just as bad as you. At least he did when he thought no one was watching. Then your mother appeared and he changed before my eyes into a happy groom. She ushered him through to the kitchen. Something about the cake." Millie shrugged. "I know what I saw, but are you sure he doesn't want this as much as you don't?"

"How can he want to marry me, Millie? We had some kind of relationship, which started to go sour before I even knew Stryker existed. Patrick doesn't want me, and I know he's only going ahead because of pressure from his father. I suspect he's also going ahead because it takes the pressure off of him and once married, he can go out after what or who he really wants."

Millie frowned but I ignored her.

"I guess I better go back to the house."

"Not so fast." Millie stood and tugged me up to face her. "What was all that about Patrick? Do you know something you're not sharing?" She tipped her head to the side and waited.

"I don't know anything." I grabbed her arm and tugged her out of the boathouse. "I suspect something that's all."

"You going to share?"

"Not yet." I shook my head. "Let me go and find Patrick. I want to talk to him before tomorrow. See if there's some way of ending this whole mess that doesn't include getting married."

"Don't hold your breath, Evie. His father's an asshole."

"I know."

CHAPTER 21

EXHAUSTED OF PLAYING A part, he tugged his tie free from around his neck and locked the bedroom door.

No interruptions.

He moved slowly to his lover who already laid naked on the large bed, waiting for him to slip his cock inside.

The buttons slowly slipped free from his dress shirt as he teased his lover with the slow removal of the garment.

"Please, hurry. It's been too long," his lover moaned, hands fisted in the bedding.

"It has been too long, but soon we won't have to hide. Soon I'll be free to be with you." He inhaled as he shucked the shirt and started on his pants. "I'm doing this for *us*, not just me. I hope you know that."

His lover nodded and then gasped when he knelt on the bed, and started to caress along legs that he craved to have wrapped around his waist.

"I don't have any reason to believe that tomorrow won't go as planned. Just promise me," he groaned, licking between his lover's legs," that you'll stay close to me." He gave another swipe with his tongue and pushing his lovers legs open wide, he took hold of his weeping shaft, impaling his lover.

He stilled, fighting for breath. "I will only be able to get through tomorrow if you're close…promise me."

"I promise…please make love to me."

With legs quivering, his balls as hard as his fucking cock, he slowly slipped free before he touched home base again.

As their lips sealed together he knew he'd do anything to protect his lover…

CHAPTER 22

STRYKER

"WE'RE LANDING IN THIRTY minutes so we need to finish our talk," Carter sat across the table and placed a folder in front of me. He sat forward, his arms on the table.

"I thought you'd already told me everything?" I frowned.

"I left out the part about your father helping Evie and Millie."

"What the fuck." I pushed away from the table and tried to pace in the small confines of the private jet, but failed. I couldn't even stand up straight so I dropped back down.

"You finished?" Carter asked, amused.

My father.

I dropped my head and wanted to ignore Carter, but he was too big to be ignored.

"He loves you, Jake. He never stopped."

"No." I shook my head and tried not to listen but he wouldn't stop.

"Yes. I've seen his house. Been inside. One room is full of pictures of you, and him. He has a picture of you and him enlarged on the kitchen wall. You're a child so no one would recognize you if they didn't know your connection to him."

"Then why? If everything you're saying is the truth, why did he do it? Why'd he sell me? I can't accept anything else. All this time I've had my anger that's been fueled by his betrayal. What will I have if it's all been a lie?"

You couldn't find the anger when you saw him the other night.

"Jake, you'll have your father back."

"I don't—"

"Think before you speak," Carter suggested.

I met Carter's gaze while my mind was in turmoil.

Are you sure?

Sighing, heavily, I asked, "Tell me why?"

"He's asked that he be the one to tell you. Evie, Millie, and myself know why. Evie wanted to be angry with him on your behalf, but after she saw his photographs of you, and heard what he had to say, I don't think she could get there. Everything he's done, he's done to get you back." Carter sat back, but looked to be anything but happy. "Look, he's going to be meeting us when we land. I'm going to take over the driving while he sits in the back with you and talks. Just give him a chance."

What I wanted was to have Evie with me when I talked to him. Coming out and saying that to Carter would make me look like a pussy so I kept my mouth shut. "I don't want my head full of crap when I'm going to be up against...I don't know...when we show up at Evie's parents' place."

"You're head won't be full with crap. It might be spinning, and I know you and your father will have to work at getting to know one another again, but I truly believe he did everything he thought he could back then."

I looked out of the window as we dropped altitude and wondered what the hell he'd have to say. I wasn't sure anything could make up for letting them have me. I was a fourteen-year-old boy when I last saw him. I became a man pretty quickly because I didn't have the choice.

"I'm not sure any explanation will make amends for what I went through as a boy because of what he did."

"I understand, but at least you can hear him out, and then decide. Otherwise, you'll spend the rest of your life curious about what happened...I'd listen."

I offered a mirthless laugh. "I guess I won't have much choice but to listen."

"What about Evie and Millie? All you've done is tell me about you, and my father. I want to know the plan to go and get Evie."

"By tomorrow, everything should be in place so we'll move in before the wedding."

"They'll know that I'm going for Evie. At least, Patrick will know where I'm headed."

"It doesn't matter. We're landing under radar and once we're in the car I have somewhere to stash you." Carter grinned. "It's somewhere that Declan Fitzwilliam might consider, but would never look."

I raised a brow.

"We're the over night guests of Millie's daddy, Jordan Michaels, except Millie has no idea. So I'd appreciate you keeping that news to yourself."

"I can, but why would Millie be pissed at us staying with her family?"

He sighed. "Whenever I mentioned her parents, she'd change the subject. I actually already knew who they were, especially her father, but I wanted her to tell me. She promised to do so when I returned. Except, I left your father's house to go and help you and ended up being dragged to Chicago. She's probably wondering where the hell I am."

"I take it her father does a lot of dealings like Declan?"

"Not anymore. At least what anyone can prove. He's a much better man than Declan has ever been or ever will be. So let's just leave it at that... I'll give you some peace until we land. It will be hectic enough for you once we do." Carter moved toward the back of the plane and stayed there.

I rubbed my brow wanting the whole damn thing over with. I wanted Evie in my arms without any worry that we'd be ripped apart. I wanted and needed her by my side for the rest of our lives.

Just her smile was enough to make me feel happy. My skin always felt fevered at her touch. And I was sure that I acted like an adolescent teenager with how quickly my cock responded to her.

Even thoughts of her had me hard and aching. Like now. I slipped my hand into my jeans and made myself comfortable, as I tried to turn my thoughts around to something else.

My father.

He must really have something to say if Evie couldn't bring herself to hate him. But what? What could he say to remove the image of him running away and leaving me in that dark alley? I always hoped that he'd come back for me. Tell me it had all been a misunderstanding. He never came and eventually my dreams died and became nightmares. I'd eventually lost all hope and started hating my father.

I wasn't sure that years of hate could turn into something else.

EVIE

WANTING TO TALK TO Patrick, I waited until he went up to the guest room for the night so then his father wouldn't catch us talking. His father was still downstairs and I certainly wanted to avoid him.

Patrick had been in there for about an hour so I figured it was time. Like before, I didn't know what to say to make him walk away from me, but it was worth a try.

There was a connecting door between our rooms, and I didn't think that Patrick knew about it. It didn't look like a door and had been decorated in the same wooden design around both rooms. To blend in.

Using the small key, I unlocked it and quietly opened the door. Patrick's room was quiet and there was no sign of him. I looked behind the door as well.

Bathroom.

The shower came on and then I heard something. As though someone had banged into the shower door. I wasn't going look. Patrick might get ideas if I followed him into the bathroom.

I paced back and forth near the bed and then I froze.

There were voices.

Male voices in the bathroom.

My heart beat erratically at the thought of what was going on in there. I'd had my suspicions, but…

Curiosity got the better of me as I crept closer to the bathroom. There was a gap in the door, and, I looked.

My eyes widened in shock. The same man that was always with Patrick was naked, facing the shower wall with his legs spread. I didn't miss his bobbing erection either.

I quickly turned to look at Patrick who was also naked, erect, and…oh.

He held his cock and pressed into the man in front of him.

I quickly turned away and tried to catch my breath. Somehow, I thought I'd feel good knowing that I was right, but I didn't.

Quickly getting back to my room, I closed and locked the door and sagged to the floor.

At least now I knew why Patrick would be going through with the wedding. His father would kill him if he knew he was gay. What a way to cover it up by marrying a woman.

I just wish I'd discovered I was right without having to witness them having sex in the shower. It was now an image I wouldn't be able to get out of my head anytime soon.

"Hey, Evie. Open up."

I scrambled to my feet and unlocked my bedroom door. The minute I did, Millie fell into the room, out of breath.

"Why'd you lock your room?" She frowned. "And why are you flushed?" Her eyes narrowed.

"I'm fine, but why are you acting like you've run a mile?"

She tugged me over to the window. "Look." She pointed to the garden.

"What?"

"Glasshouse. See something now?" She turned my head and my heart stopped.

"What's going on?"

"Some meeting of sorts. I think it's something bad."

"Oh Millie, calm down. We're safe in here."

"I'm sleeping with you tonight." Millie turned and used the bathroom before she climbed into my bed. "I'm waiting."

I laughed.

Shoving my pajamas on, I climbed into bed beside her and lay looking up at the ceiling. "Just like old times."

Millie smiled and turned on to her side. "I want the truth. Why were you flushed?"

Groaning, I turned to face her. "I used the secret door to go into Patrick's room," I whispered. "I wanted to talk to him without his father being around. I just didn't expect to see what I did."

She poked me in the shoulder. "All of it."

I could feel the flush coating my cheeks again. "He was in the shower."

"So, was he playing with himself?"

I choked on a laugh. "He wasn't alone."

She froze. "What?"

"Millie, he was having sex in the shower with another man. With Oliver"

"No way."

"Yes, way. I saw it with my own eyes."

"And you didn't come and get me so I could watch."

"Millie." I swatted her arm. "Be serious."

"I am. Two guys going at it is hot as hell. I mean two cocks to play with."

My eyes widened in surprise. "I don't know what to say to that."

Millie rolled her eyes. "Were they both hard?"

I opened my mouth to answer, but nothing came out.

"Evie, that's so not fair." She pouted.

"You do realize that you sound like a two year old, right?"

"Well, at least it's taking your mind off the wedding."

I flopped to my back. "The wedding isn't far from my mind…neither is Jake."

Millie intertwined her fingers with mine. "I hope, when he's free, that you'll call him Jake."

Tears slipped down my face. "When he's free I won't see him, Millie."

"Surely you don't expect him to go on his way without coming after you. Because no way will that man accept you being with someone else."

"That's what I'm afraid of. What if he comes after me and Declan does something to prevent him from getting close?"

"That happens then regardless of what everyone wants, I'll get my dad involved. I shouldn't have listened to you and Carter. My dad would have gotten Stryker free without this farce of a wedding."

I blew out a breath and wiped at my face. "Let's try and sleep." I turned over, praying for sleep, but not really believing it would come any time soon.

Patrick obviously needed to marry a woman to hide his true sexual orientation, so I didn't think that I'd get any help from him. I sure as heck didn't want to get my father involved because Declan was a dangerous man.

Maybe Millie's father could do something after all.

CHAPTER 23

STRYKER

DRESSED IN A MONKEY suit, I stood in front of the mirror in the bedroom not recognizing myself. My casual clothes were in a heap on the bed and I longed to put them back on. That wasn't the plan though. I wasn't sure about the whole plan, but someone who was part of the wedding had supplied us with official wedding invitations so that we could get on the property.

Security would be tight and I hoped that the false ID Carter had come up with would hold. I doubted that anyone would recognize me unless they looked close enough.

My hair had been cropped in an army cut, which made my head feel damn cold. It certainly changed the way I looked after having slightly longer hair for so long.

The bowtie around my neck felt more like a noose, but before I ripped it off, I kept telling myself that this was all for Evie.

Evie who had no clue that I was already free from under Declan, but soon would. I just hoped that we got there before it was too late.

My nerves were shot to hell and the lack of sleep hadn't helped. Millie's father, Jordan, had been a surprise in itself. I'd expected a hard-core criminal like Declan. Instead we'd found a successful businessman who knew what he was talking about, and who wanted nothing more than to bury Declan.

Carter and I had nearly come to blows when we'd arrived last night though. I'd wanted to get in touch with Evie to let her know that I was free and coming for her, but Carter told me it would be safer if she had no idea. I agreed, grudgingly. I'd just wanted to charge in there and take her with me. Keep her safe.

"Fuck." I clenched my fists wanting to hit something, or someone.

"Hold it in, man." Carter started fussing with my tie so I raised a brow in amusement. He grinned. "We don't want attention on you, and with the mess around your neck people would do a double take."

"You need to get out more than I do," I grumbled. "And how the fuck do people wear these without choking to fucking death?"

"There." He moved to the door. "Not many people who wear these things have a neck as thick as yours…we need to go and meet up with my people."

I raised a brow. "No way can I involve Jordan more than I already have. My people are the law, Jake. They can't know that I asked Jordan for help."

"Why did you?"

Carter looked away. "We needed somewhere to sleep." He shrugged.

"Hum...so it had nothing to do with Millie? You didn't want to check her old man out in person to make sure your girl would be good?"

He sighed. "I wanted to see if the rumors of him being one of the good guys were true. It wouldn't have made any difference because Millie is under my skin. I didn't want her worrying about us meeting. So now we've met, and I'm worrying about telling her that we've met."

I chuckled. He was so damn serious that I ended up laughing my way downstairs. That soon stopped when my father met us there.

I'd listened to everything he'd said yesterday and I wanted to believe him. It was just difficult after how my life had turned out. All these years I'd thought that he didn't care and hadn't looked back, but that had been a lie. I didn't want to like him or believe him. But that was hard to do when the truth was staring me in the face. Trust though. I wasn't sure that would ever be there again.

"Son," he whispered, reminding me that I was standing there staring at him. "Are you okay?"

Inhaling, I nodded. "I'll be okay once I have Evie."

"She's a lovely girl who I know loves you. We'll get there in time, and then you'll both be together without having to look over your shoulder for Declan ever again."

"Am I missing something?" I scowled, wondering what the hell he was talking about with Declan.

"Um, perhaps I've said too much."

"Dad?" I reached out to grab his arm, but he'd disappeared, out of my reach.

I went to follow when a voice stopped me. "Leave him."

I turned and faced Jordan Michaels. "Do you know what he's talking about? About Declan?"

"The man who is in love with my daughter is with the FBI, yes?" He chuckled at my surprise. "He isn't the only one who has connections. Carter is a good man and you know that you're about to meet up with *his* men, right? Who did you think they were?"

The truth was that I hadn't given it any thought. After he'd explained the situation on the plane to me, I'd kinda switched off and missed some of what he'd said.

"They're going after Declan." I ran my hands over my hair, and heavily sighed. "I'm impatient for this all to be over."

"They have gathered enough evidence of his illegal activities to put him away for a long time. Your father has agreed to testify, and I'm presuming, if asked, that you will do so." He raised a brow in question.

I nodded.

"I thought as much. From what I know, Carter hadn't been the only one on the inside." He smiled. "Now, I plan on keeping your father here so he doesn't get caught in the crossfire as he is a star witness. He won't like it, but that's how it is going to go down. In exchange, I want you to help keep my daughter safe. She is strong willed and won't hesitate to get in the middle of chaos."

I smiled. "I promise, although I should imagine she's the first person that Carter will go to protect."

"Yes." Jordan disappeared into his office, and when I turned to head out, I found my father and Carter watching me.

"You heard."

"Yes," my father said. "I don't like being told to stay here, but when he put it like 'star witness' I had to agree that he was right, just…be careful." He stepped forward and hugged me.

The first time in ten years.

I went to push him away, but found my arms wrapped around him as I returned his hug.

"I love you, son." With those words, he disappeared upstairs.

Carter cleared his throat. "We need to leave."

With one last glance upstairs, I followed Carter out of the house to the SUV.

EVIE

MY MOTHER HAD DREADFUL taste in dresses, which was why I looked like a meringue. The bodice was fitted and beaded, and the only thing right with what I wore. The skirt had layers and layers of frills, which did remind me of a dessert or little Bo Peep. I wasn't really bothered because the wedding was a farce so it held little interest for me.

The thick veil hid my distress as Millie entered the room in the pink bridesmaid dress that my mother had also chosen. At least, her dress was plain silk and looked lovely on her.

"Your father is waiting for you." She took my hands into hers. "God, your hands are so cold." She tried to rub some warmth into them.

"I'm so cold." My voice broke on a sob that I tried to control.

"Evie?"

"I have to do this. I know that. Will you promise me something?" I clutched her hands tightly to me as she nodded. "Promise me that you'll find Jake and tell him how much I love him. I need him to know that I'm doing this for him. I don't want him to think that I used him or don't care."

"Oh Evie." She hugged me close. "I promise he already knows, and if he doesn't then he will have no doubt once I've spoken to him."

I swallowed back my sorrow and pulled away from her. I straightened my spine, closed my eyes and inhaled. "Let's get this over with."

Millie followed me out of the door and downstairs to where my father waited. He looked handsome in his tuxedo, and I wished with all my heart that I were about to walk up the aisle to Jake.

My father moved close and grasped my shoulders. He rested his lips against my forehead, over the veil, and whispered, "I love you, Evie." He sighed heavily, and placed my arm through his.

I cast a glance back to Millie who looked just as unhappy as I was. I knew that she worried about Carter and I hoped that, after today, she'd get to be with him. I prayed one of us got our happily ever after.

It didn't take as long as I'd hoped to reach the seating outside.

Everyone turned to look at me, and as I scanned the guests who I didn't know, I saw Declan at the front beside his wife. He looked agitated and constantly looked around him, as though he waited for someone or something to happen.

Patrick stood at the top of the makeshift aisle, and beside him was Oliver, the man who he'd been showering with. The man looked just as unhappy as Patrick did. My groom—the thought was like ashes in my mouth—offered me a wry smile before he passed a quick glance to his father.

My nerves had already been jumping but now they jumped higher than ever. Something more was going on here and seeing how Declan and Patrick acted got my hackles up.

I tried to have sympathy for Patrick because, in a way, he was in a similar situation as I was. Neither of us could marry the man we loved.

The music suddenly started as my father got me moving toward Patrick.

I caught my mother looking happy as anything so I avoided looking at her.

The closer we got to the minister, the more my stomach turned. My hand shook in my father's arm as my grip tightened on him, not wanting him to let me go.

He patted my hand as he handed me over to Patrick, who looked just as sick as I felt.

"I'm sorry, Evie," he whispered.

I looked at Oliver with Patrick, and realized that he was close to tears. He tried to fight them with anger, but I didn't think he'd last much longer.

The minister started to talk, but I had no idea what he was saying because blood rushed through my ears.

Taking a step back, I felt my father behind me.

He turned me to face him and raised the veil. "I can't let you do this, honey." He smiled and wiped my tears with his thumb before he pulled me close. "He's free, Evie. Jake is safe with the FBI," my father whispered.

I stilled. "What?"

He met my questioning gaze. "He isn't in any trouble. He's safe, baby girl… Is he your prince, honey?"

Through tears, I whispered, "Yes."

"What the fuck!" Declan roared from behind us.

"Dad, no." Patrick went to step around us but froze when his dad waved a gun. "What?"

The guests started to run as chaos erupted around us. Guests fell as others fell over them and my heart dropped to my toes.

"There will be a wedding," Declan said very slowly. He pointed his weapon at the minister. "You. Marry them now."

The poor man quivered in his shoes, and the bible in his hands shook so badly that I was surprised it didn't drop to the floor. "Um, it doesn't work that way," the Minister mumbled.

"You value your life, then you'll make it work that way." Declan sneered.

"Patrick, take your fiancée's hand and stand in front of the minister."

Patrick made no move.

"Now, son," Declan growled.

"Dad, it's over. You might still try and force us, but the fact is that probably most of those guests will have called the cops. So whether or not I marry Evie won't matter anymore. You won't have a senator in the family, and as soon as you're taken away our wedding will be annulled. There's no point in it."

Patrick's father went bright red in the face, and looked

ready to boil over. His features were twisted in rage and pure hate ran through him.

I held my breath and witnessed the change in Declan almost immediately. I wasn't fooled as he calmed, but with a steady hand he raised the gun. Not at my family, or me, but at his own son.

"Dad?" Patrick questioned, his voice quivered.

"You think I don't know about you…and *him*," he spat, the gun moved to Patrick's lover, but his gaze held his son in place. "You're a disgrace to this family."

"Fuck you," Patrick replied.

"No, fuck you, *son.*"

Before Declan could pull the trigger my dad pushed me behind him and leapt forward. Patrick dived on top of his lover, and took him and Millie—who stood next to Oliver—to the ground.

My mother grabbed my arm and tried to tug me behind the chair she crouched behind, but I couldn't move as I watched my father fight for control of the gun.

As I watched, Declan had the upper hand. He was a bigger man than my father, so without thinking, I stayed on my knees and crawled forward.

Close beside them, I grabbed a chair and standing over them, swung the chair toward Declan's back. But he turned, swiveling the gun toward me. My blood turned to ice seconds before Patrick knocked my legs out from under me as the weapon discharged.

Seconds later, there was another shot followed by a wail as though an animal had been hurt. I turned and noticed my mother's stricken expression.

My head whipped around to my father who lay on his

back, blood covered his shirt and seeped out from his jacket.

No!

Declan had started to run toward the trees and I briefly registered him dropping to his knees as men appeared from the direction that he ran.

But all my attention was back on my father as I quickly crawled to him. He was covered in blood as I ripped his jacket open.

So much blood.

"Daddy," I cried, as I tried to open his shirt. "Please."

"Evangeline," he called, faintly.

I needed something to try and stop the bleeding.

My dress.

I gathered the front of my dress and pressed it to his stomach.

"Fuck, Evie. I'm so damn sorry. I've called for help. Tell me what to do." Patrick kneeled beside me, frantic. Millie dropped to the other side, her face streaked with tears.

"I don't know what to do," I cried. "I don't know how to help him."

CHAPTER 24

STRYKER

HEARING THE GUN SHOT, my feet started to carry me through the forest before I could even think. I just knew that Evie needed me. But hearing the second, I thought I was going to puke with fright.

We'd met up with Carter's 'friends', who happened to be men and woman of the FBI wearing combat gear. I knew the minute that Carter gave the signal to go in, it was seconds after I started to move.

We burst through the trees and there the fucker was, running toward us thinking that he would be safe in that direction. Arrogant asshole.

My fear for Evie overrode the vengeance I wanted to inflict on Declan. The Feds could have him. I needed to find Evie.

I couldn't see her anywhere, and as Carter came up beside me, he grabbed my arm and gave a tug. We changed direction and went to where people were down on the ground.

My heart somersaulted in my chest when I saw the wedding dress.

Evie.

She was on the floor and as I ran closer, Patrick met my gaze, briefly. All I could see was the blood all over Evie; her hands, neck, a bit on her face, but it was the dress that was covered.

Carter dropped to his knees beside Millie, wrapped his arm around her and kissed her on the forehead in relief.

"Evie?" I mumbled, and then her eyes were on mine.

Tears filled her eyes and with a look of hopelessness, her face crumbled as large racking sobs broke her.

"Where are you hurt?" I asked, kneeling next to her, her face cupped in my hands. "Evangeline, please. Are you hurt?"

"It isn't hers," Patrick said, instantly putting my mind at rest.

I moved her further away as the medic who was with us took over the care of the man on the ground…obviously her father.

My legs felt weak so I dropped to the ground and cradled Evie on my lap, letting her cry until she gave one long shudder and quieted.

"Evie, right?" the paramedic questioned.

I nodded in response for her.

"You're father's alive but we need to airlift him to the hospital. There's no room in the copter, but you can meet up with him at the hospital."

"I'll see that she gets there with her mom."

"Okay."

Minutes later, I still held her tightly in my arms. My face buried in her neck while I breathed her in.

She was mine now.

Mine to love.

Mine to protect.

I wasn't going to give her up for anything.

"Jake."

Hearing my *real* name on her lips caused emotion to rise up inside me.

She lifted her tear-stained face and caressed me with her gaze. "I can't believe you're here." She reached up, but before she touched my head, she pulled her hands back. "Your beautiful hair. It's gone…and I'm covered with my father's blood," her voice trembled as her hands shook.

"It'll grow back." I kissed her eyes. "Let's get you and your mom up to the house so you both can quickly change before we go to the hospital." I stood, unable to let go of Evie. "C'mon."

I noticed Carter's boss talking to Patrick and Oliver, who sat huddled together. Patrick had his arm wrapped around who I presumed to be his mother.

Until thirty minutes ago, I'd had no idea that Patrick had been the insider. I'd been shocked and I knew Evie would be too.

I searched for Carter, who I found helping Evie's mother. Millie was on the other side, helping the woman move toward the house.

Carter glanced back and caught my gaze as I followed with Evie. "Meet outside the house in ten minutes. I'll drive us all to the hospital," he shouted.

Evie walked faster as I kept my arm around her.

Once the door to her room closed, Evie stood,

unmoving for maybe a minute before she dashed for the bathroom.

I quickly followed and watched as she turned the shower on and started to tug on her dress. "I can't get it off." She panicked. "Help me. I need it off. I need the blood off me."

Hand on her hips, I turned her away from me and made quick work of getting her out of the dress. Before it fell to the floor she'd shoved her panties down her legs, so I helped and removed her bra.

She jumped in the shower and started to scrub the blood from her skin, in a furious back and forth motion.

Shucking the tuxedo jacket, I ripped the bowtie from around my neck, the shirt from my body, and dumped the lot on top of her dress. Grabbing her hand, I stopped her motion. "You're going to be red raw if you carry on. It's gone, Evie. Look." I held her hand in front of her face. "It's gone."

Her head bowed and her body shook as she inhaled and slowly exhaled. Then my Evie was back.

"Pass me a towel, please. I need to dress."

I grabbed a large bath towel and wrapped it around her body, which I tried not to think about. So not appropriate right now, but it was difficult not to.

She was naked, wet, and in my arms. What the hell should I have expected? Evie pressed into me and caught her breath when she felt my arousal. "I'm sorry." I dropped my head to her shoulder. "I want you. I've missed you. But now isn't the time for this."

"I know." She turned and caressed my face. "I can touch you now."

"You can touch me whenever you want to because I'm not letting you go. Ever."

She smiled, reached up and planted a quick, albeit wet, kiss to my lips before she raced into her room.

I tried hard not to grin, but it was difficult. I had my freedom, and what I'd wanted the most, Evie. Our happiness would have to wait though, now that we raced for the hospital.

Evie looked pale as she shoved her feet into boots. She worried, which went without saying. I wished that there was something I could do to take all her pain away.

Dressed now and ready to go in fitted jeans, T-shirt and a sweater in her hand, she turned to me. "I'm ready."

I moved toward her. "Just remember I'm with you. You don't have to do anything alone, okay?"

"You're mine, Jake." She smiled. "I'm glad your name comes so easily to my tongue. I've always tried to think of you as Stryker so that I wouldn't slip up. But you're both, and you both belong to me."

"Always." I rested my forehead against hers. "Let's go because I don't want to be stuck here. I can't drive."

Her eyes widened. "I didn't even think about that." Our fingers intertwined. "We'll have to sort that out, and soon."

EVIE

WHEN WE WALKED INTO the hospital, still hand-in-hand, my mother had pulled herself together and had taken charge of making sure my father was being taken care of properly. Part of that was after Carter had informed us that my father had made it to the hospital. He'd lost a lot of blood but he'd made it so far, and now he was in theatre.

My mother showed everyone what she was really made of before she crumpled and gave in to her tears. I think at first, when she was directing everyone around that Jake had been shocked. I'd smiled because he didn't know the half of it.

It felt good to finally call Stryker by his real name of Jake. Stryker would never be forgotten but I hoped it was the past. I always wanted him to be known as Jake from now on. With my help he was going to get his life back, and his family.

But as I clutched his hand to me, I couldn't remember being more scared while we waited for information on my father. Jake kept his arm around me and wouldn't let me go anywhere without him. We'd had a discussion about the restroom, but everywhere else, I was glad that he was with me.

I loved him and for once I knew how it felt to have someone to lean on. Before I'd always been on the outside, even when I was a child growing up. I think I grew up too soon, and I do blame my father's political career on that.

He was my father though and even though I was an awkward teenager, I loved him and my mother dearly.

Just like I knew deep down that Jake loved his father, Peter, who sat on his other side. With my help, they were going to get their family back, and that included me, who would be joining them as soon as possible. I wasn't about to lose Jake for a second time.

Curled up in Jake, I noticed Millie watching me. Carter who hadn't left her side held her tightly. I was glad that my best friend had found a good man as well. She'd been looking for a while for 'the one' even when she disagreed. The fact that he was with the FBI would make for entertaining dinner conversation with her family. I told her that was one dinner I planned on being present for.

"Evie," Jake squeezed my waist.

I looked at him and then in the direction that he nodded.

A surgeon was walking down the hallway toward our family waiting room.

Jake helped me sit up and then tugged me to my feet as my mother gripped my hand. Blood rushed through my ears in panic at not being able to decide whether the surgeon held good or bad news.

"Mrs. Southwell."

"Yes." My mother's voice broke as she answered.

"Please tell us how my father is," I begged, unable to wait for the doctor to continue.

"He's a very lucky man is how he is. I managed to retrieve the bullet and it missed most of the major organs." He took my mother's hand between the two of his. "He should make a full recovery."

"But?" I knew that there was more by the way the man hesitated.

"I had to remove one of his kidneys."

He paused again before he continued, "He still has a fully functional one as of right now, and providing he follows doctor's orders, he should be back on the golf course in a few months."

"Thank you." My mother sagged back into her chair, and I wrapped myself around Jake.

"When can we see him?" my mother asked, hopefulness in her voice.

The surgeon looked sympathetic. "I can take you and your daughter back now, but only for a couple of minutes."

Jake kissed me on the top of my head. "I'll be waiting here for you."

I buried my face into his chest and breathed him into my lungs. "I know, and that's what's keeping me going right now. Knowing that you're here with me." I kissed his chest and stepped away.

My mother held out her hand, which I gladly took.

CHAPTER 25

JAKE

WHEN EVIE WENT THROUGH the large double doors in the hospital with her mother, I sank back down into the chair I'd occupied since we arrived.

I was exhausted and felt like I hadn't slept in days, which was probably close to the truth. I couldn't leave her alone and, even now, I twitched to follow her. It was on that thought that I heard chuckling next to me.

"She'll be back out here soon, son. They don't like letting people past there. I'm guessing they've only been allowed because he's a senator."

"I didn't realize I was so obvious."

"You're still my son." My father cleared his throat. "I know you will have hated me all these years, but I hope you'll visit me and let me show you everything. I can back up what I've told you with emails, photographs, and of course, the bank statements. Once the Feds have sorted the whole mess of Declan out, then we'll get your name on to that account. It's your money, Jake. Every cent is what I won because of you." His voice broke.

I hesitated before putting my arm around his shoulders. "For years I told myself that I hated you."

He nodded and his body shook with distress. "I deserved your hate."

"But, I don't hate you. Part of me wants to and feels that I should, but I can't. Knowing the truth was hard to hear at first because I wanted to believe everything was a lie. But while I've been sitting here, waiting for news on Evie's father, I realized that could have been you through there. Declan could have killed you ten years ago and I'd have never known the truth. You could have come with us today and been in there, with or instead, of Evie's father. There are a lot of could have's, and I'm so tired that I just want to move forward with Evie, and you."

My father pulled away and wiped at his face with a handkerchief. I smiled at the memory. Even back then he'd use handkerchiefs as opposed to Kleenex.

"Thank God." He let out a loud sigh.

I grinned. "So, when do I get to meet my stepmom?"

He paused and then started laughing. "Tomorrow, if you have time. She can't wait to meet you."

"I'm supposed to meet with Carter and some other agents to give an official statement of my version of events from back then, and now. But I'll let you know."

"Okay, I gave mine after you left the house this morning. An agent took me to the office and grilled me. I passed over all the evidence to them. I kept every bit of paper, so they have a lot to sort through. They don't think any charges will be brought against me, but who knows."

My heart dropped before it started its regular rhythm

again. "I think they have too big a case on Declan to worry about you."

"I hope so." He straightened in the chair. "Evie's back."

My head whipped around and, as soon as I spotted her, I moved quickly into her space. "Everything okay?"

I wanted to wrap her up in my arms, but currently she held her mother who looked to have lost all color.

"The doctor said he probably won't be awake until tomorrow morning so we're going to go home."

I swallowed because I had no idea where home was for me. I wanted it to be with Evie, but it was obvious that she couldn't leave her mom alone right now.

"I'll drop you guys off on our way to my place," Carter offered.

Evie slipped her fingers into mine, tugging me closer. "You don't mind staying at my parents' house for a few days, do you? I don't want to leave my mom alone."

No words would come so I dipped my head and kissed her lips. "I wouldn't expect anything less."

"That's good." Her gaze flickered to the side and then back on me. "Is everything okay with your father? You've both talked?"

"It will take time, but he's still my father and the only family I have…apart from you. So we'll work it out."

"I like the family part."

I grinned. "Thought you might."

EVIE

AFTER THE DAY I'D had, I'd practically fallen into bed the minute I'd showered. I'd made sure my mother was okay for the night before I'd done anything else but I was so thankful to be back in my room.

I had so much to say, to discuss with Jake about the future, but no words would come. I sensed that he had things to say to me as well, but we were both waiting for the other to start.

His arms held me in a snug embrace that made me realize he was afraid I'd disappear while he slept. No amount of reassurance would settle him and only time would show him that I'm not going anywhere.

I hadn't missed the look on his face when he thought I was leaving him to go off with my mother. He'd hid it quickly, especially as I'd rushed to tell him what was going to happen.

In part, I was glad that he had nowhere else to go because that meant he'd be with me.

He'd be with you anyway.

Sighing, I turned in his arms, pressing against him. Jake grunted when his long, hard erection settled between my legs.

"You sleeping?"

"Not really," he mumbled as his hand slid down my back to grasp a cheek. He flexed his hips and it was now my turn to moan when he breached my entrance with the head of his cock.

"Mmm…slow, Jake."

He rolled me to my back and slid all the way inside.

My back arched in pleasure while my legs tangled with his.

He caressed up my sides, sending tingles of pleasure through my blood. His hands slipped beneath my shoulders as he cupped each side of my head.

"I love you, Evangeline," he whispered.

Jake rocked his hips, the sensation I felt from my core to my tightening nipples.

His forehead dropped to mine. "You saved me, Evie. But make no mistake about this, I'm loving you because you're mine, and you're in here." He pressed his hand to his chest. "God, I love you."

His lips sealed over mine and my mind went blank. All I could do was feel. Feel him moving inside me while my arousal coated his dick, causing him to move easily back and forth.

I arched my neck and gripped his head as he moved his lips slowly down my neck, collarbone, and finally he captured a tight nipple between his teeth.

He nibbled, sucked, and consumed me with his mouth and fingers, so it was no surprise that, seconds later, I was coming so hard on his shaft that Jake caught his breath, slammed to the hilt, and then growled through his own powerful release.

Once we'd both caught our breath, Jake stayed inside me, but rolled us to our sides. His arms held me tightly and I knew it would be my favorite place.

Eventually our heartbeats settled and before I drifted off to sleep, I placed a tender kiss to his lips, and told him, "I love you, too, Jake. So much that it hurts. But you're not going to get rid of me because as soon as my father is out of the hospital you're going to gain a wife." I gave him a cheeky grin.

It took him a minute but a huge grin slit his face. "Not that I'm complaining, but isn't the guy supposed to do the asking?"

"I heard you before but I wasn't sure what page you were on with our future, so I figured I'd get the marriage out of the way."

He grabbed my bottom and tried to get me closer to him. "We're on the same page, and we'll talk about everything in the morning. For now, I need to love you again."

He rolled to his back while he settled me on him.

"Now ride me, woman."

I threw my head back and laughed, which soon turned to moans of pleasure as he grabbed my hips and rocked me on him.

Needless to say I soon forgot how tired I was.

PROLOGUE

JAKE (3 YEARS LATER)

STRIDING OUT OF THE SURF, I shook the water from my long hair and moved toward the sun lounger that was in the shade.

My gorgeous wife of two and a half years lay cooling off. She was hot and uncomfortable with her seven-month pregnant belly. To her, she looked like a beached whale, but to me, she was the most beautiful woman I'd ever seen.

Not a day went by that I didn't tell her how much she meant to me, which was why I'd brought her away for a couple of weeks after talking to her OB. I'd wanted to surprise her with our first holiday. One that I paid for out of my own salary.

Who'd have thought that I'd have a knack with computers after spending the first twenty-four years of my life without one? It had certainly paid off with help from my dad and made me feel good that I could provide for my wife, and now, our child.

The first few days after Evie's father had been shot had been difficult, more so because I was unable to drive Evie and her mom around. However, Carter had stepped in and made sure I had my license within a few weeks, and I'm sure he called in a favor to be able to have it so quickly.

With thanks to Patrick working with the Feds, they had a lot more information on Declan Fitzwilliam and his operation than they ever thought possible. Carter had mentioned that his boss thought it was his birthday with the haul they'd found. Needless to say, Declan wouldn't be seeing the outside of a prison again, unless he got lucky. Very lucky.

Luckily for Patrick, his hands weren't muddy like those of his father so with his inside help in bringing his father to justice, all he got was community service, and a husband in Oliver.

I tried not to think about the people who had been involved back then—other than my wife, and Millie and Carter—because I'd get too angry.

Pushing the past back to where it belonged, in the past, I approached Evie, and froze.

She'd taken her cover-up off and lay in a tiny red bikini. The triangles barely covered her breasts and the one between her legs was even smaller.

I swallowed, and tried to swallow again but my mouth was dry as hell.

It didn't stop there, as I moved closer her chest rose and fell with her breathing and her legs scissored together.

"Mmm," she mumbled.

She killed me.

My body reacted to her moans, going rock hard in my swim trunks, which did not have the room to accommodate a monster of an erection.

I looked around and the only other couple on the beach had a windbreaker up so they couldn't be seen, or see us.

I turned my gaze back to my wife and cursed while my hand wrapped around my dick. "Fuck, Evie."

Her eyes snapped open. "Oh God, Jake. Stoke the fire." She dropped her legs to each side of the sun lounger, and arched up. "Please." Her eyes fixed on what my hand was doing, her breathing more erratic.

One more glance around the beach, I thought, what the hell, and dropped my trunks as I kneeled between her spread thighs.

"Hurry." Evie started to untie one side of her little panties so my hand went to the other.

Tugging the small triangle down, I ran my finger through her arousal, and felt my dick respond as I touched her bare pussy lips.

"Sit on me. You need to be comfortable." I quickly sat and rearranged Evie so that she faced away from me, her legs spread over my thighs. I slowly brought her down and prayed for strength.

"God, I'm so close. Move."

Reaching around, I slipped my hand inside her tiny bikini bra so that I could roll and tug on her nipples. My other hand went to her pussy, which I stroked while my hips rocked in time with hers.

"Oh God."

My dick felt like it was being squeezed in a vice as she convulsed around me, panting. Seconds later, I followed her into orgasm, only to have her ripple around me for a second time. Her body finally went lax, satisfied.

She rose and the feel of my dick sliding out of her had me hard and throbbing, again.

Evie smiled, and straddling my thighs as she wrapped her arms around my neck while my dick pressed up against her belly.

"We need to go back to the room," I whispered, raining kisses down her neck. I placed the longest kiss on the top of her swollen belly. Our child. Tears formed in my eyes at how happy Evie had made me by loving me and giving me a family that I'd always protect.

Kissing each bared nipple, I traveled back up to her sweet lips, placing a light kiss to them when she smiled.

"I want you inside me again. Here. On the beach."

"Evie," I groaned in warning. "Our room is less than a hundred yards away."

She grinned, and rubbed the slit at the head of my dick.

I twitched and leaked with arousal and wouldn't be able to walk until I'd been satisfied. My wife was a damn tease, and knew it as well.

I loved her so fucking much, and she was my whole world.

EVIE (4 MONTHS LATER)

I'D WOKEN MISSING THE warmth of my husband's arms holding me close, but when I opened my eyes, they filled with tears.

He sat in the corner of the room on the rocking chair with our two-month-old daughter, Reagan, cuddled against his chest.

She slept, but Jake didn't. As he rocked, his gaze was solely focused on Reagan while he whispered words that I couldn't hear to her.

My heart felt filled to bursting with the love that would overwhelm me at unexpected times, just like now.

Jake had been through so much, and he'd worked so hard to give us our own beautiful home, which had meant the world to him that he'd been able to do that.

We lived comfortably with thanks to my first and only published non-fiction book doing so well, about what happened over three years ago. Jake's father had also transferred the money he'd saved for Jake over to him once everything had settled down. Jake hadn't wanted to take it, but his father and Carter had persuaded him to in the end.

I smiled thinking about Carter. He was in a panic over Millie being close to her due date with their first child. The big, tough FBI guy was scared of childbirth. I shouldn't find it amusing because Jake had been terrified, but he'd explained it was me being in pain that terrified him, and not the actual birth. That's what I thought was wrong with Carter, and told Millie to try and get him to talk to her about it.

My focus returned to Jake with our daughter so I couldn't resist any longer and climbed out of bed. The rustling of the bedcover alerted Jake to the fact that I was awake and as I crossed the room to them his cheeks heated in embarrassment.

"How much did you hear," he whispered, holding my gaze.

I smiled and curved my arm around his neck as I stood

beside the rocking chair. "I couldn't hear anything. You whispered so quietly."

He held my gaze for a few more seconds before he patted his lap. "Curl up on here with us."

I was careful to not wake Reagan as I curled up on his lap. His arm went around my back as we both settled in watching our beautiful child.

"I can never find the words to tell you what you and Reagan mean to me." He dropped his head to mine. "I love you, Evangeline. My Evie."

"I love you too, Jake Rivers."

THE END

DEAR READER

If you liked *Stryker,* I would appreciate it, if you would help others enjoy this book too by recommending it to your friends, family, and book clubs by writing an honest, positive review on Amazon, Barnes and Noble, Kobo, iBook Store, Goodreads, etc.

ACKNOWLEDGMENTS

Image Copyright ~ Luis Rafael
Cover Model ~ Assad Lawrence-Shalhoub
Cover Design ~ Louisa Maggio, LM Creations
Editor: Sirena Van Schaik
BETA Reader: Emma Clifton, Kathrin Magyar, Lynne Garlick, Nadine Winningham, Sonya Covert & Stacie Mayer-Hamburger

OTHER BOOKS BY LEXI BUCHANAN

Bad Boy Rockers

Book 1: Sizzle

Book 2: Spicy

Book 3: Sultry

Book 4: Savor

Book 5: Sinful

Book 6: Silent Night (Novella)

McKenzie Brothers

Book 1: Seduce

Book 1.5: The Wedding (Novella)

Book 2: Rapture

Book 3: Delight

Book 4: Entice

Book 5: Cherished

Book 5.5: A McKenzie Christmas (Novella)

De La Fuente Family (McKenzie Spinoff)

Book 1: Love in Montana

Book 2: Love in Purgatory

Book 3: Love in Bloom

Book 4: Love in Country

Book 5: Love in Flame

Book 6: Love in Game

Book 7: Love in Education

McKenzie Cousins

(McKenzie Spinoff)

Book 1: Baby Makes Three

Book 2: A Business Decision

Book 3: Secret Kisses

Book4: Kissing Cousins

Jackson Hole

Book 1: From This Moment

Book 1.5: When we Meet (Novella, in the back of From This Moment)

Book 2: New Beginning (coming soon)

Romantic Suspense

Lawful

Stryker

Standalone Novella's

One Dance

Educate Me

Pure

Holiday Season

Kissing Under the Mistletoe

A Soldier's Christmas

Written as Rona Jameson

Come Back to Me
Summer at Rose Cottage
Twenty Eight Days

THE MYSTERY OF ROSE DEGAN
written as Lexi Buchanan

Set in the beautiful coastal town of Cape Elizabeth, Maine, 'The Mystery of Rose Degan' explores two love stories—one lost in time and the other flourishing in the present. McKenzie (Mack) Harper needs to get away and the small cottage just outside of Cape Elizabeth is the perfect location to unwind and bond with her six-year-old nephew, Lucas. It's here at this quaint summer rental that Mack discovers a diary dated March 4th, 1947, which pulls her into a world of love and heartache.

Each entry into the diary is brought to life through the words written by nineteen-year-old, Rose Degan, who falls in love with a man her parents disapprove of. Her heart knows what and whom it wants, Jacob Evans, a fire fighter in Cape Elizabeth. He hasn't been in town long when they meet on the cliffs while she watches the rescue of a crew from a collier ship that went aground during a fierce storm.

Back in the present, Mack discovers that Jacob is still alive and tries to find him. She leaves a message that falls into the hands of Jacob's grandson, Dean Evans. With his curiosity piqued, Dean decides that the mystery woman, along with her diary, is an excellent excuse to slip away from home, earning a break from his mother's matchmaking shenanigans—a grandchild being her sole focus.

All these characters come together in a story of love and friendship. It shows that love and family can transcend time.

Available at online retailers.

TWENTY EIGHT DAYS, ROMANTIC SUSPENSE
written as Rona Jameson

Sentenced to death...

All hope gone...

Until he receives a visit from victim #6

Condemned for a crime he didn't commit, Quinten Peterson sat on death row praying for a miracle. He just never expected his angel of mercy to be the girl he fell in love with so long ago.

The press called her a victim, but Saige Lockwood was a survivor. And she had twenty-eight days to discover the truth about what really happened to her that fateful night, eight years ago.

With time running out, Saige desperately needed to unlock her memories . . . before it was too late.

Available at online retailers.

COME BACK TO ME

written as Rona Jameson

A whispered plea transcends time.

When Esmé Rogers meets Luke Carlisle in 1987, she never expected to end up on board the Titanic for its maiden voyage from Southampton to New York in 1912. But what started with confusion and questions turns into the greatest love of her life.

As the date of the ill-fated sinking of the ocean liner approaches, Esmé questions whether or not she should try and change history. However, one question keeps coming back to haunt her: Does she survive?

With frigid waters and a predestined collision on the horizon, can she change the fate of those she loves?

Available at online retailers.

ABOUT THE AUTHOR

Lexi Buchanan is the pseudonym of Rona Jameson. Lexi is a New York Times and USA Today bestselling author of romance.

She's a wife and mother who moved with her family to Ireland, in 2010.

Her love of reading sweet romance is what eventually drew her to writing and self-publishing her first book in 2012. Since then she has self-published more than thirty books.

Her first signing was in New York in 2013, and since then she's been to signings in: Belfast, Boston, Dublin, Las Vegas, London, Los Angeles, Nashville, New York, Norfolk VA, and Oxford, to meet readers. This is one of her favorite parts of being an author and she tries to attend at least three signings a year, with at least one, in the United States.

Thank you to each and every one of you for your continued support.

For more information:
www.lexibuchanan.com
ronajameson.com
authorlexibuchanan@gmail.com

Made in the USA
Middletown, DE
12 May 2018